MURDER AT CASTLE VYNE

LOUISE MARLEY

Storm

This is a work of fiction. Names, characters, business, events and incidents are the products of the author's imagination. Any resemblance to actual persons, living or dead, or actual events is purely coincidental.

Copyright © Louise Marley, 2025

The moral right of the author has been asserted.

All rights reserved. No part of this book may be reproduced or used in any manner without the prior written permission of the copyright owner.

To request permissions, contact the publisher at rights@stormpublishing.co

Ebook ISBN: 978-1-83700-213-9
Paperback ISBN: 978-1-83700-214-6

Cover design: Ghost
Cover images: Shutterstock

Published by Storm Publishing.
For further information, visit:
www.stormpublishing.co

ALSO BY LOUISE MARLEY

Murder at Raven's Edge
Murder at Ravenswood House
Murder at Raven's Hollow

*To Novelistas Ink
for their wonderful support*

PROLOGUE

Fourteen years previously

Leaning out of her bedroom window, sixteen-year-old Natalie Grove watched a cascade of shimmering fireworks light up the night sky. Tonight was the regatta, where everyone gathered at the marina to watch the yachts sail down the river. Wistfully, she stood on tiptoe, hoping to catch a glimpse of one of the illuminated boats or even the funfair. When everyone was talking about it at school tomorrow, she wanted to be able to drop in enough detail to make her classmates believe she'd been there.

But as she craned her neck, she caught a flash of movement below and heard the click of the front door closing.

Down in the garden, a slight figure ran along the path.

Sarah?

As though she'd spoken the name aloud, her sister paused with one hand on the gate and glanced back at the lodge.

Where was she going?

To the regatta? Without her?

Natalie's fingers tightened on the windowsill. It was so

unfair. Why was *she* always the one to get left behind? She was only two years younger than Sarah.

A man stepped from beneath the shadowy trees.

Sarah ran towards him, flinging her arms around his neck. He lifted her up, whirling her around before setting her back on her feet and hugging her close.

Natalie frowned. Who was *he*?

But before Natalie could think to call out, Sarah had taken hold of his hand and followed him into the dark.

When Natalie woke the following morning, she was lying on top of her bed, still wearing her clothes from the night before. She'd also failed to set her alarm, which meant she was now late for school.

She changed into her uniform, tied back her blonde hair and, without bothering to check the mirror (she'd never achieve the perfection of Sarah in a million years, so why try?), yanked open her door, only to come face to face with her mother.

'Oh... Hi, Mum!'

'Sarah's not in her bed,' Magda Grove announced, peering over her head as though expecting Sarah to be hiding in Natalie's room. 'Do *you* know where she is?'

Inside her head, Natalie saw a replay of Sarah running down the garden path, pausing only to look back at the Lodge. 'Did she leave early for school?'

'Her bed hasn't been slept in, but her clothes are still in her wardrobe. What do I always say to you girls? If you're going to take risks like this, don't get caught. You get caught, you bring us all down. Don't expect me to save your necks.'

'Dad doesn't have to know—'

Magda rolled her eyes. 'The front door was unlocked and the gate unlatched. Of course he *knows*. So if *you* know anything, you'd better tell me now. Is it a boy?'

Natalie remembered the boy – *man* – from last night, but Sarah wouldn't thank her for sharing that kind of secret, so she said instead, 'Where do you think she is?'

Magda raised an eyebrow. 'You tell me.'

Natalie's attention wandered to the door of her sister's room. As usual, it was firmly closed.

'Go ahead,' Magda sighed. 'Take a look. See what you think. But if she's run off with some idiot boy...'

That'd never happen. Despite everything, Sarah was far too sensible to run away.

Wasn't she?

Natalie pushed open the door to Sarah's bedroom, half expecting her sister to jump out at her. As close as they were, Sarah hated Natalie sneaking in and 'borrowing' her things. But, when the door swung shut, Natalie was entirely alone in a room practically identical to her own.

Sarah's bed hadn't been slept in, that much was clear, and Natalie had made enough forays into her sister's wardrobe to know there wasn't anything missing, apart from the green dress and matching cropped cardie she'd seen her wearing last night. Neatly stacked at the bottom of the wardrobe were shoeboxes with photos stuck on the side, illustrating what each one contained. High-heeled boots, strappy sandals in varying shades, sensible work shoes – even a pair of walking boots.

Walking boots? Sarah never walked anywhere!

Natalie tugged the box out and flipped off the lid.

Obviously there were no boots inside, only a thick sheaf of paper with a notebook on top.

She tucked the notebook into the waistband of her skirt to read later and flicked through the loose paper. Sarah's ambition was to be a writer, so it was unsurprising that the wodge of paper turned out to be a story she was working on, immaculately typed in double-lined spacing.

Natalie tried shoving the paper back into the box, but a

sheet of black card beneath it rucked up and it wouldn't smooth back into place.

Was something else here?

A secret hidden within a secret?

She peeled the card away.

The remainder of the box was filled with cash.

A floorboard creaked. Natalie glanced nervously towards the door, but it remained shut.

She turned back to the box. Packed beneath the card were little bundles of ten-pound notes. Were they fake? She took one out and turned it over.

Beneath that was another bundle and then another. They certainly looked real. There must be over a thousand pounds. How had Sarah got hold of *this* kind of money? Anything she earned modelling for Sir Henry Vyne went straight into a trust fund, as agreed by their parents, which she couldn't touch until she was twenty-one.

Had she *stolen* it?

Hearing another warning creak, closer this time, Natalie shoved the lid back onto the box and stuffed it into the wardrobe. There was hardly enough time for her to close the door, before she heard the muffled sound of her father's voice speaking with her mother, and then he came in.

John Grove was wearing his scruffy work clothes, his jaw unshaven. His silver-grey eyes, the mirror of hers, narrowed suspiciously. 'What are you up to?'

'I came to see if Sarah's clothes had gone.'

'Have they?' he asked.

'I can't see that anything is missing, only the clothes she was wearing last night.'

The sharp edge of her sister's notebook dug accusingly into her waist.

Her father turned his attention to the old-fashioned

wardrobe. 'It doesn't make sense that she would disappear like this. Does it make sense to you?'

She shook her head, but did he really want an answer?

'Where is she? Does she have a boyfriend? Has she run off with him?'

Why was *that* the first thing her parents thought of?

Why would her sister *want* to run away? Their home life wasn't great, but to leave this cash behind? It wasn't logical.

'Sarah has a lot of friends,' Natalie said, careful to sound casual. 'Some of them are boys.'

Now her father was roughly pulling out the boxes of shoes, systematically opening and discarding them. The box containing the cash slid towards the back, unnoticed. How long before he found it? What would he say when he discovered the money? Did he know it was there? Was *that* what he was looking for?

And why would Sarah need to hide cash in her wardrobe like it was some big secret?

Her father glanced back over his shoulder. 'Why are you still here? Get off to school.'

'Yes, Dad.'

She scurried out of the bedroom and found her mother waiting outside.

'Well?' said her mother.

'Sarah hasn't taken any clothes...' Should she tell Magda the truth? 'I found some money...'

'*Money*? How much money?'

'Um... a few hundred pounds, I think.'

A few thousand...

Natalie had always believed that her mother considered her daughters an inconvenience and wasn't particularly bothered what they did, provided it didn't impact on her own life. She kept every emotion in check, good or bad, revealing nothing more than the tiniest frown to show displeasure. Now, however, Magda appeared utterly shocked.

This was bad. This was *very* bad.

'Mum, what's happened? Where's Sarah?'

Her mother shook her head and turned away, muttering, 'You'd better get off to school before your dad finds you still here.'

Dad: the ultimate threat.

There was no point arguing. Natalie went to grab her school bag from her room and headed out of the house.

She followed the same path as Sarah had the night before, through the little wooden gate and onto the castle driveway, which in turn led under a massive stone archway and onto the main road.

The pavement was on the other side, but, as she stepped onto the road, a rustling from the trees made her instinctively glance back. Was someone there, watching her from the shelter of the ancient oaks?

'Sarah?' she called. 'Is that you?'

A squeal of brakes and a flash of white abruptly returned her to the present. She tried to jump out of the way, but her foot slipped and she ended up flat on her back in the gutter.

A car had swerved to a halt a few metres away. She didn't know enough about cars to recognise the type, but it was small and old.

The driver's door opened and footsteps headed in her direction.

'Are you all right?'

Natalie blinked away the rain as a man's face loomed towards her. He had pale skin and auburn hair brushed back from a high forehead. Like her, he wasn't wearing a coat and his navy sweater and dark trousers were gradually becoming soaked. While she was still trying to work out what had happened, his large hand gripped hers and hauled her to her feet.

Was she all right? After her inelegant slide into the gutter, one sleeve of her school sweatshirt had been pushed upwards, exposing the white shirt beneath. Except it was no longer white but dotted crimson. She'd scraped her elbow when she'd fallen.

'Get in my car,' he said. 'I have a first-aid kit.' When she hesitated – did he think her a *complete* idiot? – he pointed at the logo of the old-fashioned sailing ship printed on her sweatshirt. 'I'm Simon Waters – *Mr* Waters – I teach at Calahurst Community School. You're in my drama class. Don't you recognise me?'

He thought she was Sarah.

Wasn't that the story of her life?

'Are you *sure* you're all right?' he asked again. He held up his hand. 'How many fingers am I holding up?'

Oh, for goodness sake!

'I'm *fine*, but I've got to get to school or I'll be late.'

'You can't go to school, Sarah. You're hurt and probably in shock.'

She tapped her chest. 'I'm *Natalie*, not Sarah.'

But his attention had been drawn to the castle gateway. 'You live *here*?'

He must be new or he'd know exactly who she was.

'My father's the head gardener at Castle Vyne,' she said, 'but we live at the Lodge.'

'Are your parents home now?'

Was that a hopeful note in his voice?

'No, they're at work. I'll see the nurse when I get to school.'

He raised an eyebrow. 'Sure you will.'

Apparently he'd been a teacher for too long.

'Why don't you give me a lift?' she said.

The fairground was close to the school...

To speed things along, she walked over to his car and tugged at the handle on the passenger door.

It didn't open.

'Allow me,' he said sardonically, unlocking the door and holding it open. Fat drops of rain splattered the upholstery. She slid in before he changed his mind.

He got in the driver's side, reaching past her to undo the glove compartment. He found the first-aid kit – a green plastic box – and handed it to her. She opened it, used an anti-bacterial wipe to clean the scrape on her elbow and then pressed a square piece of gauze against it.

'Are you going to tell me what this is about, Sarah?'

Where should she start?

Perhaps with the obvious.

'I'm not Sarah. I'm her sister, Natalie,' she repeated.

He frowned. 'You look so similar...'

Like she'd never heard *that* before.

'Could you take me to the fairground, please? That's where Sarah is. I need to persuade her to come to school.'

'Nice try, but the Sixth Form are on work experience this week.'

What was he, a human lie detector?

'No, she's at the fairground.'

'Is it even open at this time of the morning? Perhaps I should discuss this with your parents?' He glanced over his shoulder at the castle gate. 'You said your father works here?'

Why had she told him that? 'It's an enormous estate. Dad could be anywhere.'

'I suppose if I take you to school, you could discuss it with the Head?'

'The fairground is on the way,' she said. 'We could check there first?'

He was silent for a moment and then muttered, '*Fine*, but as soon as we've collected Sarah, I'm taking you both to school.'

'Deal.'

It was the best she could hope for.

The funfair had been set up in one of the fields bordering the village. It would have taken Natalie ten minutes to walk the distance from the Lodge. In a car, it took seconds. The rain was easing off too. She couldn't have hoped for a better result.

Mr Waters parked beside the gate and they got out. The gate was shut and a poster advertising the fair had been ripped off it. Four tiny triangles of coloured paper, still attached to shiny drawing pins, were the only sign it had been there.

Well, that was weird...

She undid the latch, gave the gate a hefty shove and entered the field.

The ground sloped gently downhill, and the drizzling rain was being blown straight towards her, so it took a moment for her to understand the field was empty. There was nothing left at all, only trampled grass and churned mud to show where the stalls and rides had been.

The fair had gone.

Mr Waters came to stand beside her. He'd pulled a cheap-looking, navy-blue raincoat over his sweater. A few strands of dark-auburn hair had escaped from his hood and become plastered against his forehead. For the first time, she noticed he wore spectacles, now heavily dotted with raindrops.

'I can't see a funfair,' he said, stating the obvious.

'It *was* here.' Did he think she was making it up? 'Now it isn't.'

'They must have packed up and left.'

'It was booked for three days.'

'Perhaps the three days are up?'

Natalie remembered the poster pinned to the gate. There had been three dates written on it: Yesterday, today and tomorrow.

'It must have left early.' But why would an entire funfair,

booked in advance, pack everything up and ship out in the middle of the night?

'Let's go back to the car,' he said. 'We're getting soaked.'

As this sounded more productive than hanging around a muddy field, Natalie followed him.

Once inside the car, he pushed back the hood of his coat, took a handkerchief out of his pocket and began to clean his spectacles.

'Well?' he said.

'I think Sarah has run away with the fair.'

Should she have told him that?

'I didn't think people did that any more.' He held his spectacles to the light, presumably checking for smears. 'Your sister has a flair for the dramatic.' He slid the spectacles back on. She could see little squares of light reflected in the glass. His hazel eyes were watching her closely. 'What next?'

It was nice to be asked, but her plan hadn't got a 'next' part to it.

She shrugged.

'I can take you to school,' he said, 'or I can take you home. Which would you prefer?'

'Where do you think the fair's gone?'

'I haven't the slightest idea' – he flicked back the cuff of his anorak to check his watch – 'but if you want me to take you to school, we're going to be very, very late.'

'I have to find Sarah.'

Preferably before their father did.

'I don't think that's your job,' he said gently. 'Why don't I take you home?'

Did she have a choice?

He started the car and used the mini roundabout at the top of the high street to turn around, heading back up the hill and past the great stone wall surrounding the castle. She assumed he'd drop her off outside the gate. Instead, he drove through it.

There was a police patrol car parked directly outside the Lodge.

He pulled up behind it.

They both stared at the car.

'That's not good,' Natalie said.

'I'm sure everything is fine,' he said, in the kind of voice that adults used when everything wasn't.

'Dad must have told them Sarah's missing.' To an outsider, this might seem obvious, but her father and the local police had 'history'. The kind of history where the police would be the last people you'd call.

'Why don't I go in first and explain where you've been?' Mr Waters suggested.

That was fine by her.

Natalie watched him walk down the path and knock on the door. A uniformed police officer opened it. The officer didn't appear pleased to see him. They exchanged a few words. Mr Waters pointed to Natalie waiting in the car. The officer hesitated, then stood back to let him inside. The door closed.

Natalie slumped back in the seat. What should she do now? Go indoors and risk an inquisition about why she wasn't at school? Or take a walk through the castle garden until the adults finished their discussion?

Actually, now the rain was easing off, that wasn't a bad idea. It wasn't as though she could get any soggier.

After a long wet summer, the path through the woods to the garden had become overgrown and hard to follow. The trees grew thickly overhead, blocking out the light, their fallen leaves creating a pungently rotting carpet beneath her feet. Occasionally, she caught glimpses of an old brick path and followed it through a copse of yew trees, to where a tall gate had been set into an ancient wall.

'The secret garden', Sarah always called it and, as children, they'd often played there.

Smiling at the memory, Natalie undid the latch.

Most of the flower beds had already been cut back by her father, ready for autumn, leaving only swathes of Michaelmas daisies amidst the last of the summer's roses.

She headed across the wet grass to where a terrace had been laid in the shelter of the wall and a gazebo overlooked three large ornamental ponds filled with water lilies.

One of the gardeners had left a sweater on the ground beside the central pond. Natalie poked it with her foot. Why did it seem familiar?

She glanced towards the pond. The dark water was smooth and unrippled. The petals of the white and pink water lilies appeared so perfect they could have been carved from wax. But something protruded through the round glossy leaves. Something shaped like a foot.

Natalie moved closer, her gaze travelling the length of the pool. Through the murky water, she could discern a knee, a pale thigh, a ripple of green fabric—

Floating a few centimetres below the surface was a woman wearing a pretty dress, her weight partially supported by the mass of flowers. Her skin was almost as pale as the petals that surrounded her, her hair such a light blonde it could have been spun silver.

Sarah...

ONE

Present

Rose Court was a gothic revival house on the edge of the village of Calahurst. Built of red brick and Portland stone, it had gargoyles on the roof, far too many gables and several large bay windows. The house had once been the residence of a retired schoolmaster and his spinster sisters, famous for its rose garden and beautiful view over the River Hurst. Now converted into an exclusive private care home, the view was obscured by an ugly modern extension and the rose garden had been paved over to create a car park.

Natalie Grove manoeuvred her BMW into the last available parking place as a white minibus drew up behind her, effectively blocking her in. After a matter of minutes, a ramp with a wheelchair clamped firmly onto it began to descend.

She got out to watch. 'Hi, Dad!'

The man in the wheelchair stared straight through her.

Fourteen years had passed since Sarah's murder, but their father appeared to have aged twice that. His thick, dark hair had turned white overnight, there were deep lines etched into his pale skin and the scar on his forehead – a curving silver line on his temple – was a constant reminder of the reason he was here.

A care worker unfastened John's chair from the ramp and pushed him towards her. 'There you go, Mr Grove.'

Natalie tried again. 'Where have you been, Dad? Anywhere nice?'

He didn't even glance up.

'It's not one of his good days, I'm afraid,' the care worker said, taking pity on her. He wore a green uniform with a red rose logo embroidered on the pocket and, beneath that, his name: Jason. 'The local school put on a concert for us. I *think* your father enjoyed it...'

John grunted, which could have meant anything.

'Calahurst Community School?' Natalie asked.

'That's the one,' Jason said. 'My old school. Do you know it?'

'I went there too, years ago, but I expect it's improved since my day.'

His smile was wry. 'Not really.'

Expecting him to wheel her dad through the entrance to Rose Court, she moved out of the way.

Jason, however, hesitated. 'Do you think you could take Mr Grove inside for me? We're short-staffed and I've got to go back to help with Miss Barker.'

An elderly lady was now descending the minibus from the front steps, ferociously waving her walking stick at anyone who tried to offer an arm, yet looking as though the slightest breeze would blow her over.

Go, Miss Barker!

'Sure, no problem.' Natalie took the handles of the wheelchair and pushed John up the ramp and into the gloomy reception hall, pausing only to sign her name in the visitors' book.

The blonde receptionist barely glanced up and showed zero

interest as Natalie took John past the curving wooden staircase and along the corridor towards the residents' sitting room.

She parked him in prime position in front of the TV. It hadn't been switched on and the only other occupant was an elderly man asleep in a winged-back chair. His head lolled onto his shoulder as he emitted tiny, feathery snores. A large hardback book was starting to slide from his lap.

'I've brought you some new shirts, Dad.' Natalie held up a carrier bag marked with the name of one of Norchester's more exclusive shops. She took a small packet from her handbag. 'And some of your favourite liquorice.'

She held it out to him. When he didn't take it, she carefully placed the packet within reach on a nearby table.

Why did she persist in doing this to herself? Why come here at all? He didn't care what she did. Maybe he'd prefer to be left alone? Her mother hadn't visited in years.

'Are you going now?' he said.

Was that *hope* in his voice?

Funny how he could be perfectly lucid when he wanted to be.

'No, Dad, because I'm going to sit here and talk to you. Won't that be nice?'

He scowled.

'I thought so too.' She pulled up a chair and sat beside him. 'So, what shall we talk about?'

Silence.

'We could talk about the weather? Or shall I tell you about my new book, which is due out this week? Would you like a copy? I could bring extra ones too, signed, for your friends? What do you think?'

Not that he *had* any friends, the miserable old so-and-so.

John made no indication he was even listening, but then he'd never shown any interest in her work. Most fathers would have—

Who was she fooling? John Grove had never been like most fathers.

'It's nearly fourteen years to the day since Sarah died,' she said. And almost fourteen years since his accident. 'I've ordered a wreath for her grave from the two of us. Mum's doing her own thing, as usual.'

Translation: Mum's doing *nothing*, as usual.

What a family.

His fingers, which had been resting lightly on the arms of his wheelchair, tightened.

She almost missed it.

Encouraged, she said, 'That morning, when we realised Sarah had gone, you searched her wardrobe? Do you remember?'

No response.

She tried again, asking a question she'd asked many times over the years.

'What were you looking for, Dad? Did you find it?'

He reached for the bag of liquorice, opened it and put a couple of the sweets into his mouth, before going back to staring straight ahead.

She knew why he did it. By ignoring her questions, he shifted the power back to himself.

They'd been playing *this* bait-and-switch game for years, but he *knew* something about Sarah's death, she was certain of it. What wasn't he telling her?

Was he protecting someone? The *murderer*?

Or had someone threatened him?

After fourteen years, she'd had enough. With the publication of her new book, she'd laid the perfect trail of breadcrumbs. She just had to wait for the right moment to spring the trap.

A soft thud distracted her. The man asleep in the wing-back chair had dropped his book. It was a large glossy hardback and had fallen open with the pages splayed and the spine bent back. Natalie, wincing, immediately went over to pick it up.

As she straightened the pages and placed it on the table beside him, she heard voices coming from the corridor. The staff were bringing the rest of the residents back into the home.

John hadn't shifted from where she'd left him, even though she knew he was capable of moving the wheelchair himself. He stared at the blank TV screen, his gaze unfocused and his mouth slack, back in the part he'd been playing for years – and he'd become very good at it. In the beginning, he'd had her fooled along with the doctors but she'd never understood why he persisted with it. Surely he wouldn't *want* to live in a care home if he had a choice?

Returning to his side, she said, quite casually, 'Sarah kept a diary. I found it the day she disappeared. Did you know that?'

He said nothing.

In the corridor outside, Jason and another care worker were discussing last night's football match.

Natalie lowered her voice. 'Did you know Sarah made a list of every boy she'd ever gone out with?'

She watched him carefully, waiting for the tiniest change to his expression, an indication that he understood the significance of what she was telling him.

Come on, Dad... Join the dots.

'Sarah gave them codenames. There was a "doctor", a "teacher"...' Natalie paused deliberately. 'A "gardener"... Maybe someone you worked with at the castle? Do you remember? Was there anyone she was sweet on? One of your team? Maybe *he* was the murderer?'

Surely *that* would get a response?

John tipped the remainder of the liquorice into his mouth, crumpled up the packet and dropped it onto the floor.

Bother.

'*Really*, Dad?' She bent to swipe it up. 'That's kind of petty, even for—'

A blue-veined hand grabbed her wrist. His grip was surprisingly strong. Her cry of surprise died on her lips as she glanced up and caught his intense expression.

'Let me go, Dad.'

When pulling away didn't work, she caught his long, broad-tipped fingers and began prising them off her wrist, one at a time – only for him to clamp them back down – like the 'game' he'd tormented her with as a child.

His legs might not be as strong as they'd been, but the muscles in his arms remained powerful. He pulled her closer, until her face was centimetres from his, his breath warm on her cheek. His eyes met hers and she saw the intelligence behind them. Pale grey eyes, the exact same shape and colour as her own.

It was her curse. Whenever she looked into a mirror, she'd see the person she hated most in the world staring right back.

'I know what you did,' he said, quite calmly. 'You can't play the innocent with me.'

What did *that* mean?

Had she heard him correctly?

There was a blur of green, someone caught her round the ribcage and hauled her away, at once breaking her father's hold.

'Did he hurt you, Ms Grove?' Jason was peering at her. 'Are you all right?'

She nodded, hardly able to speak.

'I'm so sorry! Mr Grove has never done anything like that before. We wouldn't have left you alone together if we'd known. He's usually such a quiet, well-behaved patient...'

A sneaky, lying, badly behaved patient, more like.

Although, maybe he was only like that with her?

John was now sitting in his wheelchair as though nothing had happened.

What *was* going on inside his head?

Behind him, another care worker was ready to make a move if he tried anything else.

'Are you OK, Ms Grove?' Jason said again, slightly louder this time. Presumably he thought she was in some kind of shock.

To be honest, she was. Had the last few moments actually taken place? Had her father really accused her of... what, exactly? *Murdering* her *sister*?

'I'm all right,' she said, before Jason could ask his question a third time. 'It was a surprise, that's all.'

She shouldn't have taunted her father. Did she think he was going to sit there and take it? Yes, she'd hoped he might blurt out the truth, but she hadn't thought through the consequences.

Jason smiled, somewhat uncertainly. 'I don't think he meant you any harm, Ms Grove.'

She took a cautious step towards her father to collect her bags, watching him all the while. His eyes didn't flicker in her direction once.

'OK, Dad,' she said. 'I've got to go now. Maybe I'll see you next week?'

But John Grove never took his eyes from the blank TV screen, apparently tuned out and engrossed in a world of his own.

The perfect patient?

The perfect fraud!

After all these years, her father was still very much in control.

TWO

As she left the community room, Natalie realised she'd inadvertently picked up the carrier bag containing her father's new T-shirts along with her handbag.

It was tempting to chuck them into the nearest bin, but she took the carrier bag to his room, dropping it carelessly onto a table set directly in the centre of a bay window. She knew her father liked to sit there and watch the world go past. No wonder; the room itself was a sterile environment with nothing personal, not even photographs.

For the first time, Natalie wondered what had happened to her father's belongings, his precious gardening books and horticultural awards? Had her mother placed them in storage? Taken them to the nearest dump? *That* seemed more likely.

Somewhere in the distance, she heard the familiar theme tune to *Friends*. It had been Sarah's favourite TV show. Feeling goosebumps prickle her skin, Natalie turned and for a split second thought she saw Sarah standing in front of her, smiling...

Before realising it was only her reflection in the window.

Sadly, she moved away – too quickly. Her hip knocked against the table, the movement sending a potted plant skidding across the polished wood. She made a grab for it, but a tall, dark-haired man was there before her, catching the plant and restoring it to the table.

How long had he been standing there, watching her?

'Hello, Charles,' she said.

'Natalie.' Charles Fitzpatrick dusted soil from his hands but didn't wipe them on his clothes. Evidently they were too expensive to spoil. 'How are you?'

'I'm fine.' Unable to help herself (it was like an itch she couldn't ignore), Natalie straightened the pot so it was centrally positioned on the table. The plant was a citrus, complete with lemons so large they looked ready to drop. 'This is beautiful. Where did it come from?'

There was only the slightest hesitation before Charles shrugged. 'A visitor brought it.'

She looked up sharply. 'My father doesn't have visitors.'

'A relative?'

What was the point of having that visitors' book if strangers were allowed to wander in off the street, claiming a relationship?

'My father has no relatives, apart from myself.' Charles *knew* that.

'Would you like me to make further enquiries?' As always, Charles spoke quietly and politely – but she knew he was lying. Charles Fitzpatrick knew *exactly* who'd given the plant to her father, but for the moment he wasn't sharing.

Who was he protecting?

Could the visitor have been her mother?

That idea was so ridiculous she almost laughed out loud.

'It doesn't matter.' She moved towards the door, eager to leave.

His hand lightly touched her shoulder. 'Wait, there's something we need to discuss in my office.'

She jerked back.

He snatched his hand away. 'I'm sorry, I didn't think—'

'What do you need to "discuss"? Can't we talk about it here?'

'Where anyone can overhear the conversation?'

In his office they'd be alone – something she'd managed to avoid for years.

'Natalie?' She could see the pleading in his eyes. 'I wouldn't ask if I didn't believe it was important. I know how you feel about me. I know I destroyed your trust and I'm so sorry...'

That was one way of putting it...

But she was a woman of thirty, no longer a starry-eyed teenager imagining herself in love with a handsome young doctor, so she allowed him to lead the way along the labyrinth of dimly lit corridors, to the stout wooden door which had his name written on it, and a long list of letters after that. Reception was only a few metres distant. She could see the sun shining through the double glass doors, creating a perfect rectangle of light in the centre of the polished tiled floor.

Freedom, a few steps away...

As though reading her mind, he said, 'I think I'm correct in saying you'd rather speak with me directly, than through my solicitor?'

Solicitor?

It was unlike Charles to issue threats, but she kept her mouth shut and stepped into his office – trying not to shiver as the door swung shut with an ominous clunk.

Fourteen years ago, this room had seemed smaller, darker and more oppressive. The dark-green wallpaper remained unchanged, along with the heavy Victorian furniture. In those days, there'd always been a nurse present. Today they were alone.

'Take a seat,' he said cheerfully.

She moved further into the room, ticking off each memory as it came back. There were the shelves with the hundreds of books, which stretched from floor to ceiling; the squashy green chesterfield, with its leather almost worn away; and the glass case containing souvenirs from his grandfather's time in the military, which always gave her the creeps.

Natalie sat in the nearest chair, assuming Charles would sit behind his desk, to keep their meeting on this new formal footing and distance themselves from the past. Instead, he cleared a space amongst the paperwork cluttering his desk and sat on one corner – as he always used to do.

Fixing those dark-brown eyes directly on her, he thankfully came right to the point.

'Over the past few days, I've had to field many calls from friends and colleagues, who are aware of my connection with your family,' he said. 'Apparently you've written a book about your sister's murder, in which you frequently refer to a character you call "the doctor". They are, understandably, concerned that this character is based on me.'

Who were these 'friends and colleagues' who knew what she'd written before it had been published? The only thing online at the moment was the blurb.

'The character in my book is a junior doctor at a hospital,' she said, 'not a psychiatrist, and the book is fiction.'

'The murder victim is a teenage girl, who's found floating in a lily pond,' he said, reproval evident in his voice.

'No, she's an older woman, discovered in a bluebell wood. Honestly, Charles! Do you really believe my publishers want to risk being sued? I'm a thriller writer. I've always written books about fictional characters being fictionally murdered. By horrible coincidence, my sister was murdered. This means that whenever I give a promotional interview I'm forced to answer stupid questions about how it ruined my life. If I'm lucky, I can get away with explaining how I use my emotions to identify with the characters in my book, but they *are* only characters. Your well-meaning friends are confusing fiction with reality.'

Before he could respond, there was a knock on the door and in walked the same blonde receptionist she'd met earlier, carrying a tray.

'Thank you, Summer.' He waited for the girl to leave and close the door behind her, before turning his attention back to Natalie. 'Would you like a cup of tea?'

'No, thank you.' She watched him pour the tea from a pot into a porcelain cup.

Anyone else would have used a mug.

'I need you to send me two copies of your book,' he said, in a way that sounded rehearsed. 'One for me and one for my solicitor.'

Again with the solicitor.

'If that's what you want. I'll put them in the post tomorrow morning. Would you like them sent here or to your home address?'

'Here would be fine, thank you.' He sighed. 'I'm sorry, Natalie, but try to look at it from my point of view. I've had a hard enough time trying to keep this place afloat in the current economic climate, without juicy rumours hitting the press that I seduce my patients.'

She couldn't help it. 'Even if you do?'

'Once! It was a terrible error of judgement, for which I paid dearly. I was young, newly qualified and incredibly naive. I took you on as a personal favour to Sir Henry Vyne, even though I was completely out of my depth and thought myself in love with you.'

Love? Was he *serious?*

'That's not what I would have called it.'

'OK... I had feelings for you that were *completely inappropriate* and I didn't know how to deal with them. I apologised and offered financial compensation, which you turned down—'

She'd been heartbroken at what she'd seen as his betrayal. 'Hush money.'

'It wasn't *intended* to be—' He broke off and sighed. 'After fourteen years, why are we still having this argument? Let's get back to Sarah's murder, what are you trying to achieve by raking it up again with this book?'

Raking it up? For her, it had never gone away.

'I need to find out who murdered my sister,' she said flatly. 'I can't write about her story properly, using the names and locations that appear in her diary, because no publisher would touch it for fear of being sued, so it has to be fictionalised.'

She hesitated, waiting for him to make some comment about *his* feelings and how Sarah's death had affected *him* (he'd once dated Sarah), but he had the grace to remain silent. He even appeared sympathetic.

'Ever since my first book was published,' she continued, 'I've had to give interviews endlessly talking about how Sarah died. How she looked when I found her, how it destroyed my family and wrecked my life. How do they *think* it affected me? Watching her walk through that garden gate, to never see her again... Well, enough of *that*. Now I'm going to tell Sarah's story *my way* – and bring closure to this once and for all.'

He frowned. 'Are you still having nightmares about her murder? Oh, Natalie! I can help with that. You could see one of my colleagues?'

'No, thank you. I've had enough therapy to last a lifetime.'

'There are many effective medications and therapies available for PTSD. It's not like the old days.'

Medication...

She remembered the way her father had looked when he'd grabbed her wrist, the way his eyes had been in sharp focus, the intelligence behind them. The cunning...

Charles was still talking. 'I can make an appointment for you to see one of our counsellors, in the strictest confidence—'

She waved his words aside. 'Have you changed my father's medication?'

'What? Why would you say that?'

'For someone suffering from incurable brain damage, he's occasionally remarkably lucid.'

'I don't understand. What does that have to do with your—'

'Could my father be pretending?'

His sigh was pure exasperation. 'John sustained head injuries in a car accident and he's paralysed from the waist down. He was seen by several specialists at the time. You can't *fake* something like that.'

'He has some feeling in his legs,' she said, 'and there was talk at one time that he might get better—'

'From the spinal injury, certainly. He has something called a cauda equine lesion, but if there's not been any improvement over the last fourteen years, he's unlikely to start walking now. Why are you *asking* me this?'

'What about the head injury?'

With yet another sigh, Charles picked up a spiral-bound notebook from his desk, using a pencil to scribble a quick diagram. He held it up, so she could see he had drawn a cartoon of a man's head, divided into sections.

'The brain is made of many parts,' he said, jabbing at the diagram with the pencil. 'It can be divided into four areas, the largest of which is the cerebrum. The front section of the cerebrum is called the frontal lobe and is involved in speech, thought, emotion, memory and skilled movement. Because of its position and size, the frontal lobe is vulnerable to injury. Are you with me so far?'

She inclined her head.

'You father had a series of neuropsychological tests following his accident and also at regular intervals since.'

As she already knew this, she made no comment.

'John can remember events from his past but not the accident itself – although it's not unusual for patients to block traumatic events from their memories. We've noticed that John sometimes becomes confused, particularly if stressed. This could be because he has problems organising his thoughts and then communicating them to others. He also has trouble concentrating, which means he loses interest in keeping a conversation going, as it takes so much effort for him.'

Charles dropped the notebook back onto the desk. 'Patients with frontal lobe damage show little spontaneous facial expression and can have trouble reacting to their environment. I understand why you're confused. If John is having a good day, his concentration improves. He understands more and can therefore communicate more. On bad days – and, to be fair, John does suffer from very severe headaches that would make anyone feel down – he isn't interested in making what we would call "small talk". Combined with his lack of facial expression, this can make him appear worse than he actually is. Does that answer your question?'

'These tests, are they foolproof?'

'I should think so, yes. Your father has his moods and whims in the same way we all do. If he's feeling frustrated, his symptoms may appear worse. If he's not in any pain and is feeling relaxed, his symptoms would be vastly improved. I have to tell you that most improvements in this kind of traumatic brain injury usually appear in the first few years. After fourteen years… Well, I'm sorry, but this is as good as he's going to get.'

'He's definitely not faking?'

'Why do you keep suggesting that? It's ridiculous. What would the man gain from this kind of deception – and over such a long period of time?'

It was exactly the same question she'd asked herself.

THREE

After her visit to Rose Court, all Natalie wanted to do was collapse in front of the TV with a mug of strong coffee. Unfortunately, instead of whisking her up from the underground car park to her apartment, the lift stopped at ground level and opened onto reception. She jammed her finger on the button, but, as the doors finally slid together, a size eight boot wedged itself between them, delaying her further.

'Hi, Ms Grove!' Phil, the porter, squeezed his bulk through the narrow gap. 'Look what's turned up.' He tapped his thumb against the side of the cardboard box he carried. 'I reckon it's your new book.'

As the top of the box had been sealed with tape printed with the name of her publisher, it was not a difficult deduction to make.

'Thank you, Phil.' She pushed her bag onto her shoulder and held out her arms. 'That's so kind of you, but I can take it from here.'

'You think I'm going to let you lug *this* all the way up to your apartment? No way. You'd be doing me out of a job for a start.'

'Would you like a copy?'

'I have one on order, Ms Grove. Don't deprive me of the fun of it dropping through my letter box. I have my entire weekend planned around it.'

'Then I hope you enjoy reading it.'

'I always enjoy your books,' he said, with all sincerity.

It made her want to cry. 'Thank you,' she said. 'That's so kind of you to say so.'

There was a slightly awkward pause.

When the lift arrived at her floor, she held out her arms to take the box, but he breezed straight past her to wait outside her apartment.

She unlocked the door and waved him through.

'Where do you want them?' He indicated the nearest door, which was her study. 'In here?'

'That would be perfect.'

He pushed open the door with his elbow and dumped the box on her desk. 'Is there anything else I can do for you?'

'No, but thank you for your trouble.'

'You're welcome.' As he turned to leave, he glanced around the room, his attention snagging on the large oil painting displayed on the wall above her desk. The canvas was entirely filled by a lush magnolia tree, its falling blossoms almost hiding the laughing woman dancing amongst them, her slender arms outstretched as she tried to catch each whirling petal. 'Isn't that a Henry Vyne?'

'Yes.' She had several of his paintings scattered about the apartment. Most people were too polite to comment, but Phil was local, so he would know Sir Henry Vyne was famous for his paintings of—

'One of his "flower girls" series,' Phil said. 'You don't see many of those about nowadays. It's a shame.'

She hesitated, not willing to lie but unable to tell the truth.

'I bought it to remind me of someone,' she said, before the silence was a reply in itself.

The girl in the painting was Sarah. It was not there to *remind* (as if she could ever forget), but to motivate her into bringing Sarah's killer to justice.

His easy smile faded. 'I'm sorry for your loss.'

She nodded, unwilling to talk about it.

After he'd gone, Natalie turned her attention to the parcel. It had been sealed with tape. Too impatient to fetch scissors, she used her keys to slice through it.

Inside was a short note from her editor's assistant, which she put aside to read later. Beneath a layer of bubble wrap were twenty copies of her new novel. Beautiful glossy hardbacks. They even had that new book smell.

The cover design was similar to her previous novels – matt black, with one single bluebell picked out in silver. Natalie was so thrilled, she could have kissed it – and perhaps would have done if she hadn't heard voices.

Phil must have stopped to speak to someone on his way out. Was it Simon? Here to take her to the theatre already?

The key rattled in the lock at the same moment she realised the significance of the book in her hand. The book that Simon was completely unaware she'd written.

Oh, no...

Hurriedly, she shoved it back into the box, ripped away the tape emblazoned with the publisher's name and chucked it into the bin. There was no time to hide the box, and no place to hide it anyway, so she dropped a couple of files on top and hoped for the best.

She was pulling the study door closed as Simon entered the apartment.

He was wearing a dark-grey T-shirt, jeans and trainers. Even doing his best to appear the hip twenty-something he imagined himself to be, he still looked like the thirty-something drama teacher he actually was.

'Hi, Simon!' She leant forward and kissed him.

'You look guilty.' He smiled as she pulled away. 'What have you been up to?' Before she had chance to answer, he added, 'I suppose you've been at Rose Court, baiting your poor father?'

She stiffened. Despite confiding in him that the fear of her father and the disinterest of her mother had made her childhood hell, she still had the impression that, while Simon didn't quite believe she'd made it all up, he seemed to think she'd exaggerated.

'He knows something about Sarah's murder,' she said. 'I'm sure he does. I can't understand why he's kept quiet all these years.'

Simon's sigh bordered on exasperated. 'That makes no sense at all. You know your father idolised Sarah. He'd do anything to help find her killer. Are you sure you're not jealous?'

'*Jealous?*'

'I know you always felt Sarah was the favourite child, but you're going to have to let it go.' Simon checked his reflection in the mirror behind her, smoothing his auburn hair until it lay flat. 'You can't compete with a dead girl. We know the truth about Sarah, but, as far as John's concerned, Sarah was always the perfect daughter and now she's going to stay that way.'

The truth?

'What "truth" would that be?' Natalie enquired sharply.

He turned his attention from the mirror and gazed down at her, apparently surprised by the question. 'All those boyfriends and the way she played them off against each other.'

What was he *talking* about?

'Sarah was eighteen years old. She enjoyed going out and having fun. So what?'

'And ended up dead.'

He was implying it was *Sarah's* fault? What was *wrong* with him? All these years they'd been together and he'd never spoken about Sarah in this way before.

'That had nothing to do with her, but everything to do with the creep who murdered her!' Natalie scooped up her bag and would have headed for the door, but, with an unexpected creak, the door to her study swung open.

Simon now had an uninterrupted view of her desk. 'What's in the box?'

She couldn't believe her bad luck.

'What box?' she asked innocently.

He raised an eyebrow. 'The one on your desk?'

'Is it important?'

He stared at her in patent disbelief.

Evidently it was.

It was a bit too early to suggest it had something to do with Christmas, so she said, 'The box contains china. I ordered it online. It's a new dinner service, in white, with a blue border—'

He held up his hand to stop her talking, as though she was one of his students. 'Why isn't it in the kitchen?'

'Phil brought it up a couple of minutes ago. Maybe you passed him outside? I didn't want to make him hang about, so I asked him to put it on the first available surface. Which was' – she gestured in the direction of her study – 'my desk.'

'You let Phil into your study?'

That was a valid point. She never let anyone into her study, not even Simon.

'He carried that heavy box all the way up from the lobby. It seemed mean to make him take it to the other end of the apartment to put it in the kitchen.'

'You can't invite strangers into your home like that, Natalie. Anything could have happened.'

They both knew to which 'anything' he was referring.

'It was *Phil*.'

'You can't trust *anyone*.'

Maybe that was true – but was it any way to live?

She took a deep breath. 'Simon, I know you only want to protect me, but perhaps we need to get a few things straight? If I want to invite Phil into my apartment, I shall. If I want to order new china without your approval, I shall.'

'Natalie—'

'If you want to check it over, go ahead. Unpack it, if it's bothering you that much. It has to be washed before I can put it away, and right now I'm too busy. But if you want to go to the theatre and see this play, let's stop talking and leave before we miss it.'

She stepped around him and out through the main door to her apartment, which slammed, leaving her on the other side of it. A calculated risk or certain disaster? She jabbed the call button on the lift. Any other man would have fallen over the wretched box and not realised its significance.

Simon, damn him, saw everything.

Far below, she heard machinery whirr as the lift began its ascent. The illuminated numbers above her head counted up. She was tapping her foot on the tiled floor, faster and faster, without even realising she was doing it.

Where was he? Unpacking the box? What would he say when he saw her book?

Anyone who knew her would be able to work out that she'd based the story on her sister's murder. The similarities were there if one looked hard enough – switching water lilies with bluebells was no disguise at all. Her publisher had even made her sign a disclaimer, ensuring she took all responsibility should anyone instigate legal action.

Obviously, Simon would have to read the book sometime.

Preferably when she wasn't around to listen to his lecture about how stupid she was.

Why had she left him alone with the box?

She glanced back at her apartment. The door remained resolutely shut.

Damn.

She'd better go back inside and face him.

Natalie had just opened her bag, with the intention of retrieving her keys, when she heard her apartment door softly open and close, followed by the light, bouncy tread of someone wearing trainers. She let her bag drop to her side and pressed the lift call button once again, trying to keep her breathing even.

From the corner of her eye, she could see Simon as a smudge of grey against the white painted walls, but she didn't take her eyes from those illuminated numbers.

The silence stretched out.

'I can't believe you let Phil into your study,' he grumbled.

She hid her smile. 'Why not? If you took the trouble to talk to him, you'd realise he's a nice man.'

'You never let people into your study.'

Not *that* again. Why couldn't he let it go?

'Sure I do,' she said.

Just not you.

'You don't. You're quite eccentric about it. As for that magnolia painting, you've turned it into a freaky shrine to your sister. Phil must have thought you were very strange.'

Everyone thought she was strange, but that wasn't the point – and what did it matter anyway? It was her painting, her choice to display it – Phil hadn't even recognised the girl as Sarah. Most people didn't.

Most people had forgotten her.

The lift arrived and Natalie stepped inside, hardly bothering to check he'd followed before pressing the 'B'.

'You make me out to be some kind of obsessive,' she said.

She'd meant it as a joke, but his hand shot between the closing doors and held them apart long enough to step back into the lobby.

She watched in astonishment. 'Where are you going?'

'I'm taking the stairs,' he threw back. 'I can't deal with you when you're in this kind of mood. I'll go to the play on my own.'

'But—'

'There's no point arguing. We'll talk tomorrow when we've both calmed down.'

She thought she'd handled it pretty well, but, in any case, 'I'm going to London tomorrow!'

'Then we'll talk the day after that.' He strode off towards the stairs.

Natalie jumped out of the lift before the door swooshed shut.

'Maybe I don't want to talk!' she called after him.

He turned slowly. 'What's the matter with you today? Everything I say is wrong.'

'You're speaking to me in the same tone you use on your students.'

'Sometimes you act like one!'

'And why are we always going out? Occasionally I'd like to stay in.'

He flung out his arms, exasperated. 'And do what?'

He'd called her bluff.

'I don't know... Watch TV—'

Simon, damn him, was looking at his watch. 'If I don't leave now, the theatre will close the door and I won't be able to get in until the interval.'

'Fine,' she said, well aware she sounded like a sulky teenager. 'If you don't want to stay in with me, maybe I'll call Alicia and see if she'd like to come over.'

'You do that,' he said.

While she was aware Simon didn't like either Alicia or her husband, there was a distinctly malicious gleam in his eyes.

Why couldn't he just come out and *say* it?

But, OK, she'd bite. 'What are you not telling me?'

'I think it's more what Alicia is not telling *you*.'

'Simon!'

He held up his hands. 'Her mother is reopening Castle Vyne to the public.'

'*What?*'

'The walled garden is being restored – and that includes the lily ponds.'

Her chest tightened, making it hard to breathe. 'Lady Vyne can't do that...'

He shrugged. 'She already has. A new head gardener has moved into the Lodge and the garden will be open from Easter next year – to any ghoul who wants to see where your sister was murdered.'

FOUR

Fourteen years previously

John Grove's accident happened a month after Sarah's death. His car had gone over the cliff at Port Rell and fallen twenty metres onto a sandy beach. If it'd hit rock, he'd never have survived, but the soft sand acted as a cushion, leaving him paralysed from the waist down and with serious head injuries – but alive. This, as everyone had said at the time, was the important thing.

With her father incapacitated, Natalie thought she and her mother would have to find somewhere else to live. Instead, she came home from school one day and found Sir Henry Vyne sitting in the kitchen, talking closely with her mother and drinking coffee from her father's favourite mug.

For a man in his fifties, he was striking in appearance, having the red hair and pale blue eyes typical of all the Vyne family. He was also tall – a fact Natalie realised when, ever the gentleman, he got to his feet as she entered the kitchen.

'Little Natalie,' he smiled.

Natalie flicked her gaze between the two, recalling how

close Magda had been sitting to him, how he'd been sprawled in the chair as though he owned the place (which he did) and how her mother was back in her immaculate mask of make-up for the first time in days, if not weeks.

Oh no, it couldn't be?

Sir Henry *and her mother?*

'How are you coping, sweetheart?' Sir Henry patted Natalie on the shoulder.

'OK,' she muttered. How did he think she was coping? Her beloved sister was dead and no one seemed to be trying very hard to find out who'd killed her – no one even wanted to *talk* about her. It was as though she'd ceased to exist the moment she was murdered.

'Such a terrible tragedy,' he was saying. 'First your sister and now your father... You will let me know if it all becomes too much? I know of an excellent counsellor – a protégé of mine. I'm sure he'd be able to help.'

Nothing would bring her sister back, so what good would talking about her feelings do? She glanced towards her mother, expecting her to say something along those lines herself, but Magda's expression, as always, was a mask of disinterest.

Sir Henry was standing so close to her, Natalie could smell the faint mustiness of the castle on his clothes and the tobacco on his breath. She could see a pulled thread in the tweed coat he wore and the hint of ginger stubble on his chin.

Belatedly realising he was expecting a reply, she muttered, 'Thank you.'

He smiled benevolently, then turned his attention back to her mother. 'That's agreed then, Maggie? Things can carry on, with the same arrangement as before. Whatever you may have heard from Cla— er, to the contrary, the Lodge is yours for as long as you want it.'

He paused, as though expecting Magda to make some comment, or at least thank him. When neither was forthcoming, he took his coat from the back of the chair, winked at Natalie and left through the back door. Before it closed, a blast of cold air sent a swarm of dead leaves swirling into the kitchen.

Natalie took his place at the kitchen table. 'Does that mean we can stay here, Mum?'

A fresh start might be better for everyone but, realistically, where would they go? They had no income and she didn't believe for one moment that her parents had savings. They weren't those kind of people. Briefly, she wondered what had happened to the bundles of cash she'd found in Sarah's wardrobe. When she'd last checked, a few days ago, the box the money had been inside had vanished.

Magda's cold blue eyes remained fixed upon her daughter, as though seeing her for the first time. She was wearing one of Sarah's pink sweaters, as well as her jeans and, although she cradled a coffee mug in her hands, she didn't appear to have drunk from it.

Natalie tried again. 'Will Sir Henry keep Dad's job open?'

She knew this to be a stupid question as soon as she asked it. Her father was lying in a hospital, barely breathing unaided. How could he continue to work as a gardener? Even if he did regain consciousness, the doctor had said he'd remain in a wheelchair for the rest of his life. He'd need constant care and, if they weren't going to do it, they'd have to pay someone else.

This led Natalie to ask a second question with more urgency. 'Mum, what are we going to do about money?'

'I'll have to get a job and you' – her gaze raked Natalie from head to foot – 'you need to smarten yourself up. Sir Henry has requested you help him with some admin work. As the castle's open to the public, you'll have to dress accordingly.'

'Why me?' Whenever she'd visited the castle to see Alicia, he'd been hidden away in his studio. Occasionally, she'd glimpsed him in the garden, talking to her father. Obviously, he knew she existed, but beyond that? 'I hardly know him.'

'It seems as though you've made a good impression.' Her mother said the words as though she couldn't believe it either.

'What will I have to do?'

'Filing, I assume! Perhaps typing letters? How should I know? I'm sure he'll tell you what he wants. You should be grateful. He's offering you the work as a favour to me, because he knows we need the money.'

If that was true, why wasn't her mother happier about it? Something wasn't right.

'What about school?' Natalie asked.

'We're talking weekends, *obviously*.'

'It won't leave much time for study.'

Her mother crashed the mug onto the table, splashing coffee everywhere. Natalie hardly had time to grab a tea towel to soak up the mess when Magda forced her chair back from the table, slamming down both hands.

'For goodness' sake, girl! We're looking ruin in the face and all you care about is *schoolwork*? Step up and earn your keep or we'll be out on the street!'

Her mother yanked open the kitchen door and was gone.

If her mother returned that evening, Natalie didn't hear her. The following morning, Magda was back in the kitchen, as immaculately and unsuitably dressed as ever, in a red floral dress and high heels, sweeping the floor, filling the washing machine and doing the rest of the chores as though the past few weeks had never happened.

This time, Natalie kept her thoughts to herself.

It was how they got through the next two years.

No one was charged with Sarah's murder, mainly because the main suspect disappeared. All her belongings were packed neatly into boxes, along with the many photographs that had been scattered around the house. For a few months, the boxes remained heaped in her old bedroom, gathering a grey film of dust. Then they vanished.

Natalie went to work for Sir Henry, and her mother got a job at the local beauty salon and then another at the wine bar at the marina. Regardless of her frosty demeanour, Magda had no trouble attracting new admirers, which was perhaps why Sir Henry, despite agreeing to let them live at the Lodge rent-free, never visited again.

Nor did he employ another head gardener. After John was moved into long-term care, Sir Henry closed the castle grounds to the public and took up blasting the local wildlife to death instead. Shortly before Natalie left to go to university, he was dead too.

Natalie liked to think it was divine retribution for all those poor birds he'd shot, but the mundane reality had been some kind of accident while cleaning his gun. The baronetcy passed to his younger brother. The castle, the grounds and the little that remained of his personal fortune went to his wife, to be held in trust for his only child, Alicia.

FIVE

Present

Alicia Vyne Fitzpatrick always bought pink roses for Sarah's grave. Had they been her favourite? Alicia had no idea. They were a bright, cheery colour and they helped soften the sharp ache she'd felt in her heart since her best friend had died. Soften, but not erase completely.

The roses were beautiful against Sarah's white headstone. It was a shame no one ever saw them. Natalie could never bring herself to visit her sister's grave and, as far as Alicia was aware, neither did anyone else. Perhaps no one knew the grave was here, hidden away behind this little church, the stone engraved with only one word: *Sarah*.

Alicia had often wondered what Sarah would have been like if she'd lived. Would they have gone to university together and been bridesmaids at each other's weddings? Would they have remained friends? Sarah had been the kind of girl who'd have gone places and done amazing things. Alicia had the idea that both she and Calahurst were likely to have been left trailing in Sarah's wake years ago.

Dispirited, Alicia took this week's pink roses out of their wrapping and tried to arrange them in the little stone vase on Sarah's grave. Whatever she did, the roses looked as though they'd been plonked in. In the end, she gave up, checking that the marble chippings were free of weeds and picking up a stray cigarette butt that had fallen amongst them. Then she stepped back to say a prayer for the friend she'd lost forever, trying not to cry.

The fading sunlight warmed her back. Summer was clinging on, despite the leaves of the surrounding trees glinting gold. Alicia's children had been back at school for several weeks now and the nights were drawing in. A few more months and it would be Christmas.

As Alicia stood there with her eyes closed, an unexpected rustling broke into her thoughts. It sounded exactly as though someone was forcing a path through the long grass surrounding the graves. At first, she ignored it, assuming the noise was caused by a dog or local children, but as it drew closer, she was unable to concentrate on her prayer.

Her eyes flicked open to glare at the intruder – only to find an empty churchyard.

How... strange...

The churchyard boundary was marked by a low stone wall and enclosed on three sides by trees. Behind her were the little wooden lych-gate and the road that led into Calahurst village. To the right were the woods where the locals liked to walk their dogs. Directly ahead was another gate that led through the trees and up the hill towards the castle. On the left, separated from the churchyard by a straggly hedge, was The Old Rectory – a beautiful Georgian house where Alicia now lived with her husband, James, and their two children.

As the sun set, the churchyard had grown bright with a golden light and it was hard to see past the shadows of the ancient trees. The Civil War had been fought in these woods almost four hundred years ago and there were some who believed the ghosts of the soldiers still lingered.

Alicia, being a practical sort of person, didn't believe in ghosts.

Did she?

She remained still, but there was no sound of wildlife or traffic. The gate leading to the road hung open, but, as there was no wind, it remained motionless, so it couldn't have been that.

Was someone standing amongst the trees? Watching her?

She strode towards the little stone wall that marked the boundary. 'Hello? Is somebody in there?'

Was that a rustle of leaves or only her imagination?

A lingering scent of smoke? Had the castle gardeners lit a bonfire?

But who'd be out in the woods at twilight other than a local dog walker?

She turned away – just as a grey blur shot from beneath the canopy of trees, almost brushing the top of her head.

Alicia shrieked and ducked – before spotting a fat grey bird land on one of the gravestones.

Was *that* all it had been? A *pigeon*?

The bird preened itself, supremely unconcerned.

Grumbling beneath her breath, Alicia picked her way back through the long grass to the path. She didn't have time to stand around spooking herself. She was already late collecting her children from the after-school drama club.

It took a matter of minutes to reach the lych-gate, but, before she left, Alicia gave the churchyard one last look to reassure herself that there really was no one there, before stepping out onto the pavement and ensuring the gate was firmly closed behind her.

It was only after she walked the short distance along the pavement to The Old Rectory that she remembered.

She'd not been the one to leave the gate open…

SIX

Natalie drove away from her apartment at a speed that was excessive, even for her. As the marina diminished in her rearview mirror, she saw her own reflection, white-faced and angry. The BMW shot around the war memorial at the top of the hill, scarcely on two wheels. She hit the straight and accelerated. The stone gateway of Castle Vyne was ahead of her, closer with every second. As the car bumped over a pothole, she realised her fury was likely to cause an accident and slammed on the brakes. The BMW went into a short skid and ended up on the grass verge, perfectly parallel to the castle wall. She abandoned the car and walked through the huge stone gateway.

In the fading light, the Lodge resembled something imagined by Jacob and Wilhelm Grimm and was exactly as she remembered, but then a building of this age and history was never going to be allowed to rot. The only mystery was why it had taken Clare Vyne so long to save it from neglect.

The little wooden fence had been replaced and stretched the entire front of the garden. The grass had been cut, although it had the shaggy appearance of a meadow rather than a lawn.

The slabs of stone that led to the front door had been cleaned to remove decades of grime. She'd never seen them that pale before and, for the first time, made the connection with the ruined medieval chapel beside the castle. It was clear where the slabs had originated from.

Nudging open the gate with her foot, Natalie walked up the path. The two little windows tucked beneath the thatch followed her progress like malevolent eyes. As a child, this had given her the creeps. As an adult, it was hard to shake off the sensation that she was being watched.

The scent of fresh paint and brick dust lingered in the air. Up close, the diamond-paned windows gleamed and the brass letter box shone. She traced its outline with her finger, remembering when she'd thought it a mouth, ready to bite an unwary finger.

The flat-roofed porch, built by her father, had been demolished, but his trellis still framed the door. The climbing rose was long gone, but another could be planted in its place. She glanced up at the window to her old bedroom. Had it really been just twelve years since she'd left to go to college? She began to feel overwhelmed with memories. The night she'd climbed out of her window to go to the fair. The night she'd met Geraint Llewellyn. The night her sister had died. Everything had started here.

She still held her keys in her hand. Her car key, her apartment key and three older keys she could never bring herself to throw away. She slotted one of these into the lock and was disconcerted to find it fitted.

Quickly, she pulled the key out and slipped it into her pocket. What was she doing? Hoping to lay old ghosts? It wasn't going to happen. She took a step back. What had she been thinking? Her family no longer lived here. She'd have been breaking into someone's home!

Framed by the golden leaves of the autumn forest, the cottage became ordinary again – picture-book pretty, nothing sinister at all.

'I'm not coming back,' she said out loud. Then, with more force, 'I'm not coming back, do you hear me?' Feeling confidence surge through her, she let her feet take her across the castle drive and into the woods, following a familiar path through the trees.

She was not wearing the best footwear for an outdoor hike. The earth was soft but not muddy and gave way to rough-hewn cobblestones, then red bricks arranged in a herringbone pattern. At this point, she stopped watching her feet and looked up. Directly before her was a wrought-iron gate, set between two neatly clipped yew hedges. It was chained and padlocked.

Was she disappointed or relieved?

She pressed her face against the gate. It was cold against her skin, smaller than she remembered and freshly painted. The yew hedge on either side had been ruthlessly clipped back, revealing glimpses of weathered brick.

The 'secret' walled garden.

How long had it been since she'd stood here?

Beyond the gate was an expanse of lawn and several large trees, casting long dark shadows. In the distance was the glimmer of moonlight on water. Or was that only her imagination?

After years of neglect, surely the ponds would have to be drained, cleaned and repaired before they could be restocked and filled with water?

She felt disappointed and then angry. It was only a garden, what had she expected? That it would be frozen in time? That there would be people standing in huddles, some in uniforms, some in coveralls, all talking in whispers? That the terrace would be illuminated by the flashes of cameras? Did she think she'd see a young girl floating in the water, her eyes staring sightlessly at the sky?

Did she really believe she could go back in time to save Sarah?

Natalie's lashes were damp. She rubbed the back of her hand across her eyes and felt a cold breeze stroke the nape of her neck. Shivering, she stepped back from the gate. The heel of her boot caught on a loose brick and wobbled. Instinctively, she reached out to steady herself and caught a handful of yew. The sharp jab of pain brought her back to the real world. One of the twigs had nicked her skin and now it was bleeding. When she licked away the little ball of blood, another oozed into its place.

She sighed. It was time to go.

She took a different route back to her car. Trying to stumble along an overgrown woodland trail in the dark wouldn't be smart. So she continued along the path as it led up towards the castle. From here, she'd be able to walk through the garden and back to the drive. If she kept to the shadows, she wouldn't be seen. She didn't want to get into any kind of conversation about why she'd revisited the place where her sister had been murdered.

Lights were beginning to pop on all over the castle. Alicia's mother, Lady Vyne, was working at her laptop, her slim silhouette easily identifiable in the huge window of the library. She had paused to chat to her assistant, Rob. No, not chat; the conversation was too intense for that. He rested one hand on her shoulder as he leant towards her, their lips only centimetres apart.

Natalie quickly turned away. The sun had set and it was too cold to hang around. She turned right, taking the garden path between a grove of ancient yews. These grew so thickly, the branches drawing together above her head made it seem darker.

Directly ahead was the chapel. Only two walls of it remained – red brick on the inside, pale stone for the exterior.

'Reimagined' in Victorian times as a folly, her father had helped the illusion by planting shrubs and flowers amongst the fallen stones. Now there was no floor, only earth and grass, and one remaining window, which gave a fine view of the castle.

Natalie stopped, peering through the darkness.

A man stood on the other side of the chapel, directly in its shadow. His hair was dark and so were his clothes.

Who was *he*? The Vyne family had always been happy to let the villagers walk all over the estate, provided their privacy was not compromised, but it was too late to be taking a walk and there was no evidence of a dog. There was also something in the way he stared impassively at the castle that made Natalie think it would be better for her if he didn't know she was here.

She took a step backwards, intending to disappear into the woods, but, as her foot made contact with the ground, a distinct crack disturbed the silence.

The only twig in the vicinity and she'd trodden on it.

Cliché or not, the man glanced back through the chapel window.

'Who's there?' he said.

Natalie took another couple of steps back and made such a racket with her boots scuffing up the loose stones on the path that she gave up trying to be quiet and hit the woodland track running.

'Hey, come back!'

Surely he wasn't serious?

She sprinted through the yew grove and down the path towards the walled garden, slipping and sliding all the way. Her boots were low-heeled but not designed for woodland rambles. He was close behind, cursing at the uneven ground. And that was another thing. If his intentions had been honourable, would he risk frightening her by chasing after her?

Once past the walled garden, the path levelled off and she caught glimpses of white lights through the trees as the street lamps flickered on one by one. The path grew narrower, brambles catching at her clothes.

He was drawing closer. Soon he'd be able to reach out and—

Suddenly, her feet were running over tarmac, past the old Lodge and through the stone arch of the castle gate. Her car was in front of her, parked on the grass verge, exactly where she'd left it. She thrust her hand in her pocket for her keys. There was a brief moment of panic when she failed to locate them, then their cold metal dug into her fingers and she dragged them out, squeezing hard on the fob for her car until she heard the reassuring click of the central locking disengage.

As her fingers closed over the door handle, she risked glancing back – and saw him fall out through the undergrowth and onto the castle drive, in much the same way as she'd done a moment earlier. He straightened, checking to see which direction she'd taken, and then saw her standing on the grass beside her car. As she watched, too terrified to move, his expression changed to one of shock. Then he said something – a word that she didn't quite catch – and held out his hand.

It was all the motivation she needed. She wrenched at the handle and almost fell into the car, locking the door as soon as it shut.

Her relief vanished the moment his hand slammed against the side window.

Horrified, she watched his palm slide down the glass before she heard the door handle rattle.

Why was she still here? What if next time it wasn't his hand but a rock?

Starting the car caused him to thump on the window again. Although it drowned out his voice, she saw his lips forming the word 'please'.

'Please' what? 'Please open the door'? As though that was going to happen!

She slid the car into gear, released the handbrake and put

her foot on the accelerator. The tyres skidded briefly, got a grip and the car shot across the grass, causing him to jump out of the way. She barely had time to jerk the steering wheel around to avoid a collision with one side of the castle gate, before the car swung around the drive and bumped back onto the road heading towards Calahurst.

Hardly daring to believe she'd got away, she glanced in her rear-view mirror. She could see him plainly in the light from the street lamp, standing beside the castle gate, staring after her.

It was only then she realised what he'd said when he'd seen her.

'Sarah.'

Natalie pulled into the basement car park of her apartment block, half-expecting to see another car draw up behind her. Had it really happened? Her hands still trembling, she took her phone from her bag and kept hold of it as she went up in the lift, in case she needed to call the police.

She didn't relax until she'd closed her door and made a mug of strong coffee.

After which she switched on her laptop and did something she'd never thought of doing before. She typed 'Geraint Llewellyn' into a search engine.

There were several pages of entries. It appeared Geraint shared his name with an opera singer, a couple of rugby players and several random Welshmen. Further down the page, other familiar names began to appear: Calahurst. Castle Vyne. Sarah Grove.

It was a shock to see her sister's name on screen. What should she do? Click on a site or let the past stay buried?

She moved the cursor across the screen, hovering over a couple of entries before picking one.

The screen went black.

Natalie put down her cup and leant forward. Had her laptop crashed?

The screen flashed, torn apart by a jagged streak of lightning. Great – cheesy special effects. Natalie stabbed the back button.

The second site was also dedicated to true crime but more clinical, with facts that were well-researched and mostly accurate. She scrolled through the menu. Sarah was listed under 'S' and subtitled 'the girl in the lily pond'.

The link took her to another page, with Sarah's picture at the top. It was a school photograph, released to the press at the time of the murder. With her white-blonde hair, Sarah appeared vaguely other-worldly. There were more pictures too, of Castle Vyne and the famous garden. These were slightly blurry and amateurish. Presumably the author had taken them himself.

The photograph of the castle showed the south wall burning with scarlet Virginia creeper, so it must have been taken in the autumn. The photograph of the lily pond had no lilies in it and the water was mud-coloured and only a few centimetres deep. *That* picture had been taken more recently. The photographer would have had to climb over the padlocked gate to get it.

Right at the bottom of the screen was another picture, but a drawing, not a photograph. It was a sketch done by a police artist of a man in his early twenties, with overlong dark hair, light brown skin and a direct gaze. It was not accurate. Natalie could have given a better description, but no one had thought to ask her.

That knot of fear returned to twist her stomach. It wasn't credible. There had been a massive manhunt, a search of every fairground in the UK, every port checked and his picture circulated throughout Europe. For fourteen years there had been nothing – no trail of evidence, no positive sightings – it was as though he'd vanished into another dimension. Yet tonight she'd seen him standing in the castle grounds as though nothing had happened.

Geraint Llewellyn.

Her sister's murderer had returned to Calahurst.

SEVEN

Fourteen years previously

Why should Sarah have all the fun?

Natalie waited for her sister to disappear into the darkness before climbing onto her bedroom windowsill. From there, it was a matter of slipping through the window and onto the flat roof of the porch beyond. Her father had planted climbing roses up a trellis, but there was no time for an elegant descent. Swinging her legs over the edge, she lowered herself into the garden, ran down the path and hurdled the gate rather than wasting time opening it.

There was a long line of traffic on the road to the village and a steady stream of people walking along the pavement. Natalie quickened her pace, pulling up the hood on her cardigan in case her sister should glance back and see her, but Sarah and her boyfriend were lost in a world of their own. His arm was curved around Sarah's waist and his hand tucked into the back pocket of her jeans. From the back, all Natalie could see of him was that he was tall and had dark hair cut short.

Outside the village, a police officer was stopping traffic to allow pedestrians to cross over to the field where the funfair had been set up. There was only one entrance – a narrow muddy path leading across a ditch and through an open gate, with a long queue of people waiting to get in.

Natalie dropped back to allow Sarah and her boyfriend to go through and then attempted to sneak to the front of the queue, counting on her age and lack of height to let her pass unnoticed. It didn't work. She was unceremoniously shoved to the back. By the time she'd passed through the gap in the hedge and elbowed her way out of the crowd, Sarah had gone.

The fair was crammed with people jostling to be first in the queues for the rides. There were plenty to choose from: traditional fairground rides such as dodgems and the waltzers, and other rides she didn't recognise with names like 'The Destructor' and 'Afterburner' – the kind of rides where you had to be strapped in before being flung around. They had the longest queues.

Waiting in line for The Destructor were some of the kids from school. Natalie paused to watch them laugh and joke around, moving quickly away before they saw 'poor little Nat'.

The Destructor was the last significant ride. As the crowds thinned, Natalie could still hear the repetitive bass of its music, but this part of the field was dark and silent. There was one last ride, completely deserted, painted grey and almost indistinguishable from the shadows. She walked to the front, stepping carefully over thick electric cables snaking through the grass. The paintwork was peeling, but its lights flickered defiantly against the dark.

'Hello, *cariad*.'

Natalie jumped.

Behind the glass window of a paybox was a teenage boy, not much older than her. His black T-shirt (emblazoned with the name of some indie band she'd never heard of) helped him blend into the dark.

She pushed back her hood. 'Hi, can you help me? I'm trying to find my sister.'

He shrugged. 'I've not seen a soul. No one comes out this far.'

What was that accent? Scottish? Irish?

'Thanks, anyway.' She flipped up her hood and would have walked away – she *should* have walked away – if he hadn't said:

'Aren't you going to have a go on the ride?'

It was the last thing she wanted to do. The ride was old-fashioned, rickety and seriously cheesy. Was it supposed to be a gothic castle? The entrance resembled a portcullis, complete with fake spikes hovering over a narrow track.

A *track*?

Of course... It was a ghost train!

Kind of appropriate that they'd stuck it out here in the dark.

'What do you think?' he asked.

'Sorry, not my thing.'

He grinned. 'Too scary for you, huh?'

How young did he think she was?

She fixed her eyes on his, in case he was in any doubt of her sincerity. 'It's a kid's train,' she told him. 'It goes around in the dark and stuff comes out at you. Vampires, ghosts – skeletons too, I expect – all made out of plastic and papier mâché. I bet there are even rubber bats and fake cobwebs strung up from the ceiling. Am I right?'

'You can believe that if you want to,' he shrugged. 'If it makes you feel safe.'

She rolled her eyes. There were two carriages waiting on the tracks and she could hear others rattling around inside, accompanied by the ubiquitous screams. The carriages appeared uncomfortably small and roughly painted, built to resemble giant skulls. Apart from the metal platform, the whole thing was nothing more than huge sections of plywood bolted together, designed to be flat-packed onto a lorry.

Still, *he* was kind of cute...

Maybe it wouldn't hurt to flirt a little?

She walked up to the paybox and leant on the counter. Now they were centimetres apart, with only the glass between them, she could see him more clearly. His eyes were a curious light green with dark shadows beneath them, but he was older than she'd thought. Not a boy of her own age, but an adult. Could he be twenty? Twenty-one? Those four or five extra years meant he was too old for her. Her father would have a heart attack.

'OK, I'll take a ticket, but only if you come with me.'

There was a flash of interest behind those cool eyes. 'Who'd start the ride?'

'The ghost?' she suggested.

His chuckle was low and flirtatious. 'I thought you didn't believe in ghosts?'

The doors to the ride crashed open, making them both start, and two carriages rumbled through to join the others at the back of the queue. The occupants jumped down, hardly before the ride had stopped, and ran laughing into the night.

'Do you want a beer?' he asked, in a rather more matter-of-fact tone.

'What?'

'Or a coffee?' He reached behind him and flicked a switch. The ride was plunged into darkness. 'It's bloody cold tonight.'

'Um, sure,' she said. This wasn't going in quite the way she'd expected but, 'OK...'

He closed the paybox and locked it, leading her across the grass to a line of caravans parked beside the hawthorn hedge. A few had lights in their windows and some of the residents were sitting outside. They didn't give Natalie a second glance.

He led her towards a small, scruffy caravan at the end of the line.

There were no lights on.

They'd be alone.

This was *such* a bad idea.

'Is this where you live?' she asked.

'It sure is.' He leant past to unlock the door. 'Home sweet home.'

Was he being ironic? She couldn't tell.

As the door swung open, she caught a whiff of stale air, cigarettes and beer. There was a split second while she reconsidered her options, but, even though common sense was telling her to walk away, she still went up the steps.

On the inside, the caravan was functional but extremely cramped. The door led directly onto a small seating area with a table and an equally tiny kitchen. Every available surface (and there weren't many) was littered with clothes, empty drinks cans and what looked like the remains of beans on toast on two plates. Wedged beneath one of the benches, half hidden by an old blanket, was a motley collection of mobile phones.

He took off his money belt (which hardly made a sound as he dropped it onto the counter) and pushed the clutter from one of the benches. Flipping the blanket over the junk stored beneath it, he gestured for her to sit down.

'I'll put the kettle on,' he said. 'Or would you prefer a beer?'

He hadn't realised she was only sixteen, but Natalie thought she'd better stay sober all the same. This was one of those occasions where she'd need all her wits about her.

So why was she here? For a pair of pretty green eyes?

'Could I have a coffee, please?' she said.

One drink, and then she'd go.

'Sure, take a seat.' He squeezed between the junk and went into the kitchen.

Natalie sat on the bench, crashing her knee against the table as she did so. This caravan was *tiny*.

While the kettle boiled, he told her his name was Geraint Llewellyn and proceeded to make small talk about the fair.

Again, *not* what she'd expected. She nodded to be polite, but her insides were churning. What was she *doing*? Her father would kill her if he knew she'd gone to the home of a strange man.

He returned to the table with two mugs but sat opposite her. She relaxed a little, taking one of the mugs. The coffee was scalding, so she put it back on the table and searched around for something to say.

'Do you share this caravan with your girlfriend?'

A flicker of amusement showed in those green eyes. 'I live with my cousin.'

'Your female cousin?'

One corner of his mouth quirked up. 'No, Bryn's definitely a guy.'

What was so funny?

'He works here too?'

'We all do. It's a family business.'

'That's so cool. I'd love to work at a funfair. Be paid to play on rides all day? Bliss!'

His smile promptly vanished. 'It's not all rides and candyfloss.'

'Oh... Don't you enjoy it?'

'It's hard work in all weathers for very little cash.'

'Then why do it?'

His expression turned incredulous, but he checked what he'd been about to say and said, somewhat stiffly, 'It's not the sort of job I would have picked if I'd had the opportunity to choose. This is my uncle's business and, while he loves it, I...'

As though he'd said too much, Geraint shrugged and took a drink from his mug.

'OK... So what would you do, if you could do anything?'

'Why angst about it? You have to take what life chucks at you and make the best of it. There's no point dreaming for something else. That's a loser's game.'

She didn't understand what he was getting at, but, growing up in her family, she'd learnt never to push it. She reached for her mug, taking it in both hands, deliberately mirroring his position. It was one of Sarah's tricks.

Natalie could feel the heat of the coffee warm her hands. His, slightly oil-stained, were only centimetres from hers. Did she dare reach out and brush her fingers against them?

What would Sarah do?

Flirt shamelessly – as she did with everyone, male or female, whatever their age.

To Sarah, it came naturally.

But for Natalie...

She glanced at Geraint from beneath her lashes, only to realise his attention was fully on her. That was a good sign, yes? Except... his expression didn't seem right and the corner of his mouth had twitched up again, even though she'd not said anything funny.

Was he *laughing* at her? What had she done wrong?

The door crashed open, accompanied by a furious, 'What the hell's going on?'

It was impressive timing, to say the least.

'Sarah...'

Her sister had the same white-blonde hair, but her eyes were the deep blue of a Mediterranean sky compared to Natalie's colourless grey. Sarah's nose was straight, rather than tilted towards the heavens, and her lips were full. She didn't need to wear layer upon layer of carefully applied make-up to look pretty. Sarah just was.

She's the original, Natalie thought sadly. *I'm only the copy*.

For some reason, Sarah was scowling at Geraint. 'Sorry to spoil your romantic interlude,' she said, 'but you do know she's only sixteen?'

'*Sixteen?*' Even in the gloom of the caravan, there was no

mistaking his horror. 'I knew she was young but—' He looked at Natalie. 'Sixteen? *Really?*'

'Why does everyone make such a big deal about it?'

'Because I would never have invited a sixteen-year-old—' He broke off, looking from Natalie to Sarah and back again. 'This is your sister, right?' he asked Natalie. 'The one you were searching for?'

'Not searching particularly hard, obviously,' her sister said.

'*Sarah!*'

Her sister's gaze softened, but only for a moment. 'I'll deal with *you* later.'

'We were only drinking coffee,' Geraint said, his expression serious. 'Nothing happened. I knew something wasn't right from the way she was behaving, but I assumed she was at least eighteen.'

Sarah glared at him. 'Then you're an idiot. I suppose you followed me?' she added to Natalie.

Natalie nodded miserably. This had to be the most humiliating night of her life.

'What the hell were you *thinking*? Do you know what Dad will do if he catches you out at night? If he catches you *here*, with *him?*'

'*Excuse* me?' Geraint said. 'I'm sitting right here – and we were only drinking *coffee.*'

'Shut up.' Sarah didn't even look at him. 'I was talking to my *sister.*'

The stale air in the caravan seemed to be making it difficult to breathe.

Natalie shook her head, unable to form a reply.

'I'll take her home,' Geraint said calmly.

'I think *you've* done enough,' Sarah snapped, and then her gaze fell on the box of phones, stuffed beneath the couch, and her mouth tightened. 'Besides, Alicia can do that.'

For the first time, Natalie noticed another girl standing

halfway up the caravan steps. She had stunning red curls, although the effect had been ruined by a black sequinned beanie jammed over her head. In contrast to the tight clothes favoured by Sarah and Natalie, Alicia's attire could only be described as 'comfy' – slouchy jeans and a sweater that stretched to her knees. She was staring round the scruffy caravan with awe, as though she'd fallen down a rabbit hole into Wonderland.

'Alicia?' Sarah repeated testily.

Alicia turned her head. Her long curls took a moment to catch up. 'What?'

'Remember that you said you felt sick and wanted to go home?'

'Oh, I feel fine now, thanks! I expect it was that last ride on Afterburner. I shouldn't have had the candyfloss first. Or the hotdog. Or maybe it *was* the hotdog—'

Sarah raised an eyebrow and Alicia had a visible light-bulb moment and nodded, curls bouncing.

'Oh yes, very sick, possibly food poisoning. I'm on my way home right now. Would you like to come with me, Natalie?'

Natalie hesitated.

'Off you go, sweetheart,' Sarah said cheerfully, and Natalie was propelled down the caravan steps before she'd quite realised what was happening.

Alicia set off across the field in long strides.

Natalie glanced back, hoping Geraint would accompany her, only to see Sarah blocking the door to the caravan.

'Aren't you coming too?' Natalie asked her.

'Not yet. I have a proposition I'd like to discuss with your new friend.'

'So why should *I* go home?'

Sarah came down the steps and put her arm around Natalie's shoulders. Drawing her away from the light spilling through the caravan door, she said, in a low voice, 'Please, Nat, do it for me?'

Now it was Geraint leaning against the door of the caravan, arms folded, scowling.

'But I *like* him,' Natalie whispered. 'He's really cute.'

'Oh, sweetheart... He's easily in his twenties. Far too old for you!'

'But perfect for you?' She pulled herself out of Sarah's embrace. 'You want him for yourself!'

Sarah rolled her eyes. 'You know that's not true. Now *please* go home, before you get us both into trouble.'

'OK, but can you give him our phone number?'

'*Natalie*! Go home!'

'Not until you tell me what this is about.'

Sarah sighed. 'Trust me when I say I'm in real trouble, OK? The very worst.'

'You're not *pregnant*?'

'Thankfully not!' Gently, Sarah turned her away from the caravan. 'Go home with Alicia. She'll look after you. Don't worry about me. I'll be fine. Because I suspect your new friend is *exactly* the sort of person who'll be able to help me.'

EIGHT

Present

Alicia's father had given her The Old Rectory on her marriage to James Fitzpatrick. No one had much faith in the longevity of their marriage, least of all Sir Henry Vyne, because he arranged that the house should be in her name only. On her death, it would revert to whichever child (or children) didn't inherit the castle. 'A consolation prize,' he'd joked at the time.

Predictably, James hadn't thought this funny. 'Another bloody entail,' had been his only comment, but then, he was the youngest of three, with no prospect of inheriting anything.

Whatever James's feelings on the gift, they couldn't afford to turn it down. The Old Rectory was a beautiful, six-bedroomed Georgian manor house set in a large, sprawling garden. The alternative would have been to stay in the tiny apartment they'd been renting in Norchester.

They'd been eighteen when they'd married and both still at college. The gift of the house meant James could continue his teacher training and not have to worry about rent or mortgage payments. Once Lexi and Will came into their lives, Alicia stayed home to look after them and research the history of the castle.

Obsessed by painting, her father had never been much interested in the castle, only as a backdrop to his art. Alicia was surprised at how much she enjoyed the work. Every morning she'd get up early while it was still quiet, sneak downstairs and write up the previous day's research. Once the children were safely at school, she'd continue working in the local archives until it was time to collect them.

Hearing James coming down the stairs was usually her signal to start cooking breakfast, but today it was the sound of the doorbell.

Ensuring her dressing gown was securely belted, Alicia opened the front door. On the other side was a delivery man and on the ground by his feet was a large cardboard box with a picture of a floral arrangement on it.

'Sign here,' the delivery man said.

Alicia dutifully signed and took the box from him, closing the door with her foot. Attached to the box was a small envelope with a card inside. It was hard to read in the murkiness of the hall, but then James appeared and switched on the overhead light.

'"*Sorry! Love, Nat*",' he read over her shoulder. 'What's Natalie got to be sorry about?'

'I dread to think.' Alicia placed the card back on top of the box. 'Are you leaving now? You haven't had your breakfast.'

James, distracted by his reflection in the hall mirror, grimaced and quickly straightened his tie. He looked more like a banker than the head teacher of the local school, but she knew that wearing a suit helped with his confidence.

'No.' He tugged a newspaper from the letter box and held it up. 'I came to see what had happened to this.'

James was the only person she knew who still received his news the old-fashioned way.

She took the flowers into the kitchen and left them on the counter until she had the time to unpack them. Lexi and Will had helped themselves to breakfast. For once they weren't arguing, but that was because they were watching TV. As James returned to his seat, he picked up the remote and began flicking through the channels.

Will glanced up, his freckled face scowling. 'We were watching that!'

'My house, my TV,' James said. It was a regular argument. James believed television rotted children's minds.

Alicia blamed his parents.

Opening the newspaper, James turned automatically to the sports pages.

'You're not even looking at it!' Will pointed out.

Lexi (who always felt rules never applied to her) surreptitiously picked up the remote and tried to flick back to the channel they'd been watching. In error, she ended up on one of the lifestyle programmes. Before she could try again, James had swiped back the remote.

'I don't want cartoons playing while I'm trying to read.'

'You could read in the study?' Lexi suggested.

Her daughter had a point, Alicia thought, but, at thirteen, she'd developed a worrying tendency to argue with everything her parents said.

That was something those parenting manuals never warned you about: your child thinking you were an idiot.

'No, I couldn't,' James argued – and good luck to him. It was practically impossible to win an argument with Lexi. 'It's important for us to sit together at mealtimes. Sometimes it's the only chance we have to catch up on any news, talk about our achievements—'

'But we *don't* talk!' Lexi said. 'You read the paper, we watch the TV, and no one talks about anything.'

'All right, so let's talk.' James brought the remote back to table level and hit the off button. As Will was sitting between the remote and TV, nothing happened. James was about to try again when Will let out an excited shriek.

'It's Natalie! On TV!'

The kitchen TV was small, the screen needed dusting and Will's ginger head obstructed a lot of the view, but after his sister had shoved him out of the way, sure enough there was Natalie, her usual insouciant self.

'You didn't tell me Natalie was going to be on TV,' James said to Alicia.

'I didn't know. Perhaps she didn't think it was important?'

'What programme is this?'

'Prime Cuts on CLTV,' Alicia said, rather too quickly. 'Every morning Ella Carmichael reviews new books, music and films released during the week.' And once Alicia's family had left the house, she often liked to watch it. She could hardly admit that to James though. Not when she made a big fuss about how important her research was.

James frowned. 'Natalie's got a new book out? I didn't know that.'

'Me neither. I knew she was working on something, but she never tells me—'

Alicia was interrupted by a horrific screech as Will scraped his chair closer to the TV. 'I can't hear!' he protested.

James racked up the volume as the camera flipped to the TV presenter, who was holding a book at the camera.

Four heads craned forward to read the title.

Like all of Natalie's books, the cover was black and had her name and the title, *Obsession*, picked out in silver. Beneath was a simple etching of a flower. Was it a bluebell?

Alicia had a horrible sense of foreboding.

The TV presenter, Ella, was still talking, although she'd put the book down on a small coffee table beside the lurid pink sofa she and Natalie were sitting on.

'You must get tired of people asking you this question, but do you ever base the plots of your books on what happened to your family?' Ella asked. 'I'm speaking, of course, of the tragic death of your sister, who was murdered at the age of eighteen.'

Alicia held her breath. How would Natalie react to that?

She needn't have worried. Her friend hardly paused before answering, 'I never grow tired of talking about my sister. I adored her and I was devastated when she was killed. However, my books are complete fiction.'

Hmm, Alicia thought. She'd often recognised scenes from their childhood recycled into Natalie's work.

'Have you ever thought about writing a biography of your sister's life?' Ella asked.

'My speciality is fiction,' Natalie repeated politely. 'So I'd hardly know how to go about it.'

'You must have been only a child at the time of Sarah's death?'

'I'd just turned sixteen.'

'So much of what happened would have been kept from you?'

'Children understand a lot more than adults give them credit for. I was always aware of what was being said and what was going on. Adults would talk in front of me and think I wouldn't grasp what they were saying. But I did.'

'You were the one who found her body?'

'Yes.'

'How did that make you feel?'

Even beneath the TV make-up, Alicia could see Natalie's skin blanch. How did they *think* it made her feel?

The silence stretched on. Ella made no attempt to fill it, waiting patiently until Natalie had to either answer or tactfully evade the question.

'Everything I've done, the person I've become, has been influenced by my sister's death,' she said at last. 'It's tainted my entire life and I admit I've become obsessed with discovering the truth about what happened that night.'

Hence the title of the book.

Oh, dear...

'Sarah's killer was never found?' Ella asked.

'No,' Natalie replied.

'There was extensive press coverage at the time. The police issued a warrant for the arrest of a fairground worker named Geraint Llewellyn. Did you ever meet him?'

'No, he was Sarah's friend, not mine.'

Alicia frowned. It was such a long time ago, but she was sure she remembered—

'You must really miss her,' Ella said.

'She meant everything to me,' Natalie told her. 'She was a typical big sister. One minute moaning at me for borrowing her clothes; the next, taking my side in an argument. That's the very worst thing, having to live my life without her.'

'I can't imagine what you went through, at such a young age too. How on earth did you cope?'

There was only the slightest hesitation before Natalie said, 'I saw a bereavement counsellor for a time, but there comes a point when you have to get on with your life. I have bad days, but, when I become really down, I like to re-read her diary. It feels as though she's talking directly to me. I find it soothing.'

Diary? What diary?

'What did Sarah write about in this diary?'

'The usual things: school, clothes, music, parties—'

'Did she talk about her friends?'

'Yes, Sarah was very popular.'

'Did she have any boyfriends?'

'Of course,' Natalie said. 'My sister was stunning.'

'Was Geraint Llewellyn her boyfriend?'

'No.'

'Did she ever mention him in the diary?'

Alicia shifted in her seat, uncomfortable with the direction the interview was taking. This was more of an interrogation than a friendly chat about a book.

'No,' Natalie said, after a slight pause. Her fingers were twisting together on her lap but otherwise she seemed completely calm.

'Could one of these other boyfriends have killed your sister?' Ella asked.

'The police did interview everyone at the time...'

'Does Sarah mention the names of these boyfriends in her diary?'

'Not really. It's typical teenage girl stuff. You know, "I saw 'J' at school today, he asked me out again". That kind of thing.'

'No names then?'

'Only initials or silly nicknames, like "the doctor" or "the teacher".'

'Your sister dated a *teacher*?'

Oh, hell!

Alicia seized the remote and hit the off switch. 'Time for school, kids!' she said brightly.

James stared at the blank screen as though in some kind of trance. 'I can't believe Natalie said that.'

'Perhaps we could discuss it later?' Alicia nodded in the direction of the children. Will, bored, was drawing faces with his egg yolk, but Lexi, like her father, had become completely absorbed in the interview. 'Kids, could you please get ready for school?'

Muttering beneath their breath, Lexi and Will removed themselves from the table.

'What's this about a diary?' James said. 'Isn't it evidence? Shouldn't the police have it?'

'This is the first time I've ever heard Natalie mention a diary. I didn't even know Sarah *kept* a diary and I was her best friend.'

He frowned. 'I remember Natalie saying something about a diary, a long time ago.'

Alicia wanted to scream. Why couldn't he let it go?

'I'll check with her later, if you like?' Wary that the children might be in the hall and able to overhear any conversation, she added, 'You and I can discuss this *tonight*.'

'Sarah went to Calahurst Community School. If she dated a teacher, it could be one of ours.'

'This was fourteen years ago.'

'Some of the staff have actually been there that long.'

'If it was significant, the police would have acted on it. I expect she felt obliged to mention it to drum up publicity for the new book. You know how that works.'

'If that's true, she's playing a dangerous game. Once the local press get wind of this, they're going to be camped outside the school, and then it'll be picked up by the nationals, not to mention the internet.'

'This diary might not even exist!'

'You think anyone will care about that?'

Too late, Alicia realised she should have agreed with him. Now he had the idea in his head, he fully intended to run with it.

'Natalie has accused a teacher of dating her sister and possibly murdering her too. Weren't you listening to what she was saying? The parents are going to be in uproar. Sarah went to our school. Some of the teachers were there in her day. It could be one of them. Hell, people might even think it's me! It's a public relations disaster.'

'No one's going to believe she was talking about *you*! You were eighteen when Sarah died. "Teacher" in this context could easily mean a boy with spectacles or someone who helped her with her coursework.'

'Do you imagine anyone is going to be concerned with technicalities? I thought Natalie was your friend? Why would she do this to us?'

'I don't think it was deliberate. You know how she loves to talk about Sarah.'

'For goodness' sake, Alicia! Stop thinking the best of people! Natalie sent you flowers with a note that says "Sorry" on the very morning she announces this on TV? She's thrown me under a bus – and not only me. Think about it. Who else teaches at that school? Who else was there, fourteen years ago?'

'*Simon*? But he's Natalie's boyfriend! Who on earth would believe—'

'Everyone! As far as the world's concerned, Sarah's murderer could be any one of her friends.'

NINE

Prime Cuts had gone to an ad break. The programme had another twenty minutes to run, but Natalie was no longer required. As she exited the TV studios, Siân Williams, her publicist, was waiting for her.

'You were terrific,' Siân said predictably. She was a tiny brunette with long glossy hair and a habitual frown. As though determined not to be overlooked in favour of her famous clients, she wore bright colours and ostentatious shoes, which, although adding several centimetres to her height, still didn't bring her much above five foot.

Natalie slipped on her coat, realising her fingers were still trembling, and said, 'Thank you. You're very kind.'

Siân's fragile, elfin appearance belied her frightening efficiency. 'The car is waiting outside,' she said. 'We have the bookstore appearance next and then I thought we could break for lunch. Is there anywhere in particular you'd like to eat? I didn't book anything in case you had a preference. Thai? Italian?'

'You choose.'

Siân consulted her phone. 'This afternoon we have a couple more bookstore visits, just to sign stock, followed by a radio interview, followed by dinner with Julia and the MD. Tomorrow morning we're hoping for a spot on breakfast TV, but we're waiting for confirmation.' She paused, tapping out a rhythm on the screen. 'We've other interviews lined up, but they can be done online. Some of the bigger publications may want to send a journalist to your home with a photographer. Or to a hotel, if you prefer?'

That meant *more* questions about Sarah's murder.

No one ever wanted to talk about what Sarah had been like as a person, only the horrible way in which she'd died.

I just want to go home...

The grey autumnal day didn't help. It was beginning to rain, big fat drops splashing onto a dusty pavement.

Siân took something from her bag, flicked her wrist and, like magic, a scarlet umbrella opened above Natalie's head as their car pulled up.

Siân took her arm and hustled her into the car, before sliding into the front seat.

The early start was catching up with Natalie.

In front, Siân was arguing with the driver over the quickest route to the first bookstore. Natalie closed her eyes and let them get on with it.

Let the performance begin.

The rest of the morning went well. Even Siân began to relax. The staff at the bookstore they visited appeared genuinely pleased to see her. Natalie was given a good table at the front for the signing, and the store was well-stocked with copies of *Obsession*, as well as her backlist. Her readers were happy to wait their turn for the chance to exchange a few words and take a photo. They seemed to accept the book at face value, assuming it was another Natalie Grove thriller rather than anything more personal. She didn't know whether to feel relieved or cheated in some way – but did she really want to discuss Sarah with strangers, however kind-hearted?

They stopped for lunch at a pub. It was down a side street, away from the chaos of the tourists, which she assumed was Siân's criteria for choosing it. The seating had been divided into a series of wooden booths and the jukebox played classic rock. A solitary barman was reading a book, which he slipped beneath the counter as they approached.

'What can I get for you ladies?'

Siân asked for a glass of wine.

Natalie settled for an orange juice, deciding it wouldn't be a good idea to drink alcohol before appearing on national radio, and suggested they took the booth closest to the window.

As they sat down, Siân's frown reappeared, creating a distinct crease between her eyes. When she picked up a menu, Natalie saw her hand was shaking.

She was about to ask if everything was all right, when Siân carefully replaced the menu and said, 'There's someone here who'd like to meet you. Is that OK?'

As Siân was usually the consummate professional, Natalie didn't feel she could refuse.

Taking her silence as acquiescence, Siân slid out from behind the table. 'I'll see if they're here.'

Natalie slipped her phone out of her bag. If Siân was about to turn *Misery* on her, she intended to have back-up.

To the rear of the pub came the low murmur of voices, then footsteps heading in her direction. Instinctively, she glanced up.

The phone slipped through her fingers and hit the floor.

It couldn't be...

He scooped it up and held it out to her. 'I hope it's not broken?'

As she failed to take it from him, he placed the phone carefully on the table, before sliding into the seat opposite her.

'Hello, Natalie,' he said.

He wore the same faded jeans and leather jacket he'd worn last night. In daylight, his hair was dark brown with no sign of grey, but there were distinctive lines and shadows beneath the familiar green eyes.

It was disconcerting to realise he was checking her over too.

'*Geraint?*' she whispered, unable to believe what she was seeing. She'd known it was him last night, but to see him here...

'No,' he said. 'Not Geraint. I'm Bryn Llewellyn, his cousin.'

Cousin? Did he think she was stupid? The skinny youth from the fairground had grown broader, but she'd know him anywhere. But she remained silent and waited to see what would develop. Let him be the one to make the first move.

'Bryn's my brother,' Siân said.

'Your surname is Williams,' Natalie felt obliged to point out. They were related for certain, sharing the same dark hair and intense stare, but, apart from that, they weren't all that alike.

'That's my married name.'

'Don't blame Siân,' Bryn said. 'It was my idea. I never expected to meet you in the castle grounds. I wanted to see where it happened and there you were in front of me, like a ghost.'

Was he telling the truth? He was staring at her as though he couldn't believe she was real.

She knew how *that* felt. To encounter him again, after all these years... Trying to imagine what she'd say when she saw him again.

Except, it *wasn't* 'him'.

Was it?

Her phone was on the table. She could call the police, her publisher, anyone she chose. She could even shout out for the barman.

Why hadn't she done so?

'The resemblance to your sister is incredible,' he murmured.

'The colour of your hair, everything. I'd forgotten how alike you were. No wonder I thought I'd seen a ghost.'

She'd never met Bryn. How could he have 'forgotten'?

'What do you want?' she said. 'Why meet now? You've had plenty of time to get in touch.'

He took something from his satchel and laid it on the table. It was a copy of her book; well-read, if the battered jacket was anything to go by. Protruding at irregular intervals was a sheaf of coloured index markers.

Perhaps he thought she'd take it. Instead, she used her finger to turn the book ninety degrees until the cover was the correct way up. It was definitely her book, although she hardly required confirmation. Along the bottom edge were the words: 'uncorrected proof'. Proofs were usually only given to people in the publishing industry.

'Did Siân give you this?' she asked.

'It was an interesting read,' he said, 'this story about a man's obsession with his wife's murder. Parts of it were *very* familiar.'

Not the answer she'd wanted.

Ignoring the nausea tightening her stomach, she tried again. 'Is it a coincidence? That Siân's my new publicist?'

He glanced towards his sister, as though seeking approval. 'Siân's a bright girl,' he said. His Welsh accent was becoming more pronounced. *Like Geraint's.* 'She wanted to work in the media right from university. She found she had a flair for publicity and was recently hired by one of the biggest PR firms in the city. It was a coincidence that the company was hired by your publisher.'

His sincerity was spoilt by Siân not lifting her gaze from her feet.

Guilt, personified.

'Where's *Geraint*?' Natalie asked.

His gaze remained steady. 'Geraint disappeared the night your sister was killed. We want to know what happened to him.'

'So do the police,' she said. 'They think he killed my sister.'
There, she'd said it.

'The evidence was circumstantial,' he said flatly.

'Why did he run away?'

'Geraint didn't run away, he vanished. The police never found him.'

'I expect there are ways to hide from the police if you really want to,' she said.

'For fourteen years?'

'For fourteen years.'

'This is getting us nowhere,' he said. 'I thought you'd want to help.'

'How?' The word was out before Natalie could stop it. She'd meant her tone to be derisory, but it had come out wrong and now it was too late.

Eagerly, Bryn leant forward. 'I saw you on TV this morning. You said you wanted to find out the truth about what happened the night Sarah died. Did you mean that?'

'Of course I meant it!'

'Why don't we work together and pool our knowledge?'

He made it sound so reasonable.

'Why have you waited so long to come forward?' she asked.

'Like you, we thought Geraint had gone into hiding. We knew he was innocent and we wanted to protect him. But the years have passed and we've heard nothing. We think his disappearance is connected to your sister's death and the only explanation would be that he's dead too. You want to know what happened; so do we. You solve Sarah's murder, you'll find out what happened to Geraint. His name should be cleared.'

And that, when it came down to it, was all they were interested in. Not Sarah, not the murder of an innocent young woman. They only wanted to protect their cousin.

She pushed the book towards him. 'I wish you luck with that.'

He made a fist on the table, preventing the book from moving. 'Geraint didn't kill your sister. He wasn't that kind of guy.'

For the first time, she felt sorry for him – for both of them. She knew what it was like to live with that kind of obsession, to have it eating away inside you.

'They never are,' she said gently. 'But maybe it's time to face the fact—'

'No!' He uncurled his fist and slammed it on the table. 'If Geraint's dead, the person who killed him killed your sister. Why is this so hard for you to believe?'

'Because it's not true! What motive would there be to kill Geraint?'

'Perhaps he saw something—' Siân began, but her brother spoke over her.

'What does it say in the police report? What about any witness statements? You mentioned a diary this morning. Can we see it?'

'No, it's private. And there were no witnesses, only me. I was the one who found my sister. Have you any idea what that felt like? Imagine yourself as a sixteen-year-old, finding your sister dead. You'd completely lose it, right? Because that's what happened to me.'

Everyone believed she'd put it behind her and moved on. But after all these years faking it... Had she forgotten how to be 'her'?

Behind the counter, the barman was watching. He'd already lifted the counter and was about to head in their direction. She shook her head.

Bryn observed the exchange. 'It's OK, Natalie. We're on the same side.'

He sounded tense. She drew strength from it.

'I doubt it,' she told him. 'You don't care about Sarah. You're only interested in proving your cousin innocent. I can tell you what happened to Geraint. He caught the first ferry across the Channel and has been bumming round Europe ever since. Give it up. You're wasting your time.'

'He would have been in touch,' Siân protested, her voice breaking. 'He wouldn't have wanted his family to worry.'

'He didn't contact you because he didn't want to create a trail that could be followed. I know you want to believe it, but he's not dead. He's out there somewhere, laughing at everyone. Geraint murdered my sister and he thinks he's got away with it.'

But did she really believe that? The Geraint she'd met had seemed kind – but how long had they been together before Sarah had arrived? Five minutes? Ten?

Bryn didn't respond. Beside him, Siân was fighting back tears. He slid his arm around her.

The fight drained out of Natalie. Why was she taking it out on them? When had she become this horrible, cold-hearted person?

'I'm sorry,' she said. 'I really am. I'm probably the only person who can appreciate exactly how you feel. But I'm tired and you tricked me into being here. If you want to talk about this properly, to present me with a reasoned argument about why I should help you, then you can contact me through my solicitors.'

Bryn closed the book and returned it to his satchel. 'No,' he said. 'I don't think I will. I'd be wasting my time.' He took a scrap of paper from his inside pocket and, scrawling a number across it, pushed it across the table. 'In the meantime, that's *my* number. When *you* decide you want to talk, call me.'

TEN

Despite feeling ravenous earlier, Natalie felt any food would choke her. She let Siân buy sandwiches-to-go and they headed for the next bookstore. Neither spoke. Siân was nervy and on edge, perhaps anxious she was about to be fired. Natalie felt overwhelmed with guilt and uncertain how to deal with it.

She did another signing session before the car collected them from the bookstore to take them to the radio station. By the time they were heading back to her hotel, Natalie had calmed down.

'I met Geraint once,' she said, to break the frosty silence.

Siân regarded her warily.

'He seemed like a nice kid.' Geraint had been five years older than her, but in her head was forever frozen at twenty-one, just as Sarah would always be eighteen. 'It must have been hard on you, having him disappear like that?'

Siân's gaze slid away. 'Yes.'

'You've had no contact from him in all this time?'

'No.'

As the car pulled up outside her hotel, she glanced again at Siân. 'See you at the dinner with my publisher tonight?'

Siân inclined her head but said nothing.

Natalie headed up to her room to shower and change. When she arrived at the restaurant later that evening, to be effusively greeted by Julia and the rest of the editorial team, Siân was conspicuous by her absence.

The following day, another PR took over from Siân and the remainder of the book tour passed without incident. By late afternoon, Natalie was back in Calahurst. She let herself into her apartment and dumped her overnight bag in her bedroom. A large mug of coffee should wake her up and then she could relax with a book – *not* one of hers. The thought of dialling out for pizza also appealed.

Her kitchen was tidier than she remembered. She put it down to her cleaner having a blitz in her absence, until she picked up her kettle and found it still warm. The oven had been set to 'reheat' and on the centre shelf were a couple of small green cartons with the familiar gold logo of the local Indian takeaway stamped on one side.

Simon was on the sofa watching TV. On the coffee table was the remainder of his takeaway, packed neatly back into its box. Natalie could smell the coriander and cumin before she saw the carton.

'Hello,' she said, 'I wasn't expecting to see you tonight.' After the row they'd had, she hadn't expected to see him for a while.

He clicked the mute on the remote. 'You're always forgetting to eat. I thought you'd be hungry after your trip, so I bought us a couple of takeaways.' He smiled ruefully. 'You were a little later than I expected.'

'Thanks – and sorry!' She slumped onto the sofa beside him, sliding off her shoes and sinking her toes into the thick white pile of the rug. After a day crushed in high heels, it was bliss.

'I've got to take the drama club for an extra rehearsal later this evening,' he said. It was as though their argument had never happened. 'I'd cry off, but we're doing *The Wizard of Oz* this year and they've worked really hard.'

'Why don't you come back afterwards? Please?'

His mouth curved into a smile. 'After two hours of listening to Year 7 murder "Follow the Yellow Brick Road", I'll be shattered! It'll have to be another time.'

He leant forward to kiss her cheek – the kind of kiss you gave a maiden aunt. She re-angled her face so the kiss landed on the corner of her mouth. Not quite on target, but good enough. He kept his eyes open, so perhaps she wasn't entirely forgiven.

'Perhaps we could meet up at the weekend?' she suggested.

He got up from the sofa, scooping up the takeaway carton from the coffee table as he passed. 'If you think you can fit me into your schedule.'

If that was meant as a joke, he needed to work on his delivery.

'I'm sorry,' she said, unsure what she was apologising for. 'You knew I was going to London, so why did you come round?'

'I thought you might want to see me.' He disappeared in the direction of the kitchen, presumably to load his one knife, one fork and small glass tumbler into the dishwasher.

Sometimes he could be infuriating.

'I recorded your interview on Prime Cuts,' he added, returning to the sitting room. 'I made notes on your performance. When you have the time, I'll take you through them.'

'Notes?' She felt a sense of unease that took her right back to her teenage years. He'd helped her get into university, for which she'd always be grateful, but she was thirty now, not eighteen. 'I thought it went well. I sold the product, dropped in some personal stuff, talked about my family to make it relatable – everything you trained me to do.'

'Why didn't you tell me you were planning a book about your sister?'

His tone was far too casual.

She braced herself for another argument. 'You would have stopped me writing it.'

'I would have counselled caution,' he said.

'But you understand why I had to write it?'

'Not really. I appreciate you have unresolved issues regarding your sister's death, but there are other ways you could have dealt with them.'

'Like visit a counsellor?'

He grimaced. 'Charles was the "doctor" character in your story, right? Why didn't you ever tell me about your relationship with him? You were sixteen and completely traumatised. At the very least, he deserved to be struck off.'

Natalie was suddenly cold. How would Simon know that? Unless...

'You've read my book.'

'One of my ex-students works for the *Calahurst Echo*. He saw an advance review copy and phoned me for a quote. I was grateful for the heads-up. "The doctor", "the teacher", "the gardener"... When I'm doorstepped by the press, at least I now know what I'm supposed to have done. You do realise what you've accused me of, don't you? Abusing a position of trust, at the very least.'

'No one is going to think "the teacher" is you.'

'Your naivety astounds me. I'll be the first person they'll suspect. If I'm lucky, the second after James Fitzpatrick. There's nothing people love more than the rumour of a scandal, particularly if it's unsubstantiated. Those tiny provincial minds can run riot with very little evidence. You should know. You've had a lifetime of experience. And that's the problem. People will look at you and me, and think, "Ah yes, he's done it once, he must have done it before."'

Too late she remembered that if there was one thing guaranteed to wind Simon up, it was to be reminded of the way they'd originally met.

'We didn't begin a relationship until I graduated from university.'

'After reading your book, do you think anyone is going to believe that? Journalists will ask around and find out how I personally coached you through your exams, helping you get the necessary grades to get into university. They'll want to know why I went to all that trouble for you. The kinder ones might suggest I felt sorry for you after your sister died. The not-so-kind will say it was because I wanted to seduce a sixteen-year-old girl.'

'*Simon!*'

'What I find most hurtful,' he continued, 'is your utter lack of loyalty. All credit to you – you took the opportunities you were given and you ran with them. Look at everything you've achieved, all those books you've written, the millions you've sold. But do you ever consider the rest of us? Do you ever think about what it must be like to be me, stuck working at that school forever and never progressing beyond Head of English & Drama because of my relationship with you?'

Is that what had happened? She was ashamed to realise she'd never given it a thought.

'Is that why James Fitzpatrick was promoted over you? Because of silly gossip?'

'Gossip or not, the entire village believes it. The governors were quite matter-of-fact about that.'

She'd never had much to do with the locals – or anyone other than Alicia – much preferring her own company. Did people believe she'd dated Simon at sixteen? Because that would be horrible.

'Oh, Simon... I don't know what to say. I'm so sorry—'

He sighed. 'I know you are, but you've written this book and stirred everything up. What were you *expecting* to happen? Did you think that Welsh fairground worker was going to turn up after all this time and say, "Yes, I did it"? Because that's not going to happen. You've moved on from your appalling childhood and made a huge success of your life, and good for you, but now you've written this book reminding everyone who you are and where you came from. I think it's a huge mistake, I do really.'

'I'm not ashamed. Why should I be? If I'd wanted to hide from my past, I could have changed my name and moved away. This way, I can be an inspiration to others—'

'An *inspiration*?' he derided. 'Listen to yourself! You'd have been more of an inspiration if you'd done something different. As far as I remember, it was always Sarah who wanted to be a writer, not you. Yet from the moment she died, you took on her dreams and aspirations, you cut your hair in the same style, you wear the same type of clothes and even went out with the same men – Charles and James – following directly in her footsteps. It's as though you don't trust yourself to be "you".'

'That's not true—'

'Of course it's true! All I ever hear from you is Sarah, Sarah, Sarah. You need to move on from this morbid fascination you have with her death. And get rid of these horrible pictures,' he gestured towards another of Sir Henry's paintings that she'd hung on the wall. 'They make my skin crawl.'

'What? No, I can't, I won't—'

'Then let me do it for you.'

He lifted the nearest one from the wall. It was her favourite, slightly smaller than the others, a painting of Sarah sitting in an apple tree, biting into one of the fruit. She remembered Sarah telling her that she'd been so hungry, she'd actually eaten the apple. Sir Henry had been furious.

Before Natalie could get her head around what he was intending to do, Simon had raised the picture high above his head and broken the frame across his thigh.

Natalie was so shocked, she couldn't move. Simon, whom she'd loved for over eight years, whom she thought she'd known as well as she knew herself, had done *this*?

'There you are,' he said, slightly breathlessly, 'that wasn't so difficult.'

That painting had cost thousands, although she'd been able to buy it cheaply because work by Sir Henry was no longer as popular as it had been. But that wasn't the point. Simon knew how much she loved these paintings. They were practically all she had left to remember her sister.

Natalie forced herself not to react. If he knew how much she'd been affected by the broken picture, would he smash the others? It was the kind of thing her father would have done – but Simon wasn't like her father.

Was he?

Vaguely, she became aware of a stinging on the sole of her foot, where she must have trodden on a splinter, but it hardly seemed important. She waited, perfectly still, to see what he'd do next.

'This obsession you have is consuming you,' he said, and she could tell by the low, tight way he was speaking that he was so utterly furious he could hardly get the words out. 'If you want to continue with our relationship, I want all evidence of Sarah purged from this apartment. Do you understand? *Everything.* You can phone your publisher and get them to pull that book too, before someone sues you. Somewhere inside your head is the real Natalie Grove, not this pale shadow of Sarah. One day I'd like to meet her, but until that moment you can consider our relationship terminated.'

ELEVEN

Simon wanted her to choose between him and Sarah?

Natalie chose Sarah.

Not that she'd had the chance to tell him. Without another word, he'd left, leaving her to pick up the pieces of broken frame – luckily the painting didn't appear to be damaged – and wonder at his insensitivity. Maybe he was trying to make a point, but he *knew* how much these paintings meant to her. If he was unhappy with her behaviour, they could have worked through it. Why did he have to be so nasty, so *cruel*?

How had she ended up with a man like her father?

Maybe she *should* see a therapist, if only to stop her making the same mistake again.

In the meantime, she was better off without him, although it would feel strange to be single after all this time. To have no one to confide in, to consult or to answer to.

Strange... but also liberating.

But when she dropped the pieces of broken frame into the kitchen bin, she saw a note on the table, a single sheet of paper written in Simon's hand.

Charles phoned – urgent.

The number listed was for Charles's mobile phone, but he didn't answer until the seventh ring.

'Speaking,' he said, without bothering to state his name.

'Hi, it's Natalie,' she said. Her foot was still stinging. She lifted it up to check on the plaster she'd hastily slapped over the wound left after she'd dug the splinter out. It was grubby but still intact. She switched off the oven, hobbled into the sitting room and dropped onto the sofa.

'Thank you for returning my call. Your father says he wants to talk to you. It's up to you whether you see him. Visiting time is almost over, but I'll tell the staff to expect you. I'm working late tonight. We can talk more then if you wish.' The line went dead.

Her shoes lay on the floor beside the sofa. She ignored those and slid on a pair of trainers, heading for the door.

It wasn't as though she had anything better to do.

John was alone in his room. He was in his wheelchair, staring through the window, even though there was nothing out there but the dark. A copy of her book lay on the table beside him.

She picked it up. 'Where did you get this?'

He didn't turn his head, or even acknowledge her presence, so she dropped the book back onto the table. It skidded across the polished wood and came to rest against the ceramic pot that held his citrus plant. The glossy green leaves quivered, but the lemons didn't fall. John didn't even turn his head.

'I told you I'd give you a copy. Why did you buy one?'

His hands moved from his lap to grip the wheels of the wheelchair and manoeuvred it round to face her.

She tried again. 'Did someone give it to you?'

He let his gaze drop to the citrus plant and pulled the

ceramic pot a few centimetres towards him, so it returned to its central position.

'Does it make you look bad?' he said. 'Me, buying my own copy? Your mother always worried about what other people thought.'

He picked up the book, flipping through the pages until he reached the back, pausing at the black and white photograph of Natalie on the inside cover. Then he shut it abruptly.

'I thought you wanted to see me?' she said. 'I thought it was urgent?'

The book was dropped back onto the table. 'Not urgent,' he said. 'Important.'

She waited.

'I did follow your career,' he continued. 'I never read your other books – fiction ain't my thing – but this one was different. You can pretend all you like that it's made up, that it's about a man trying to find out who killed his wife, but I see what's there. It's about you and Sarah.'

That was the entire point, but Natalie kept quiet. This was the first proper conversation she'd had with her father since he'd begun this charade. She didn't want him to close up again. Not until she'd extracted every last piece of information from him.

'I knew you were writing it,' he said. 'I knew you were asking everyone questions, nosing around like the police. Didn't get very far, did you.'

It was true that she'd revisited those who'd given evidence at Sarah's inquest and asked them to tell their stories again. It wasn't a secret; she didn't care who knew, yet her father was locked away in here with no visitors except for herself.

'Who told you I was asking questions?'

'You're an idiot,' he said. 'Digging over stuff that's better left buried.'

Why did everyone keep *telling* her that?

'Don't you *want* to know what happened to Sarah?' she

said. 'Sometimes I think I'm the only person in the world who cares.'

His face reset to inscrutable. 'Sarah's dead. Knowing the details won't bring her back.'

'It'll help me achieve closure,' she said automatically. Although, to be honest, after all these years, she wasn't entirely sure why she was persisting with this. Knowing the truth *wasn't* going to bring Sarah back.

'*Closure*? Don't quote that doctor at me! I get enough of his rubbish during the week.'

'OK, OK; it will help me get on with the rest of my life. Does that suit you better?'

For a moment, he said nothing, then, 'On TV, you talked about Sarah having a boyfriend who was a gardener? Did he work at the castle? Did I know him?'

It was a predictable question. John had always hated the idea of his daughters maturing into young women, wearing make-up and forming relationships.

But she needed to speed things up a little.

'"The gardener", "the teacher", "the doctor" – these are all names that appear in Sarah's diary. They're the code names of Sarah's old boyfriends. Who do *you* think he was?'

'*Diary?*' Unexpectedly, he laughed. It transformed his sunken features, revealing a brief glimpse of the handsome man he'd once been. 'You got all this from a *diary*? You're twice the fool I thought you to be. This isn't about Sarah, it never was.'

It was as though she had something stuck in her throat, making it hard to breathe.

'Then what *is* it about?'

'I never wanted to get married,' he said.

The abrupt change of subject sent her head spinning but if she kept quiet and let this play out?

'It wasn't my idea,' he said. 'Your mum said she was up the duff and, fool that I was, I believed her and offered to do the right thing. I didn't know she was carrying on with *him*, that devil up at the castle. Now, *he* was never going to do the right thing.'

'Sir Henry was Sarah's father?' Natalie couldn't believe it.

John grinned. 'Oh, no. I reckon she *told* him Sarah was his kid. The silly bint thought she could marry him and live at the castle – happily ever after, like a fairy story. But I had the last laugh. You're both my kids all right. You're both the spitting image of me. Besides, Sarah was born a full year after we married – so I guess that makes me the sucker.'

Natalie waited, but nothing was forthcoming. No more explanations, no excuses, no regrets. Her father broke eye contact.

'Look,' he said, shifting slightly in the wheelchair, 'We've said what we had to say. You've got it off your chest. You don't need to come again.'

Was that what he thought this was all about?

'You don't want to visit me,' he continued. 'I know that. I understand. You hate me. Fair enough. I was a terrible father. I deserved what I got. But what I don't understand is why you keep coming back. Revenge? You've got to let it go, girl.' He prodded the soil in the pot that held his citrus plant, to test whether it needed watering. 'Save yourself the bother, all right? Or you'll end up bitter and twisted like your mother, constantly trying to impress people who really couldn't care less.'

Resolution was slipping through her fingers. 'You had a visitor, do you remember?'

'No.'

'They brought you this plant.'

He wiped the soil from his fingers onto his trousers. 'It was a present.'

'From whom?'

He waved a dismissive hand. 'What does it matter?'

'It matters to me.'

'It's irrelevant.' He wheeled himself back to his favourite position in the window. 'What if you did find out who killed Sarah? You reckon it's going to change anything? You reckon your life's going to be any better? Take it from me; you've got to let it go. *Vengeance is mine, I will repay, saith the Lord.* You'd do well to keep that in mind.'

'I *can't*. I can't let it go! I've got to find out who did it!'

'Then you're a fool, because once they know you're onto them—' He broke off and sighed. 'Burn the diary. That's my advice, before anyone else gets hurt. Burn it, shred it, *destroy* it.'

As he drew level with the window, the wheelchair ceased all motion. It was as though a switch had been flicked and whatever electrical impulses had been coursing through his brain now crashed. His eyes slipped out of focus, the angle of his head seemed to slip forward and to the side.

Tentatively, she shook his shoulder. 'Dad?'

There was a movement behind her. Jason, the handsome care worker she'd met on her previous visit, had come into the room carrying a tray with a jug of water and a plastic beaker.

'Oh, hi, Miss Grove. Is everything OK?'

'Two minutes before you walked through the door, my father and I were having a perfectly lucid conversation,' Natalie told him, 'and then he heard your footsteps in the corridor.'

'John was talking?' Jason only seemed mildly interested. 'What about?'

'He had a visitor—'

'If you don't want people to visit your father, you should have told us.' Jason transferred the jug and beaker onto the table. 'I'll give you a few more moments, but visiting time is over.'

She waited until his plimsolls padded away down the corridor before turning her attention back to John.

'Who came to see you, Dad?'

She'd not expected an answer but was hoping for a reaction.

She got nothing. *Was* he faking?

'You know something about Sarah's death, something that could help. Why won't you tell me?'

Already, she could hear voices in the distance, then more footsteps. Jason's rubber-soled plimsolls had been joined by the tap of Charles Fitzpatrick's leather shoes. By concentrating on that, she missed what her father said.

'What?'

'You said you wanted to know who came to see me?' he sneered. 'You think it's so significant?'

She didn't dare speak in case he withdrew into himself once more.

'I suppose you could call them my nemesis,' he said, and then he sighed. 'You ain't the only one out for revenge, girl. I did warn you. You've got competition.'

TWELVE

Fourteen years previously

The fair had fallen eerily silent. The lights were on and the music still played, but only a few villagers remained and the workers were beginning to pack up.

Natalie headed for the gap in the hedge, where everyone was queuing to walk through the exit. Typically, Alicia joined the end of the queue. Natalie impatiently barged through to the front and out onto the road.

'Wait for me!' Alicia called.

'Go back to the fair,' Natalie shouted back. 'I don't need a babysitter.'

'I'm trying to help!'

Natalie was about to tell Alicia to leave her alone when she stepped off the grass verge and collided with a tall, dark-haired teenager standing beside a red sports car, hazard lights flashing.

'Come *on*, Sarah,' he gestured towards the open door. 'Hurry *up*. I'm blocking the traffic.'

It was tempting, but, 'I'm Natalie,' she sighed, aware of

Alicia finally catching up, stumbling out of the crowd, quite out of breath. 'Sarah's decided to stay on.'

'Like that, is it?' He looked her up and down, his lips curving in appreciation. 'So... Little Nat, all grown up?'

Alicia slapped his head. 'Eyes front, James Fitzpatrick. She's only sixteen.'

'Why does everyone make such a big deal of it?' Natalie grumbled, clambering into the back of the car. 'I'm only two years younger than you. Stop treating me like a child.'

'Then stop behaving like one,' Alicia said.

Jamie started up the car and then checked his rear-view mirror. Their eyes met. His gaze lingered a split second too long, before sliding back to the traffic.

'I came to warn you,' he told Alicia. 'Sarah's dad turned up at the pub, crazier than usual. He wanted to know if anyone had seen her. Obviously no one was going to tell him anything, we all know what he's like, but the bar was full of tourists and Sarah's blonde hair is distinctive. It didn't take long for someone to mention they'd seen her at the fair.'

'Sarah said she had permission to go!'

'Then your darling Sarah is lying again.'

'He definitely said "Sarah"?' Alicia asked. 'Are you sure about that?'

Jamie hesitated. 'Mr Grove said "daughter". He didn't say which one. I assumed he meant Sarah.'

Natalie moaned and leant over. If her father knew she'd sneaked out...

Jamie caught her movement in his mirror. 'Really, Nat? What were you *thinking*? You know what he's like.'

'Jamie,' Alicia lowered her voice. 'A little sympathy?'

'The whole village knows what he's like. Why does your father still employ him?'

'As far as my father is concerned, John Grove is an excellent horticulturist.'

'And a terrible human.'

'All my father cares about is painting,' Alicia sighed. 'Anything else is irrelevant.'

Natalie kept her gaze on the view outside the window. She didn't know what was worse. That the whole village knew their family's personal business or that no one did anything to help.

'What about Sarah?' Jamie was saying. 'We ought to find her before Mr Grove does.'

Alicia shrugged. 'Sarah can take care of herself – it's the boys she dates you need to worry about. If I have to provide a shoulder for them to cry on, one more time...'

Natalie zoned out. The road to the village was practically empty. All the parked cars had gone, leaving deep ruts in the grass verges to show where they'd been.

'We don't *have* to take Nat home,' she heard Jamie say and quickly sat up.

'Where else are we going to take her?' Alicia asked. 'Back to your place? Your mother would love that. She's worse than mine.'

'I was thinking of Social Services.'

Natalie slumped back. The last time a social worker had turned up, after a tip-off from the school, her father had launched into his Father-of-the-Year routine. The social worker had gone away, happily reassured, with a deluxe hamper from the Castle Vyne gift shop safely stowed in the boot of her car.

'Best not to get involved,' Alicia said flatly.

'Like your father?' Jamie derided. 'How can you call yourself Sarah's friend?'

'John Grove is a renowned horticulturist with friends in high places, including both our fathers. Think about it. Who are Social Services more likely to believe? A couple of teenagers or Sir Henry Vyne?'

Reinforcing Natalie's view that the only person capable of helping her was herself.

She leant between the front seats. The way Alicia started guiltily, you'd have thought she'd forgotten Natalie was there.

'I'll be fine,' Natalie told them, with enough confidence to almost believe it herself. 'You don't need to worry about me.'

The stone gateway of Castle Vyne loomed into view, gleaming white in the headlights of Jamie's car.

'Drop me here,' she said. 'I'll sneak through my bedroom window and pretend I've never left.'

'If you're certain...' Jamie slowed the car, mounted the grass verge and stopped.

Alicia got out first, flipped up the seat and helped Natalie out of the back.

'Are you sure you're going to be all right?' Alicia asked. 'I know my mother can be a pain, but I'm sure my father would try to help you and Sarah if we explained it to him.'

She shook her head. 'I'll be fine.'

It was a lie and they both knew it.

The other girl seemed reluctant to leave her.

'Go.' Natalie gave her a shove towards the car. 'Before my dad turns up and catches us all standing here.'

'Good point.' Alicia quickly got back into the car. 'But if you have any trouble...' She lowered her voice so Jamie couldn't hear. 'Any trouble at all, you call me, is that clear?'

Before Alicia could say any more on the subject, Natalie slammed the door and stepped back onto the verge to allow Jamie to drive off, waiting for his car to turn in through the huge stone gateway.

By the time she walked beneath the arch, the lights from Jamie's car had vanished towards the castle and she was standing alone outside the Lodge.

THIRTEEN

Present

It was late by the time Natalie got home. She should've taken a couple of painkillers and collapsed into bed, but she knew she'd never sleep. The conversation she'd had with her father was stuck on repeat inside her head. Instead, she left her car in the basement and took the side exit out onto the marina.

Calahurst was a pretty place to live, with its cobblestone streets and smart Georgian houses, and popular with both tourists and the sailing crowd. Natalie walked past two late-night cafés, a bar and a busy nightclub, until she came to a club called Remedy. Located in a converted boathouse, the interior had been painted black and was strewn with fairy lights. At one end was a rudimentary stage, at the other a bar. Between them was a small dance floor. It was too dark to hook up and the beer and company wasn't great. The only reason anyone went to Remedy was for the music.

As usual, the club was packed. Tonight, a dark-haired woman was singing soulfully about doomed love. Everyone stood in the area known as the dance floor, even though no one ever danced.

After watching the woman's set, Natalie headed for the bar and ordered a rum and cola, gulping down half as soon as the barman placed it in front of her.

On stage, a band launched into something more upbeat. The barman turned his attention to the man in the woollen hat standing next to Natalie. Cheered by the warmth of the alcohol, she scanned the room to see if there was anyone she knew. Surprisingly, there was – and it was the last person she expected to see.

He caught her attention because, in a sea of rumpled black and grey, his shirt was white and pristine. He'd unbuttoned it a couple of notches in an attempt to blend in but looked as though he'd have been happier presiding over a meeting of shareholders.

There were three other chairs at his table. Two were empty, although there were assorted glasses to show they'd once been occupied. In the third seat was a young woman with pale blonde hair. They weren't regulars or they'd have realised no one ever sat at a table.

Natalie picked up her drink and turned sideways to squeeze a path towards them. They didn't see her approach.

'Hi, James,' she said, keeping her head close to his, so he could hear her above the music. As always, his formal name sounded strange on her tongue. To her, he'd always be Jamie. 'This is a surprise.'

'Nat?' James Fitzpatrick glanced up and smiled. 'What are *you* doing here?'

'Enjoying the music. I often come here. It's basically my local.' At his blank look, she added, 'I live at the marina, remember?'

'Oh, yeah. So you do. I forgot.'

This wasn't doing much for her self-confidence. Neither

were the pitying looks sent in her direction from the blonde. Still, who else was she going to talk to? Some random man at the bar? That would be sad.

Despite the two empty seats, Natalie pulled another from the table behind, wedging it between James and the blonde.

'What about you?' she asked. She'd have thought the wine bar two doors down would have been more his thing. 'Aren't you worried about your image?'

He laughed. 'What image would that be? Staid, boring headmaster? Thanks, Nat. You always know how to wound me. Can I get you a drink?'

She raised her glass. 'Got one, thanks.'

'Well, I could do with another.' He opened his wallet, peeled out a couple of twenties and handed them to the little blonde. 'Summer, could you do me a huge favour? I'll have another beer and be sure to get yourself and your friends something too. Please ensure the drinks are *non*-alcoholic for those under-age.'

Summer curled her fingers around the notes and rose to her feet, looking between the two of them, apparently suspicious that she was being dismissed so obviously.

Natalie waited until Summer was out of earshot and then came straight to the point.

'Are you dating your brother's teenage receptionist?'

'*Obviously* not.' He rolled his eyes. 'Honestly, Nat. You've known me half my life. Do you *really* think I'd do that to Alicia? Give me some credit at least. Summer Ellis is twenty-two and she's here with her boyfriend and her brother, *not* me. We were left alone when the others went to chat with their friends.' He waved in the direction of the dance floor. 'Some of my students have formed themselves into a band and will be performing later – or sooner, hopefully. I'm not sure how much of this I can take. It's not my sort of music at all. Summer's younger brother is in the band, along with her boyfriend, which is why *she's* here. They're surprisingly good. Simon would have come along to support them, but he's busy rehearsing *The Wizard of Oz* with the drama club, as I'm sure you already know, so I said I'd do it.'

There was a commotion on the dance floor as a group of boisterous teenagers forced their way through the crowd, aiming for their table. This was the band James had been talking about?

She slid out of her chair, murmuring, 'Good luck with the baby-sitting,' and grinning as James rolled his eyes. It was well past time to leave anyway, particularly as Summer had now returned with a tray of drinks for her friends.

Natalie left her own glass behind. It was still half full, but, after the day she'd had, she shouldn't be drinking alcohol anyway.

Outside, the warm air held the hint of a storm to come. The wind had got up, causing the yachts to bob frantically up and down on their moorings, shredding the reflection of the pretty lights around the marina. Although it was early, the pubs and clubs were emptying onto the street. Natalie crossed the road with the intention of avoiding the tourists but had hardly reached the pavement when she began to feel odd.

The railings that kept the tourists from falling into the marina were in front of her. She leant against them, taking several deep breaths. Her head was swirling. It must be the heat, coupled with a long, stressful day. She could hardly have got drunk on half a rum and cola!

The pavement shifted beneath her feet. She gripped the railing. Despite the coolness of the breeze, sweat dripped from her forehead. Did she have food poisoning?

She took a few more steps and almost collapsed.

What was *wrong* with her?

People gave her curious glances as they hurried past. Thick dark clouds hung low in the sky, promising a downpour. She knew she shouldn't linger, but what choice did she have? Her apartment block was only a few metres away, yet she could hardly put one foot in front of the other.

It began to dawn on her that the clubs were emptying too early. The marina was packed with people – but they were all walking in the same direction – towards the high street and up the hill.

She caught the attention of the next person to walk past. 'What's going on?'

The woman's eyes glittered with excitement. 'There's a fire on the hill. We're going to watch.'

Wildfires were commonplace in the King's Forest District. Mostly they took place in the summer months, although the weather had been dry for the past few weeks. If the fire was a big one, it would prove devastating to the local community. How could *that* be considered entertainment?

Fortunately, before she could say so, the woman hurried to catch up with her friends.

Natalie stayed close to the railing in case she was inadvertently knocked over. She lost count of the number of people who carelessly bumped against her in their rush to see what was happening.

Wretched ghouls.

Even the locals were coming out of their homes to see what was going on.

She could smell the bitter scent of smoke and hear the wail of an emergency vehicle siren. This wasn't good.

A teenage girl crossed the road in front of her, struggling to negotiate the cobblestones in her high heels. She had unusual white-blonde hair. There was a man with her. He had his arm curved around her waist and his hand was tucked into the back pocket of her jeans. He was tall, with broad shoulders, which he hunched protectively against the crowd.

The blonde girl glanced back. For the briefest moment, familiar blue eyes stared knowingly into her own.

Natalie was chilled. '*Sarah?*'

The girl's lips curved into a smile as she turned away.

'Sarah! It's me! Wait!'

The crowd shifted. The girl and her boyfriend vanished.

Natalie turned her head. Where had they gone? But there were so many people...

Carefully, she walked in the direction she'd last seen them, away from the marina and towards the gift shops and cafés on the high street, but as the road grew steeper, her foot slipped on the wet cobblestones. When she threw out her hands to prevent herself falling, the fingers of one closed around cold wet metal, keeping her upright. It was a bannister, curving alongside the stone steps to one of the cottages.

Natalie glanced up. Above her head was a sign proclaiming cream teas. She watched it swing, back and forth, back and forth, as it was caught by the wind.

Memories came flooding back.

A girl running down a moonlit path and a man who waited in the shadows.

A man with dark hair and green eyes.

Geraint Llewellyn.

She closed her eyes, no longer sure what was real.

The noise around her faded away, leaving only the creak of the sign as it moved back and forth.

Back and forth.

Back and forth.

Like a garden gate.

FOURTEEN

'Natalie? Natalie?'

The voice was a long way off.

'*Natalie*? Are you all right?'

Someone was patting her cheek, softly at first and then harder. It stung. She tried to bat them away. They caught hold of her hand. She opened her eyes, attempting to separate hallucination from reality. Familiar green eyes stared into hers.

Geraint?

No, not Geraint.

'Bryn?' She tried to bring him into focus. 'What are you doing here?'

He was crouched beside her, one hand still stroking her cheek. As soon as she spoke, he abruptly moved away from her.

'Sorry, I thought you'd blacked out,' he muttered. 'I was worried.'

'I'm OK.'

Was she though?

She looked him up and down. He was wearing the same scruffy jeans, red plaid shirt and work boots, but seemed taller than she remembered. Except she didn't remember him, did she? She'd never met him until yesterday.

Bryn. This was *Bryn.*

'You don't look OK,' he said doubtfully.

'I have a headache.'

'Are you drunk?'

Drunk?

'Don't be ridiculous. I had half a rum and cola. Hard to get drunk on *that.*'

It was a struggle to get up though.

She was still clutching the bannister. Her fingers had stiffened and were almost numb, and she'd collapsed into a sitting position on the bottom step. It was gritty. Her skirt would be filthy, but she'd got to the point where she no longer cared. What was she doing in the high street anyway?

She closed her eyes, trying to remember. She'd been to Remedy, met Jamie – *James—*

'Something's not right,' Bryn said. 'Are you ill?'

Again, he'd disrupted her train of thought. Why was he here? Did he know where she *lived*?

Her concentration drifted again. She remembered the splinter she'd trodden on and the alcohol she'd drunk. Had she taken painkillers? She couldn't remember. They wouldn't work well with the alcohol, but she was equally sure they wouldn't have caused a reaction like this.

'You don't get a reaction like that from one rum and cola,' he said, echoing her thoughts.

'Are you stalking me?' There was no hint of slurring this time. The fresh air seemed to be making her feel better.

'Why would I do that? I already know where you live. I know who your friends are. I know everything about you.'

'I think you'll find that's the very definition of stalking,' she said drily.

She had another attempt at standing up. Her foot was

painful, but, apart from that, she felt fine – remarkably focused, in fact. Had someone slipped something into her drink? She remembered the man who'd stood so close to her at the bar, the one with the woollen hat. He'd had the opportunity, but what would've been his motivation?

Motivation? Now she was thinking like a thriller writer!

Obviously no one had slipped anything into her drink. She'd just had a very tiring day.

'Let me take you home,' Bryn was saying. 'You're not well.'

She sighed. 'Did you follow me here from London?'

'I wanted to make sure you're OK—'

Perhaps he *was* trying to be kind, but she couldn't deal with him right now – and the memories that surged back every time she looked at him.

Not Geraint, *not* Geraint...

'Stay away from me,' she said and stepped backwards, into the crowd of people surging up the hill, letting their motion carry her along and effectively losing him.

Little glowing embers floated high above the street. She lifted her head to watch, thinking how pretty they were, but as they drifted towards the cobblestones, they turned to ash.

In front of her was the stone cross of the war memorial. The streets behind and to the left returned down the hill to the marina. Ahead was the road that led past the castle and towards Raven's Edge and Norchester. To her right was a wide avenue of Victorian houses, where old-fashioned street lamps twinkled amongst the trees – against the backdrop of a sinister orange glow. It was the same road where she'd visited her dad not an hour previously.

Her dad!

Natalie pushed through the milling crowd until it became a mass of bodies, tightly packed, jostling together as more joined from behind. She still couldn't see what was going on.

She slapped the shoulder of the man in front of her. Impatience made her sound imperious, which was probably why he ignored her.

'Excuse me?' She had to repeat it three times before he deigned to turn his head.

He was a great bear of a man and his irritation evident. 'Look, love,' he said. 'Stop prodding me. The police have the whole road cordoned off. You're not going anywhere.'

It was difficult to keep a hold on her patience. 'The fire? Where is it?'

'The psychiatric unit. One of the patients has sent the place up in smoke.'

Her heart took a dive. 'Rose Court?'

He'd already turned away, presenting solid broad shoulders. If only she could see what was happening, but everyone was taller, bigger and stronger. No one would let her through.

She moved sideways, off the pavement and towards the centre of the road. There were fewer people here, but the reason soon became apparent. An ambulance was attempting to force a route through. There was no siren, but the lights on the cab flashed silently, casting a cold blue light.

As the crowd parted, Natalie was squashed even tighter against the people behind; the wheels of the ambulance only a few centimetres from her toes as it pulled up behind the strip of blue and white tape.

In the narrow gap between the crowd and the ambulance, she saw a police officer winding up the tape to move it aside. The ambulance started up again with a deep rumble. Everyone moved out the way.

Everyone except Natalie. It was her chance to find out what was going on.

She kept close to the side of the ambulance as it moved slowly through the crowd, picking up speed as it drove beyond the tape. She caught the surprised expression of the police officer as she slipped past, but didn't look back, even when he shouted at her.

As the ambulance increased speed and she could no longer keep up, she ducked between a row of parked cars and onto the pavement again. She ran a bit further, taking refuge in the shadow of an overgrown hedge while she caught her breath. The air here was warm and thick with black smoke. With no breeze, it lingered, stinging her eyes and making it hard to see or even breathe.

On the pavement opposite, the police were herding local residents to safety. Some were still in their nightclothes. The road was filled with emergency vehicles. Three fire engines were struggling to keep the blaze at Rose Court under control. Another ambulance was parked directly in front of her. The doors were open and paramedics were inside, administering first aid to an elderly man. His pyjamas were tattered and scorched.

Another body was stretchered past her, the face almost hidden by an oxygen mask. Natalie recognised Mrs Barker – the feisty lady with the walking stick – and wanted to cry. All around her was chaos. She was never going to find her dad.

A man was hunched on the kerb a few metres away. He was wearing a familiar green uniform with white plimsolls.

She grabbed his shoulder. 'Jason?'

Except it wasn't Jason. A dark-skinned face stared vacantly back.

'Sorry,' she said, backing away. 'I thought you were someone else.'

Her gaze dropped to the uniform. There was a rose embroidered on his chest, with his name underneath: Ty. He was Jason's colleague, the one who'd come to her aid the day her father attacked her. He appeared to be in deep shock.

She sat on the kerb beside him. 'Hello, Ty,' she began carefully. 'Do you remember me? I'm Natalie, John Grove's daughter.' She paused to let her words sink in. 'Have you seen my father? He has a scar here' – she pointed to her forehead – 'and his hair is white. He's in a wheelchair...' She was unable to prevent her voice trembling. 'Can you tell me if he got out safely? I can't see him anywhere...'

There was no response. She could've been talking to a statue.

Tears welled in her eyes and no amount of blinking made any difference. She rubbed the back of her hand across her face. Her father had been a horrible man who'd made her childhood a misery. So why was she crying?

Unexpectedly, something brushed against her shoulder. She pushed her hair away from her eyes to see Ty's hand there, an attempt at comfort.

'Not seen Mr Grove.' His voice was dry and scratchy. 'Sorry.' His blank look returned as he refocused his attention on the flames engulfing Rose Court.

She needed to try a different tactic.

She took out her phone and dialled Charles's number. He'd know what was going on. Most likely, Charles was here somewhere, helping to evacuate the building, but there were so many people she'd never find him on her own.

Charles's phone went straight to voicemail, so she left the briefest message, asking him to call, before shoving the phone back into her bag. When she looked up, there was a familiar figure sitting on the kerb beside her.

She couldn't be bothered to be polite. 'What is it, Bryn?'

'Do you want my help or not?' he said. 'Because your attitude is really starting to annoy me.'

'*My* attitude—'

'I found the guy in charge. He's willing to talk to you. Are you interested?'

'Of course, but—'

'Then follow me,' Bryn said.

FIFTEEN

Bryn only slowed down as he approached a line of cars parked close to the police cordon. The same line Natalie had ducked between when she'd followed the ambulance.

He stopped in front of a black Audi and held open the passenger door, indicating that she should get inside.

She hesitated, bending to peer into the car. She thought he'd brought her to see Charles. Instead, a stranger sat in the driver's seat. A dark-skinned man with close-cropped hair and beard, his suit so smart he could have been the CEO for some designer brand. He was staring straight ahead, one hand resting on the steering wheel, manicured fingers tapping impatiently.

'Please get into the car,' he said, not even glancing in her direction.

'Who are you?' she asked.

'Police.'

Not the answer she'd been expecting.

Police? He wasn't like any police officer she'd ever met. His suit was too smart and his car too new. There was a pair of expensive-looking sunglasses folded neatly on the dashboard and she could hear Etta James singing softly from one of the speakers. The police officers she'd met during the research for her books were usually far scruffier. This man had style.

'Could I see your ID?' she asked.

Taking a wallet from the inside of his jacket, he flipped it open and held it up. 'Detective Chief Inspector Douglas Cameron, CID. I don't have all night. Get in the car. *Now*.' He snapped the wallet shut and returned it to his pocket.

He also had arrogance.

She hesitated. The ID appeared real enough but so would any good fake.

'The press are here,' he sighed. 'You're drawing attention to yourself. Unless that's what you want? Either way, stop wasting my time.'

She checked behind, but all she could see were the emergency vehicles and the locals, still standing behind the cordon.

'Ms Grove? If you're not going to get into the car, please shut the door. There's somewhere else I need to be.'

'OK, OK.' She slid into the passenger seat. Bryn closed it before getting into the back of the car. She heard the doors lock.

'It does that automatically,' the DCI said. 'If you want to get out, just open the door in the usual way.'

It didn't help make her feel any more relaxed.

He turned the music down but left the interior light off. Even in the dim glow cast by the street lamps outside, she could see he was younger than she'd first thought – in his mid-thirties at the most. He didn't appear *old* enough to be a DCI, except...

'I *know* you,' she said.

Surprised, he turned his head and a nearby street light caught a fleeting expression that she'd not seen for a very long time.

Pity.

Everything fell into place.

'You were there,' she said, 'the morning Sarah died. Standing outside the Lodge. You were wearing a uniform and your hair was longer, and you had no beard, but I remember you.'

'I was the one who heard you scream,' he said. 'I was the one who found you tearing through the castle grounds.'

'No, I was beside the pond with my sister.'

Did he think she'd forget something like that?

'Not then, later. You were running through the woods as though the devil himself was after you.'

That didn't seem right.

'I don't remember that,' she said.

'It was a long time ago.'

She didn't want to argue, so said instead, 'I was hoping you could tell me what's happened to my father?'

'It's not good, I'm afraid.'

'He's dead?'

The DCI nodded briefly. 'I'm sorry.'

'You're sure it's him? There's no mistake? Did you have someone identify him?'

'It was fairly conclusive. Mr Grove was in his room, still in his wheelchair.'

Had her dad been sitting in his favourite spot in the bay window, just as she'd seen him earlier? Why hadn't he tried to escape? Had he known it would be hopeless and so had not even tried?

She shivered as the enormity hit her. John Grove was dead. She'd never have to face him again. He no longer held power over her. She was free.

So why did she feel so upset – and so *angry*?

She could almost hear his voice inside her head: *'You've got to let it go, girl.'*

In the background, DCI Cameron was still talking, although she could hardly make sense of what he said. She dug her fingernails into her palms, forcing herself to concentrate, and caught a word she recognised.

'Accelerant?' she repeated. 'Are you saying the fire wasn't an accident?'

'There was no attempt to disguise it,' he said.

'Oh no...'

Despite not having eaten since lunch, the contents of Natalie's stomach wanted out. She struggled to open the door, but her feet got caught up with the straps of her bag.

'Not in the car!'

The DCI reached past and gave the door a violent shove. She swung around to lean out over the leaf-strewn gutter, taking deep breaths to calm the nausea, but the choking, smoke-filled air made her feel worse.

The conversation went on without her. She could hear Bryn, his voice low and bitter, muddled with the DCI's.

'Why did you have to tell her like *that*?'

'She needed to know the truth.'

'You could have put it more kindly!'

Natalie's head pounded, making it impossible to think.

Accelerant?

Had someone murdered her father? Because of what had happened to her sister? No, it couldn't be that simple. Fourteen years was too long to wait for revenge.

She closed her eyes, but all she could see was him.

'Nemesis...' Wasn't that what he'd said?

'What's that?' The DCI broke off in mid-argument. 'What did you say?'

Had she spoken out loud? She leant back in the seat and opened her eyes. 'I'd like to go home please. I don't feel at all well.'

He regarded her thoughtfully. 'Tell me where you live and I'll get one of my team to drop you off.'

'I'll walk,' she told him. 'I could do with the fresh air.' Perhaps it would help clear the fog from her brain.

'If that's what you want. I'll need a statement later, detailing any conversations you had with your father. There may have been something he told you, something that, with hindsight, might explain what happened.'

She remained silent.

Had John known he was going to die? Was that why it had been so urgent for him to see her this evening? But why would anyone want him dead?

'He was the head gardener at Castle Vyne at the time of your sister's death,' the DCI said.

'Yes, what of it?'

'Sarah's body was found in the grounds of Castle Vyne. Did it ever occur to you that your father might have killed her?'

Natalie found her eyes closing again, with little she could do to stop them. She felt so tired, so *ill*...

'You understand that I have to ask these questions, no matter how unpleasant?' His tone was different now, more sympathetic.

'Our father was a bully but not a murderer.'

She could tell the DCI thought she was hiding something. She should've kept silent. She'd forgotten how the police could trick even the most innocent person into tying themselves in knots, attempting to keep their story straight.

She opened her eyes. Keeping them closed might make the DCI believe she was trying to evade his questions.

Sure enough, he was still watching her.

It was tempting to get out of the car and walk away.

Would he let her?

'Your father deliberately drove his car over the cliff after Sarah's death,' the DCI said. 'Why would he do that?'

She watched the emergency crews running about the street, without actually seeing them. The blaze appeared to be under control, but smoke still billowed around the car like fog.

'It was an *accident*,' she said. 'Just one of those things that could happen to anyone.'

'You believe that?'

'*Yes.*'

The DCI said nothing, either from tact or because he was contemplating what she'd said. The silence stretched out. Did he believe her?

He took his phone from his pocket and dialled a number.

'Is that it?' she asked. 'Are we done? Can I go home now?'

'Sure.'

He held the phone to his ear, barely glancing in her direction. It was as though she'd ceased to exist.

She got out of the car, half-expecting him to run after her.

He didn't, so she began to quickly walk home.

And that was when the ground slid sideways and the darkness came back.

SIXTEEN

Natalie staggered. The cobblestones lurched towards her, before another arm slid beneath hers, hauling her up.

'I've got you,' Bryn said.

There was a moment of awkwardness as they stared at each other and then he let her go.

'Would you like to sit down?' he asked politely, indicating the kerb behind them.

'No.' Aware tiredness was making her snappy, she made a joke out of it. 'On the pavement? Not quite my thing.'

'You should've taken that lift.'

'I live five minutes' walk away. I'll be fine.'

'I'm glad to hear it,' he said. 'Come on, I'll walk you home.'

She was too tired to argue.

The police barrier tape at the end of the road was still in evidence. The officer on duty lifted it for them to pass beneath. Beyond that was the junction with the roundabout and the war memorial. The air was fresher here; the breeze whipped straight up the hill from the river.

She took a deep breath. It was like a long drink of cold water.

'Why are you in Calahurst?' she asked tiredly. '*Are* you stalking me?'

His smile was rueful. 'My company has been contracted to restore the garden at Castle Vyne.'

A few more pieces of puzzle slotted into place.

'Congratulations,' she said.

His smile turned into a grin.

'I seriously undercut the competition.'

At least he was honest.

'Do you really believe Geraint is innocent?'

The smile abruptly disappeared. 'We haven't heard from him in fourteen years. He wouldn't do that to his family.'

'He could be dead?'

'I still want to know what happened to him.'

Was Bryn's obsession with finding his cousin any different to the one she had with her sister? Maybe she should give him a break. He didn't look like a murderer.

But what did they look like anyway?

'I'm sorry about your dad,' he said. 'It must have been a shock. Are you going to be OK on your own? Shall I call someone to be with you?'

He knew she lived alone.

'I'll be fine.'

It was a lie. She was still trying to get her head around the idea that she'd never see her father again. They'd spoken only a few hours ago. How could someone be there one moment and not the next?

The moonlight glittered on the river. Where it had been hectic earlier, the marina was now deserted. The clubs and bars alongside the water were closing. A few stragglers loitered beneath the street lights, chatting, sitting on the railings – some were even singing, reluctant to end their evening. The bitter scent of smoke hung around, but was it in the air, lingering on her clothes or only inside her head?

At the foot of the hill, Bryn took a left turn and stopped outside her apartment block.

He really did know where she lived.

The ground floor was mostly in darkness, but there was a light on in the gym. A solitary figure, neatly framed by one of the windows, was pounding on the treadmill. Further along, the great glass doors revealed the reception area was deserted.

She placed her hand against the door and pushed. It was locked, with no sign of Phil in reception. Bryn was standing behind her, reflected in the glass. She knew nothing about him...

He knew everything about her.

Catching sight of her own image, pale and hollow-eyed, beside his, she forced a friendly smile before turning back to face him. 'Goodbye, Bryn,' she said firmly. 'Thank you once again for your help.'

He inclined his head. 'I'll wait to see you inside.'

She raised her hand to key the security code into the panel beside the door, but he was still watching. She made a circular motion with her finger and he got the message, turning his back so she could enter the code.

A faint click; the array of lights on the control panel switched from red to green and the entrance door slid open.

'Bye then,' she said.

Perhaps this time he'd take the hint and actually leave.

The door swished shut as she headed for the lift; her footsteps echoing. The reception desk was deserted. Was Phil doing his rounds? She pressed the call button for the lift. Reception and the street beyond the entrance were all reflected in the mirrored tiles.

Bryn *still* waited outside. He was persistent, she'd give him that.

The lift slid open and she stepped straight in. A few moments later, she was standing outside her apartment. She was about to fumble in her bag for her keys when the door swung open.

What on earth...?

She'd locked the door before she'd left, she knew she had!

Slowly she pushed it open, aiming for stealth, but the door swung back against the wall with a dull thud. Beyond, the apartment was clearly in darkness and there were no strips of light showing beneath any of the doors.

She'd left the hall light on though, she'd swear to it.

'Simon?' She couldn't face him again. 'Is that you?'

There was no response. Of course, there wouldn't be. She needed to get a grip. Simon would still be sulking and a burglar would hardly announce himself.

She flicked the switch for the hall light. Nothing happened. She tried again, flipping the switch on and off at speed.

'Perfect,' she muttered. 'Absolutely perfect.' The bulb had gone and it was unlikely she had a spare.

She checked the next light switch, which was beside the study door, and got the same result. OK, *not* the bulb. Had the fuse tripped out?

The fuse box was located in the study, high on the wall behind the door. She took her phone from her bag to use as a torch, but when she tried to open the study door, it hit against something and stuck. Had one of her many books fallen from a shelf and jammed against it?

She gave the door a violent shove. It gave slightly – and then slammed back into her.

Natalie fell against the wall and slid to the floor, all the breath knocked out of her. A shadowy figure stepped from behind the door, pausing to look her up and down, before stepping over her and into the hall. By the time it occurred to her to scream, he'd gone.

Her phone was a few metres away, glimmering in its own pool of light. She scooped it up, using it to illuminate the study.

Reassuringly empty. Nothing appeared to have been taken – even her laptop was still on her desk.

What had they been hoping to steal? The diary?

Knowing that they'd never find it, didn't prevent a little sizzle of panic, humming low in her gut. Would they be back? What should she do? Was it worth calling the police? Would they even turn up when nothing had been taken?

Hands shaking, she checked the fuse box. The red power switch had been flipped to 'off'. The intruder must have heard her arrive and hit the power to give himself time to escape.

As soon as she flicked the switch, the apartment was flooded with light, blinding her. She cursed and covered her eyes, and didn't see someone standing behind her, until she'd walked smack into them.

This time *she* did scream, but someone caught her shoulders and a familiar voice said, 'Thank goodness you're all right!'

Bryn? How had he got in? Was it a set-up? Bryn was to keep her talking while someone else broke into her apartment?

She shoved him hard. 'Get away from—' and then saw two police officers were beside him.

DCI Cameron appeared in the entrance to her apartment. 'May we come in?' he asked, blithely stepping over the threshold and walking inside before she had the chance to reply.

She threw up her hands. 'Why not? I'll put the kettle on.'

He failed to pick up on her sarcasm. 'That would be lovely, but before you get started' – he reached into his pocket and handed her a small plastic bottle – 'do you think you could pee into that?'

SEVENTEEN

Natalie turned the bottle over in her hand. It was a clear plastic vial and had a white label ready to be inscribed with her name.

'You want me to... *what?*'

The blank expression on DCI Cameron's face didn't flicker. 'We think someone may have put something into your drink.'

No prizes for guessing who'd put *that* idea in his head.

'I had my drink with me all the time. There was no opportunity—'

'Humour me.' DCI Cameron gave her a gentle push in the direction of the cloakroom. 'Speed is of the essence, Ms Grove.'

So now she was in the cloakroom with the door closed. Outside, the police were moving about the apartment. She could hear doors opening and closing as they made no effort to be either quiet or discreet. They constantly called out to each other – too muffled for her to discern exactly what was being said, until one spoke directly outside the cloakroom door.

'No sign of anyone, sir.'

They were searching for her intruder. Hadn't she seen him leave? Did they believe there was a second one too?

Natalie leant wearily against the door. The wood felt cool against the hot skin of her forehead. She could barely keep her eyes open. Would this never end?

Someone banged on the door. Abruptly, she stepped back, confused. Had she drifted off?

'Are you all right, Ms Grove?'

She muttered something appropriate through the door and then looked at the bottle. She'd better get on with it.

When she stepped back into the hall, the two uniformed officers had left, but now there was a swarm of crime scene investigators spreading throughout the apartment. It was a lot of trouble to go to for one foiled break-in. Was there something else at play?

She dangled the bottle from her fingers. 'Who wants this?'

One of the CSI officers took the bottle before she'd barely got the words out, sliding it into a clear plastic bag. 'I also need a blood sample and a strand of hair.'

She looked at DCI Cameron. 'Is he serious?'

'Let's go into the kitchen,' the DCI suggested. 'I'm afraid this is going to take a while.'

By the time the CSI officer had taken the required samples, the kettle had boiled and Bryn was spooning instant coffee into mugs. 'Milk?' he asked, holding up a bottle. *Her* bottle. She'd been reduced to being a guest in her own apartment. 'Sugar?'

'Just black, thank you.' She sat at the glass breakfast table by the window overlooking the marina. What else *could* she say?

A plate of her favourite ginger biscuits appeared in front of her. She'd been saving those for the next time Alicia came round.

At least the kitchen was tidy, although there was a lingering scent of Indian takeaway. Thank goodness she'd cleared up the pieces of broken wood and stashed Sarah's picture in her wardrobe until she could have it repaired. Heaven knew what they would've made of *that*. Had it only been a few hours ago that she'd come home and found Simon sitting on the sofa?

'You're a most interesting lady, Natalie Grove,' the DCI was saying. 'You go on television and talk about a long-forgotten murder, and within a few hours all hell breaks loose.'

Deciding a reply was not required, she took a sip of coffee. Unexpectedly, Bryn had made it exactly the way she liked. She sought him out. There were not enough chairs at the table so he was leant against one of the worktops, cradling a mug in his hand, watching her. Did the police trust him? Should she?

'We've checked your apartment,' DCI Cameron added, as though sensing her attention had wandered. 'Your intruder was working alone. He executed a tidy search and your valuables appear to be still here. What was he looking for?'

The question took her by surprise. She put down the mug and spooned sugar into it, to give herself time to think. As she stirred, she was aware of every clink of the spoon and that everyone in the room was waiting for her answer.

Admit nothing. She could almost sense her father's presence in the kitchen, even though he'd never visited her apartment. *Don't volunteer information. Don't incriminate yourself.* She remembered how he'd always hated the police. It'd never occurred to her to wonder why.

'The usual, I suppose,' she said.

'Do you have a safe for cash and jewellery?'

That one was easy. 'I don't keep cash in the apartment and I don't have much jewellery.' She took another sip from her mug. She liked her coffee black, strong and unsweetened. The sugar she'd added now rendered it undrinkable. It was an effort not to grimace. She carefully set the mug back on the table, smiling politely at the police officers. How had they got here so quickly?

'Would you know if anything was missing?' the DCI persisted.

Down the hall, she could hear the CSI officers moving from room to room.

'I suppose so.' It was easy to sound vague when she felt so weary.

'Would you be so kind as to check the apartment for me?' The tension had returned to his voice. 'Then we'll be out of your way.'

That suggestion she was happy to agree with, although it took a good hour for the forensics to be finished. The DCI and his team drank more coffee and finished off the biscuits. Bryn made a call on his phone. To Siân? As he went out into the lobby to make it, she had no idea who he was phoning.

Eventually, she was given the all-clear to check her apartment. She knew it'd be a waste of time but went through the motions to keep them happy. The police stayed in the kitchen. Bryn, however, followed her.

'Is it safe?' he asked in a low voice, once they were clear of the kitchen.

'Is what safe?'

'The diary. It's what he was looking for, wasn't it?'

She'd almost convinced herself that this had been a random break-in.

'I've no idea what you're talking about,' she said. 'This was an opportunist crime, nothing more.'

'You could be right.' She couldn't miss his sarcasm. 'After all, the intruder only had to get past the security system on the main entrance, the guard at reception, check he wasn't caught on camera and finally get through your apartment door. I assume you locked it before you went out?'

She remembered the empty reception. 'Phil! Is he all right?'

'We found him unconscious on the floor behind the front desk. Luckily he managed to press the panic button before he passed out. It was put straight through to the local police station, which was why DCI Cameron and his team were able to get here so quickly.'

She must have walked right past his unconscious body. 'Oh no, poor Phil...'

'His pride is hurt, but he's OK.'

They'd reached the sitting room. To her relief, it was as much as she'd left it. The cushions on the sofa were fluffed up, the rug lay straight against the polished wood and the pictures were perfectly aligned.

It was the pictures that caught Bryn's attention. 'Sir Henry Vyne?'

He'd recognised them?

'That's right.'

'He painted your sister?'

'He painted lots of local people.'

'But not you?'

She wanted to joke, 'Unfortunately not', but that wouldn't be true. She didn't think she'd like a painting of herself hanging on someone else's wall.

He made no further comment, but, as she walked slowly around the room checking for anything out of the ordinary, she knew he was drawing his own conclusions.

'Everything seems to be OK.' She was careful not to look at him directly. 'I think I must have arrived home shortly after the intruder broke in. He didn't have the chance to go further than my study.'

'You were lucky.'

Not *quite* how she'd have described it, but it didn't appear as though anything had been taken and she'd only suffered a few bruises.

The next room to check was the guest bedroom. It was immaculate, as usual, because it was never used. The one after that was her bedroom. Seeing her suitcase in the corner, still waiting to be unpacked, made her feel strange. Her trip to London could have been a lifetime ago.

Her study was the last room. Bryn gave the painting of Sarah dancing beneath the magnolia tree a cursory glance. As Natalie ran her fingers along the bookshelves – who'd break in to steal a book? – she saw Bryn pick something off the floor and hold it to the light. A narrow shard of wood – from the picture frame Simon had broken. He must have the most amazing eyesight.

She held her breath until he dropped it into the waste basket without comment.

As far as she could tell, nothing was out of place. Her books were still in alphabetical order. Her files – hard copies of her manuscripts and all her research notes – were neatly in place, although her shelves had acquired a layer of dust, presumably from the CSI officers checking for fingerprints.

Her attention flicked to her desk. Her laptop was where she had left it, along with a bag of sweets.

Sweets?

She scooped them up. A scrap of paper fluttered to the floor.

Bryn, unfortunately, missed nothing.

'What is it?'

'Liquorice,' she said slowly. 'It's the same brand I always buy for my father.'

But how had the bag got *here*?

This one hadn't been opened.

Bryn caught on the same time she did. 'Is it the same packet?'

'No. The intruder didn't take anything. He left this behind.'

'As a warning? Now your fingerprints are all over it!'

'You think he's going to leave fingerprints? This is the work of a professional.'

'At last, we agree on something.'

Their sniping brought DCI Cameron into the study. 'What have you found?'

She explained the significance of the bag of liquorice.

While he appeared unconvinced that it could be connected to her father, he instructed his colleague to put it into an evidence bag.

'There's nothing else? Nothing taken? Nothing untoward?'

'I don't think so.'

'Then we'll be on our way.' A signal to his colleagues and they began packing up and filing out of the apartment.

That was it?

The DCI was the last to leave. Before he did so, he paused and looked back. 'Be sure to bolt your door – and I'd recommend you change your locks.'

He thought the intruder might return? That little fizz of panic, that she'd been trying so hard to ignore, became more insistent.

'We'll be in touch,' he added, and was gone.

The door swung silently shut. Finally she was alone.

Or perhaps not...

'We need to talk,' Bryn said.

Why was *he* still here? And how had he managed to inveigle entry? Had he just tagged along, unnoticed, with the police? Was he *working* with them?

'Fine,' she said, pulling open the front door, leaving him with no excuse to remain. The officers waiting for the lift glanced round curiously. 'Two o'clock tomorrow, Tom's Coffee Shop on the waterfront.'

'OK...' He seemed surprised at her easy acquiescence but allowed himself to be hustled out. 'I'll see you there.'

After shutting the door on him, she locked and bolted it, then dragged a table in front of it. No one would be able to get through *that* without making a great deal of noise.

There was one thing left to do.

Back in her study, the slip of paper that had been left on her desk beside the liquorice had wafted beneath her desk.

Natalie crawled on her hands and knees to retrieve it.

It'd been torn from one of her notebooks and had curled slightly at the edge.

She smoothed it out on her desk.

There were just two words, written in black ink:

Destroy it

EIGHTEEN

Natalie was woken by someone hammering on her door as though endeavouring to wake the dead. She tried ignoring it, but, as they obviously weren't going away any time soon, she slid out of bed cursing. The long pink T-shirt she wore only reached about mid-thigh, so she grabbed a long cardigan to throw over it.

Sunlight streamed through the windows, warming the floorboards beneath her feet as she padded down the hall. What time was it? How long had she slept? She was so groggy, it could have been a week.

She was further confused by finding a table wedged in front of the door.

What on earth...?

The hammering started again before she'd got her head around the events of the previous night. She pulled the table away from the door and wrenched it open, fully intending to give the person on the other side a piece of her mind. She'd assumed it was Bryn, not trusting that she wouldn't stand him up. Instead, Phil stood on the other side, a cordless drill in one hand and a toolbox planted by his feet, but it was the flesh-coloured plaster on his bald head that caught her attention.

'Oh, Phil! Did the intruder do that to you?'

His easy smile faded. 'I was lucky not to need stitches.'

'I'm so sorry!'

'*He* will be, when I catch up with him. Until that happy day, I'm here to change your lock.'

'Now?'

He took in her bed hair and bare legs. 'Oh... Were you asleep?'

'Not at all, just having a lazy morning. Would you like a cup of coffee?'

Hopefully a good dose of caffeine would wake her too.

'That'd be brilliant.' He squatted to check the lock on her door, before flipping open his toolbox and setting to work.

She'd have left Phil to it, but at that moment Simon stepped out of the lift. He was wearing jeans, a thick grey sweater and his usual trainers. The overhead light glinted on his spectacles, masking his expression, but he wasn't smiling.

Natalie tensed. If she'd woken earlier, she might have left the apartment by now and avoided him.

She faked a smile, but Simon's attention was on Phil and his toolbox.

'What's going on?' he asked.

Where to start?

Phil raised his head. 'Ms Grove had a break-in last night.' He'd wrestled the lock off and was now poking at the hole with a short stubby finger. 'We're changing the lock as a security precaution.'

'What kind of lock?'

Phil held up a small cellophane packet.

Simon regarded it dismissively and said to Natalie, 'Why didn't you call me?'

So now he was a locksmith?

'It *was* the middle of the night,' she said.

And there was the little matter of her wrecked picture frame. Did he think she was going to forgive him that easily? He knew how much those paintings of Sarah meant to her.

'That doesn't matter. I'd have come straight over. Did you contact the police?'

What business was it of his?

'The police were here, yes. But how about you? Shouldn't you be at work?'

'It's my break. I heard the news about your father. Why didn't you call me?'

It hadn't occurred to her. Weren't she and Simon supposed to be 'finished'? They'd been a couple for about eight years, but after the way he'd spoken to her last night...

No, she *definitely* didn't want him back.

'So much happened yesterday evening,' she said, 'that by the time the police had left it was gone midnight.' It was as good an excuse as any.

'I'd have come over,' he said. 'You know I would.'

He reached out, as though to slide his arm about her shoulder, but she stepped aside.

Simon frowned. 'I tried phoning you several times this morning, to apologise for losing my temper and... er, you know, but there was no answer.'

'I haven't had the chance to check my phone for notifications.'

'I assure you, I did call.'

'I believe you.' Why was he getting so het up about this? 'I must have slept through it. I was absolutely shattered.'

Phil, oblivious to their tension, picked up his cordless drill and switched it on.

The high-pitched whine went right through Natalie's head.

'Thank you for coming round, Simon. It was thoughtful of you. But you don't want to be late getting back to school.'

She reversed into the apartment, to get away from the noise of the drill, assuming Simon would leave.

Instead, he followed her into the kitchen. 'I'm here because I wanted to check you were OK.'

'As you can see, I'm perfectly fine.'

'It's lunchtime and you're wearing your nightclothes!'

Who made him the sleep police?

'As I explained earlier, I had a rather fraught evening—'

'Are you alone?'

'*What?*' Did he believe she had another man? *Already?*

'Oh for goodness' sake, Simon!'

She'd promised Phil a coffee, so she put the kettle on, hoping Simon would take the hint and leave.

Her stomach rumbled, reminding her that she'd missed out on breakfast.

Simon leant against the kitchen doorway. 'I don't have time for coffee. I've got to get back to work.'

She took a couple of mugs from the dishwasher and banged them onto the counter. 'I wasn't offering you one. This is for Phil.'

'So he gets a coffee but not me?'

'I overslept and I'm running late. The caffeine is to help wake me up. As soon as Phil finishes, I'm going out.'

He stared at her. Was he waiting for an apology? When *he* was the one at fault?

'Was there anything else you wanted?'

(Perhaps that could have been said less tetchily.)

'What's the matter with you?' he asked. 'At the very least, you could be polite.'

Polite? *Polite?* She hadn't asked him to come round. She'd thought she wasn't going to see him again.

Only the rumbling of the kettle and the distant sound of the drill broke the silence.

'I appreciate it must have been a dreadful shock for you,' he added stoically. 'For your father to die so suddenly...'

'Who told you?'

'Not you, obviously.' When she didn't respond, he sighed and added, 'It was on the news.'

Great, so now she was going to be doorstepped by reporters?

She leant against the counter. She really couldn't deal with all this. To be honest, she didn't want to deal with anything – Sarah, Geraint, Bryn, her father, the police – and certainly not Simon. All she wanted was some paracetamol for her headache and a duvet day. But if she didn't keep her appointment at Tom's Coffee Shop, Bryn was likely to turn up here. And that would *really* set Simon off.

The simplest solution would be to explain everything. Simon would be happy to take control for her, just as he always did.

But she was thirty years old now, not sixteen, and she'd quite like to make her own decisions.

Simon produced a slim bouquet of flowers from behind his back. Roses, of the palest pink, just starting to open.

He held them out towards her. 'I'm sorry, Natalie. I should never have said those things to you. It was cruel and unkind. If you let me have that painting of Sarah, I'll arrange to have it reframed.'

The flowers were pretty, but she couldn't bring herself to take them. Too little, too late.

The kettle switched off. Grateful for the distraction, she began spooning instant coffee into the mug. By the time she'd poured out the hot water and milk, the flowers were lying on the counter beside her.

'You're upset,' he said. Now he was standing beside her; so close, she could feel his breath on her neck. 'You've had an appalling shock. It's only natural to feel disorientated. You should give Charles a call. Even though you're no longer his patient, I'm sure he can sort you out with something.'

Had he forgotten Charles had sweet-talked her into a clandestine relationship at the age of sixteen, when she'd been his *patient*? It was probably what had screwed her up in the first place. To give someone like that control over your mental wellbeing? Why had no one stopped him?

Because no one had cared enough to.

Then she'd traded him in for Simon, who was just as controlling in his own way.

'If I feel the need, I'll visit my own GP.' She concentrated on stirring the coffee. Did Phil take sugar? She'd not thought to ask. One simple task; that was all it had been. Make coffee. Why was it so difficult?

'Charles helped you get back on your feet last time.'

Last time...

A sharp pain brought her back to the present. Somehow she'd cut her hand.

She grabbed a tea towel and pressed it against the cut to stop the blood. In the centre of the worktop, in a pool of spilt coffee, were the shattered remains of a mug.

Simon was staring at her, horrified. 'What's *wrong* with you? Why are you behaving like this?'

If she hadn't seen his lips move, she'd have thought she was hallucinating him too.

She rather wished she was. It would have made him easier to get rid of.

'I don't know...' Coffee dripped down the side of the counter. She used the end of the tea towel to wipe it up. 'I don't know what happened. I must have zoned out for a moment...'

'You deliberately smashed that mug onto the counter! I saw you do it!'

Had she? Better add that to the list of everything else she couldn't remember.

Could it be a form of stress or was something still in her system? She certainly had plenty to be stressed about!

Simon was backing out of the kitchen as though he thought she was dangerous.

'Are you OK, Ms Grove?' Phil appeared in the doorway behind Simon. He still held his drill.

'I've had a bit of an accident.' She cheerfully held up her hand, still wrapped in the tea towel.

Within seconds, Phil had pulled away the tea towel, turned on the cold tap and thrust her hand beneath the water. 'Got a first-aid kit?' he asked Simon. 'Even another tea towel would do.'

'I don't know.' Simon glared at her. 'I don't live here.'

She gestured towards the dresser on the other side of the kitchen. 'There's one in that cupboard.' She expected Simon to fetch it, but suddenly he wasn't there any more.

'He's a keeper,' Phil muttered, retrieving the first-aid kit himself. 'It's not as bad as it looks,' he added with fake cheer, drying Natalie's hand on a piece of kitchen roll and applying a bandage. 'Press firmly on that for a bit. If it bleeds through, stick another bandage on, but don't take that one off. You won't need stitches, at least.' He pointed to the plaster on his head. 'We make a right pair, eh? Regular bookends!'

Bless him; he was trying to cheer her up.

It made her want to cry.

Phil rinsed the tea towel and hung it on a rail over the radiator, before wiping down the worktop with a sponge and placing the shattered pieces of the mug into the bin. 'Is there anything else I can do for you, Ms Grove? If I'm not back soon, they'll send out a search party. We're all a bit paranoid after last night.'

Something else that was her fault.

'You didn't have your coffee,' she said sadly.

'Maybe next time, but I've got to go.' He dropped a collection of keys onto the worktop. 'That's for your front door,' he said, 'plus a couple of spares.'

'Thanks, Phil. For everything.'

'No problem, Ms Grove.' He hesitated, glancing again at the shiny new keys on the table and then in the direction of the door Simon had just walked through. 'But this time be careful who you give 'em to, eh?'

NINETEEN

By the time Natalie arrived at the coffee shop, Bryn was at the counter placing his order. He was easily recognisable, even from the back, in his scruffy jacket, jeans and boots. He had his leather satchel too, carelessly slung over one shoulder. Was her book still inside? It was unnerving that he'd discovered so much about her, when she knew so little about him in return.

He turned his head and caught her staring.

'Hi,' he said. 'How do you like your coffee?'

She relieved him of the two china cups he held and placed them back onto the counter. 'We'll take them to go,' she told the barista, who rolled his eyes but carelessly tipped the coffees into two paper cups all the same. 'We're going on a trip,' she told Bryn.

He regarded her with suspicion. 'What kind of a trip?'

She pointed her key through the café window at the black BMW parked outside. The indicators flashed.

'A road trip,' she said. 'You want to work with me to find out who killed Sarah? We're going to start at the beginning.'

. . .

Natalie was relieved Bryn didn't question her again, but settled back into his seat and watched the village pass in a grey and white blur as they headed up the hill and towards the main road. The tinted windows made everything seem darker and gloomier than it actually was. Or was that only her mood?

By the time they entered the forest, the sun had emerged from the clouds and was glinting on the autumn leaves, which ran through every shade from deepest crimson to brilliant gold.

'Why did you stay in Calahurst?' he asked her. 'You're rich. You could live anywhere.'

She wasn't prepared for that conversation. She didn't want it either. All she wanted was to get to their destination as quickly as possible.

So she gave him a flippant reply. 'It certainly made it easier for you to find me.'

'You're surrounded by unhappy memories. I'm surprised it didn't send you crazy.'

'Better the devil you know.'

'It would send *me* crazy, living my life where everyone knew me and judged me on what I'd done in the past.'

'I guess that makes me the stronger person.'

He fixed her with a rather too astute stare. 'Are you sure about that?'

'I believe that the way you deal with your past helps you to develop as a person.'

'That sounds as though it came straight from the mouth of a shrink.'

Because it had.

Charles Fitzpatrick.

She clenched her fingers tighter around the steering wheel.

Why did Bryn find it so easy to see right through her?

'You think you've become a better person because your sister was murdered?' he said. 'Excuse me, but you're talking rubbish. Your sister is dead, gone from your life for ever. Everything she was, the person she would've been, snuffed out in an instant. It's worse than if she'd never existed. There's a permanent hole in your life where she should have been.'

There was a hole in her life all right, but it wasn't occupying a space where Sarah should have been. It was where her hopes and dreams had disappeared, wrapped in this all-encompassing obsession with finding out the truth. Writing this book had put a bow on it.

'You don't know me,' she said. 'You can't judge me or presume to know how I feel. So don't, and we'll get along fine.'

'I *do* know how you feel. I've been through it myself. Except you *know* what happened to your sister. You haven't spent your life hoping she'll walk back through your door. You have a conclusion; a finality. You have a grave.'

It was the one thing she'd never been able to do – visit Sarah's grave. Alicia left flowers regularly, but Natalie hadn't even attended Sarah's funeral. Instead, she'd crept out of the Lodge and peered over the stone wall of the churchyard as Sarah's small, slight coffin had been lowered into the earth. The only mourners had been her mother and Sir Henry Vyne.

For the first time, Natalie realised her father had been absent. Where had he been? Had the funeral been before or after his accident? It'd taken a while for the authorities to release Sarah's body, so perhaps the funeral had been afterwards? Why had she never realised the significance before?

'Are you OK?' Bryn broke her chain of thought. 'I didn't mean to upset you. I get the impression you've never really talked to anyone about this. It might help if you did.'

He sounded so kind, so caring, she could feel her eyes welling up again. First with Phil, now Bryn – as soon as anyone showed her any kindness, basically. She'd have to toughen up or he'd walk all over her.

Thankfully, as the road emerged from the forest and swooped along the edge of the moor, she realised they'd arrived.

'We're here.'

Bryn said nothing, staring at the bleak coastline before them. There was no sandy beach here, only mud and rocks where hungry herring gulls swooped low over the shallow pools, left behind when the tide had receded.

She turned the car down a single-track lane, between a long avenue of lime trees. At the end was a pretty Georgian manor house, its red brick glowing in the afternoon sunlight.

She parked close to the house beneath a cluster of chestnut trees. The leaves hung limply, dead and brown, dripping from a recent shower of rain. The gravel drive beneath them was littered with pale green and yellow shells, each one split to reveal a furry white inside. The glossy brown conkers were conspicuous by their absence.

Natalie didn't linger. She knew their approach would have been seen and that a strategy was being formed. She walked quickly across the drive towards the house. Bryn followed, but his attention was caught by something on the other side of a wire fence. It was a tennis court, where two young boys played with great enthusiasm, if not much skill.

'Natalie?' When she didn't respond, he caught her arm. 'Who lives here?'

She glanced past him, at the two boys playing tennis. They wore matching jeans and striped jerseys; their distinctive blond hair so pale it was almost white.

'My mother,' she admitted.

'Your mother is dead.'

'Yeah... People tend to think that because she'd rather have nothing to do with me.'

Was it because she reminded her mother too much of Sarah?

To avoid any further questions, she tried to pull away.

Bryn held on. 'Natalie, why are we here?'

She sighed. 'To understand the life that Sarah and I had,

you need to meet our parents. It's too late for you to meet my father, so I've brought you here to meet my mother. *If* she'll see us. I never know what mood she's going to be in.'

The door to the house opened.

'It appears we're in luck,' she said, sliding out of his grip and walking towards the house.

Bryn hesitated and she could hardly blame him. Then she heard him curse, followed by the scrunch of his footsteps in the gravel as he caught her up.

'You could have told me about your mother. We didn't have to come all the way out here.'

'Trust me, we did.'

He'd never have believed her otherwise.

She'd half-expected to be denied entry, but the man who opened the door stood aside to let her enter without saying a word. Evidently, the staff had been briefed.

Natalie was taken across the hall to a sitting room overlooking the tennis court. It was a small, pleasant enough room that didn't appear to be used very often. The walls were painted an inoffensive duck-egg blue, the furniture was old and mismatched but most likely antique, and there were a few silver sporting trophies and nondescript paintings – perhaps banished from someplace more important.

Natalie tried not to think of allegories.

Her mother stood slightly to one side of the window, ostensibly watching the boys play tennis. She wore a simple grey blouse and dark trousers, and had a delicate platinum chain around her neck that she was winding about her fingers.

It took a moment for her to turn her head, but, when she saw her daughter approach, she offered her cheek to be kissed.

'Natalie, how lovely to see you.'

Natalie reluctantly moved in for an air kiss. Magda smelt of expensive perfume. Close to, there were barely any lines or wrinkles. She certainly didn't appear old enough to be the mother of a thirty-year-old. The hunting, shooting and fishing lifestyle she'd adopted since her remarriage obviously suited her.

Was this how Sarah would have looked if she'd lived?

'Thank you for agreeing to see me,' Natalie said, blanking out that last thought.

'Perhaps next time you'll allow me to have the choice?' her mother murmured.

Natalie chose the chair nearest the fire. Old houses were always so *cold* – it was one of the reasons she'd sworn never to live in one again.

Magda seemed rather more pleased to see Bryn. 'You're the new one?' She looked him up and down. 'You're certainly an improvement on Simon. Did you know he used to be her teacher? He should have been sacked.'

'Simon was *Sarah's* teacher, Mother,' Natalie sighed. 'Never mine. I owe everything to him. He helped me get into university and he encouraged me to write my first book. He even found me a job and somewhere to live after you married Richard and I found myself unexpectedly homeless.'

Magda pretended she hadn't heard.

Bryn, thankfully, said nothing more incriminating than his name and held out his hand.

Natalie waited for the recognition of the surname, but when Magda reached out to shake his hand, her disinterested expression didn't falter.

'I'm Lady Vyne,' she said graciously. 'You may call me Magda.'

It appeared Bryn's research had some holes in it. '*You're* Lady Vyne?'

'Perhaps you thought there could be only one?' Magda glanced across the room to her daughter. 'Haven't you told him anything?'

'Not really, no.'

Where would she begin?

'Is your husband related to Sir Henry Vyne?' Bryn asked, politely filling the silence.

'They were brothers,' Magda said. 'Richard inherited the baronetcy when Henry died, as well as most of the property. Unfortunately, the Castle Vyne estate was not entailed, so Henry could leave it to whomever he pleased – and he left it to his daughter, Alicia.'

The butler was lingering in the doorway. Magda requested tea and then sat in the chair opposite Natalie. This left one end of a sofa for Bryn.

'Have you come to tell me your father's dead?' Magda asked.

Natalie supposed it was as good an excuse for her to use as any. 'You already knew?'

'A Detective Chief Inspector Cameron came to see me this morning. Apparently I was still listed as John's next of kin – perhaps from when I originally filled out the forms for Rose Court.'

'Did you ever visit him?'

'I visited him often,' Magda reproved. 'The last time was about a week ago.'

'I thought you wanted to keep that part of your life in the past?'

(Or maybe that was just Natalie.)

Magda shrugged. 'I'd prefer to forget; I make no secret of it. Just because one wants to forget something though, does not necessarily mean one can.'

'I'm surprised the two of you could find anything to talk about.'

'Talk?' Magda was astonished. 'We didn't *talk* about anything. He was my husband, I felt obliged to visit, to take him the odd gift – a plant, a book, and so forth – but, really, I could have been anybody. Since the accident, he lives – I mean, *lived*

– in a world of his own. As cruel as it sounds, perhaps his death was for the best. He certainly didn't have any kind of life in that home.'

'Are you sure?' Natalie asked.

Magda frowned. 'Am I sure of what?'

'That Dad was injured in that accident? You never felt he was... faking?'

There was only the briefest hesitation. 'The doctors made the diagnosis. Who am I to argue with professional opinion?'

'Was it you who gave him the citrus plant?'

'Yes, I even signed the visitors' book. It wasn't a secret. Surely Charles mentioned it?'

'Perhaps he thought you valued your privacy?'

'Charles thinks of no one but himself, as well you know.' She held Natalie's gaze for a fraction too long, as though tempted to say more, but then the butler returned, wheeling a trolley set for afternoon tea. The moment was gone.

While Magda delicately poured the tea, Bryn got up and walked over to the window. 'Are those your children?'

Magda gave a little laugh. 'Natalie, you seem to have told your new boyfriend very little about me.'

It was on the tip of her tongue to retort, 'I wonder why?' but with great effort, Natalie remained silent, plonking two sugar cubes into her tea and stirring vigorously. Even though she didn't like sugar and hated tea.

'They're my boys,' Magda told Bryn. 'My children with Richard. The elder one is Ricky. He's the image of his father. He's coming up to eleven and doing very well at school. His little brother is called Sven after my father. A dreadful mischief-maker but quite affectionate. They're home for half-term. As they attend a private school, they don't have the opportunity to mix with the local children, but luckily they're very close.' Magda broke off, frowning. 'Natalie, you're going to break that cup if you keep stirring your tea like that.'

Natalie abruptly put the spoon back onto the saucer.

'The police think John Grove was murdered,' Bryn said.

Natalie thought that was pushing it.

She watched for her mother's reaction.

As usual, there wasn't one.

'You must think me very cold-hearted,' Magda sighed, 'but I'm afraid his death means nothing to me. We had an unhappy marriage and, after his accident, I had the courage to divorce him. I try not to think about that part of my life. I've moved on.'

Yet she visited him 'every week'?

'Of course,' Bryn said gently. 'It must have been very difficult for you.'

'It was a dreadful time,' Magda agreed, glancing at her watch.

Natalie helped herself to a cake.

'I know that John was injured in a car accident following Sarah's death,' Bryn said, 'but how did it happen?'

Natalie's hand, which had been halfway to her mouth with the cake, froze.

'He drove his car off the cliff,' Magda said, with a complete lack of emotion. 'It was a month after my daughter's death. He'd been drinking heavily. You can draw your own conclusion. The police did.'

Natalie bit into the cake. It showered pink crumbs across her sweater. As she brushed them away with her fingers, she realised her mother hadn't finished.

With a malicious glance in her direction, Magda added, 'Of course the best person to ask about that would be Natalie. She was with him in the car at the time.'

TWENTY

Natalie and Bryn drove back to Calahurst. After twenty minutes of silence, Natalie thought she'd got away with it but, as they passed the war memorial and entered the village, Bryn said, 'Stop here.'

Was he serious? Calahurst High Street was so narrow that in places it was only wide enough for one vehicle, which was why there were double yellow lines running its entire length.

'I can't,' she said truthfully. 'It would cause an accident. I'll drop you off at the marina.'

'You're not dropping *me* off anywhere,' he said. '*We* are going to have a talk.'

Twenty minutes of having to suffer his silence, and the moment they arrived at their destination, he decided they had to talk? She didn't think so!

'No,' she told him.

'You owe me an explanation.'

They'd reached the bottom of the hill. Directly in front was the marina and, on either side, the cobblestone road that ran between the quaint little shops and the water.

Bryn indicated the tall, glass building on the left. 'Turn in here,' he said.

It was the entrance to the underground car park of her apartment.

'No,' she said again and stopped the car, turning her head to glare at him. 'We talk in the coffee shop or we don't talk at all.'

'Sure,' he said, 'let's go into the coffee shop and talk about how you escaped from your father's car *before* it went over a cliff. Because that's a story I'd really like to hear.'

Apparently there was no way of getting out of it.

Resentfully, she flicked the indicator and drove down the ramp into the car park.

It was Friday afternoon, so the car park was more than half full. There were plenty of cars but no people. Her apartment had three bays assigned to it, but she ignored those and deliberately parked beneath one of the security cameras — not that Bryn seemed particularly bothered. In fact, she had a strong suspicion he'd already rolled his eyes.

'Now what?' She had no intention of inviting him up to her apartment. Did that mean they were going to just sit here in the car?

She forced herself to relax. It had been her idea to go and see Magda, so she only had herself to blame. She should've realised the visit was never going to pass without incident. Since Sarah's death, her mother's disinterest had turned into active dislike. The question Natalie had never been able to bring herself to ask was 'Why?' Because Sir Henry had once shown interest in her? But Magda was now the wealthy Lady Vyne, with a new husband and family. Surely she was over everything that had happened in the past?

The way Natalie was 'over' it?

Perhaps they had more in common than Natalie liked to admit.

'OK.' Bryn settled himself back in the seat and closed his

eyes, as though she was about to read him a bedtime story. 'Talk. Tell me about the night your father had his accident. I want to hear every last detail, no matter how irrelevant or trivial you might think it. And, Natalie?'

'Yes?'

'Make sure you tell me the truth.'

TWENTY-ONE

Fourteen years previously

Natalie lay in bed, fully clothed, waiting for the house to fall silent and the downstairs clock to chime midnight, before climbing through her bedroom window and onto the roof of the porch, using the metal trellis to negotiate the last couple of metres. It had been raining and the trellis left flakes of black paint and rust on her jeans. She wore silver sandals, stolen from Sarah's wardrobe, but they had higher heels than she was used to, so she jammed them into her jacket pockets and climbed down the trellis barefoot. It was only as she ran down the garden path, and sharp stones cut into her feet, that she remembered to slip the shoes back on.

The little gate didn't creak because she'd taken the time to oil the hinges the day before. When she passed through it, she didn't look back. When she reached the trees, Jamie Fitzpatrick was already waiting, but she shoved him away when he tried to hug her.

'What's up with you?' he grumbled.

'Not here,' she told him. 'Not now. Someone might see.'

'Who?' He threw out his hands in exasperation.

'Stop whining and come *on*,' she said.

'*Whining?*'

He'd parked his car a short distance away, as she'd asked. It'd been a mistake. An expensive sports car, fire-engine red, was *not* going to blend into the background. She ran ahead, to jump quickly inside, but it was locked and he was some distance behind, jogging gently, puffing slightly.

'You're certainly very keen!' He grinned, to show he was joking, but within seconds they were driving through the forest at such speed she felt as though she was being pressed back against the seat.

'Slow down,' she told him. 'You'll attract attention.'

'Hurry up, slow down – you're as bossy as your sister.' But Jamie eased his foot from the accelerator.

The signpost to Norchester flashed past. That had not been part of the plan.

'Where are you taking me?'

'Where do you think?' he said. 'My apartment in Norchester.'

Although the rent was paid by his father and, until very recently, he'd shared it with someone else.

'Will Alicia be there?'

'Alicia and I have always been very on/off,' he said. 'Right now it's definitely off. She finished with me last weekend and is coming to collect her stuff next weekend – otherwise I'd never have asked you out. Give me *some* credit. I'm not a complete bastard.'

Natalie wasn't entirely convinced but, 'Did Alicia find out about you and Sarah? Is that why she dumped you?'

His fingers tightened on the wheel. 'How do *you* know about Sarah?'

'My sister had a diary.'

'And you, being her snoopy little sister, have read it.' He

sighed. 'Sarah and I made a mistake. I don't know what we were thinking. We drank a little too much at a party, we got a little too friendly – and soon realised we'd both made an enormous mistake. It only happened once and Alicia knows nothing about it. She'd be very hurt if she found out, so *please* don't tell her. She thought the world of Sarah.'

Why would Natalie want to hurt Alicia, who'd always been very sweet to her, even if Natalie had never appreciated it at the time?

But wasn't that exactly what Natalie was doing now? Being Jamie's next 'enormous mistake'?

'Is Alicia still in love with you?'

He grimaced. 'Hardly. I had to listen to exactly what she thought of me – she'd actually written a list – with *bullet points*, can you believe? – and it wasn't a pleasant experience.'

'Are you still in love with her?'

'Who knows – it's hard to switch those kinds of feelings off abruptly – but are you sure you want to have this conversation? I thought it'd be fun to go out – it'd cheer us both up. I don't want to make you do anything you don't want to do – but you're the one who said you didn't want to be seen in public. Shall I turn around and take you home?'

Jamie was honest – a little *too* honest – she'd give him that. He was also handsome, fun to be with and his family was very rich. She'd be a fool to say 'no'. But doing this seemed so wrong – like going out with her brother – if she'd had one.

She watched the forest retreat from the suburbs of Norchester and the winding country lanes straighten into a city street. Jamie parked in a mews behind the cathedral, its gothic spires making the surrounding Georgian houses appear small and squat. Every shop was aimed with the tourist in mind – designer boutiques, an art gallery, a café with exorbitant prices... The roads even had cobblestones, like the villages in the forest. How quaint – and how impossible to walk on in her borrowed high-heeled sandals. She slipped them off, letting them dangle from her fingers as she ran to catch up with Jamie.

His apartment was over the art gallery and had its own entrance, with stairs leading up to a small landing where a tiny window overlooked the city lights. Once inside, it was hard not to be reminded of Alicia, from the Sophie Kinsella novels on the bookcase, the *Titanic* DVD on top of the television and the chocolate wrappers in the bin.

Jamie disappeared into the kitchen and emerged with a bottle of surprisingly expensive champagne. Natalie couldn't help a wry smile. He was handsome and good-natured, which was why she was happy for him to slide her jacket from her shoulders and kiss her. It was nice. He was a good kisser – but at the back of her mind was the nagging suspicion that he might be Sarah's murderer, which was one of the reasons she'd accepted his offer of a date in the first place.

Finding out what had happened to Sarah meant everything to her. If she had to kiss every man that Sarah had ever dated, to sweet-talk them into revealing the truth, she'd do it.

She hoped it wasn't Jamie though. She liked him a little *too* much.

How had she got herself into this?

She liked him, *really* liked him, but his recent split with Alicia didn't sit well with her. She didn't want to be the rebound relationship – but she also didn't have the luxury of being picky. This was *James Fitzpatrick*!

And she had a really loud conscience.

She pulled away. 'Jamie...'

He picked up the bottle of champagne and opened it, pouring it into two glasses and then holding one out for her.

She shook her head. 'I'm sorry, Jamie.'

He glanced down at the glass and frowned. 'Oh, I didn't think. Would you prefer a glass of water? Coffee?'

'I mean I can't do this – and I think we'll both regret it if we go ahead.'

'Oh,' he said, carefully putting the glass down. 'Fair enough.'

She hadn't expected him to agree so quickly!

Perhaps he hadn't quite got over Alicia after all.

'Would you like me to take you home? Or we could just watch a film?'

'Maybe it would be best if you took me home. I'm sorry.'

'You've nothing to be sorry about,' he said. And then, just as she thought he was behaving a little *too* perfectly, added, 'Shame about the champagne though.'

She hid a smile as she slipped her coat back on, then froze as something crashed against the door.

'What the—?' began Jamie.

At the second crash, the door flew open and there was her father, filling the space with his bulk.

'Bloody hell,' Jamie said. He was still holding one of the champagne glasses. A fact that didn't go unnoticed by her father.

John Grove looked him up and down, his face expressionless.

'Sir, I can explain,' Jamie said hastily. 'It's not how it looks.'

It was completely how it looked, but John ignored him and turned to Natalie. 'Get in the car.'

She really didn't want to leave Jamie alone with him, but when her father made a step towards her, she turned and ran through the open door – like a coward, she told herself later.

His car had been abandoned directly outside, the motor still running. As she stood there, wondering what to do, he appeared beside her, yanked open the back passenger door, snarled, 'Get in!' and shoved her onto the seat.

By the time she'd worked out which way was up, the car was in motion. She stared through the back window, hoping to see Jamie run out onto the road – not to rescue her, but just so she'd know he was OK.

The street remained deserted.

She slumped back into the seat and caught her father's reflection in the rear-view mirror watching her.

'Did you hurt him?' she asked.

'Of course I didn't hurt him! Do you think I want the Fitzpatrick family breathing down my neck and pressing assault charges? I put the frighteners on him though. Bloody rich kid thinks he can do what he likes. Not with *my* daughter.'

John seemed quite pleased by this, so Natalie hoped he was telling the truth and kept quiet to avoid antagonising him further. She had no idea where they were. It was dark and, although she could see trees flashing past the window, they could be anywhere in the King's Forest District.

After about ten minutes, her father said, 'From now on, you don't leave the house unless it's for school, is that clear?'

She was grounded? OK, it was hardly surprising.

'Once your exams are finished, you can work for me. We'll call it an apprenticeship.'

What?

'But I'm going to college!'

And then university. That was her dream.

'No, you'll be working in the glasshouses, where I can keep an eye on you.'

'No chance,' she said without thinking. 'When I leave college, I'm off to university and *you* can't stop me.'

John slammed his foot onto the brake. The car went into a sideways skid, the tyres shrieking across the tarmac.

Her first thought was that he'd crashed, but when she reached across to the door, it was flung open. She raised her head in time to see her father reach in and grab a handful of her sweater to haul her out. Instinctively, she lifted her arms to push him away and her sweater suddenly slid up. She had a split second to duck her head before her sweater slithered free and she was left sprawled across the back seat of the car in her vest top and jeans.

He stared at her sweater, still in his hand, then dropped it to make another grab for her. This time, she was prepared, scrambling over the seat and out of the opposite door. Falling backwards onto the tarmac, she kicked the door shut to stop him following her, then rolled over and struggled to her feet, breaking into a run.

They'd stopped somewhere on the coastal road between Norchester and Port Rell, high on the cliff with the harbour lights below. She could smell the salt on the air and feel the wind coming up from the river. A short distance behind her was a row of terraced fishermen's cottages and, as she stumbled towards them, she saw their lights flicker on, one by one.

The door to the nearest cottage opened, revealing the silhouette of a man against the interior light.

'Please,' she croaked. 'You've got to help me.'

But he pushed her aside and ran out onto the road.

What the—?

Other residents were emerging from their cottages, shouting and waving at something happening behind her.

What was going on?

Natalie glanced back.

Just in time to see the car, with her father still on the back seat, roll over the edge of the cliff.

TWENTY-TWO

While Natalie told her story, Bryn stared silently through the windscreen at the brick wall of the car park as though he wasn't even listening. The yellow overhead lighting made his skin appear sallow and emphasised the dark circles beneath his eyes. He looked as though he hadn't had a decent night's sleep in a week.

When he did finally speak, he didn't say what she expected.

'It wasn't your fault. It was an accident.'

'It was *completely* my fault,' she said. 'Dad had been drinking and was in one of his rages. He didn't pull up the handbrake when he parked. The police discovered that when they carried out an inspection on the wreckage of the car.'

'So that's why you're the only person who doesn't believe he drove over that cliff deliberately. You were there.'

'Why *would* he want to kill himself?'

'His beloved daughter was dead, he'd argued with you, and threatened James Fitzpatrick – whose influential family might have persuaded Sir Henry to give him the sack. If that happened, his life and career would have been ruined.'

'Dad only wanted to frighten me.'

'John Grove was a monster and I can't believe you're making excuses for him.'

'I'm not, but...' She trailed off.

Wasn't that exactly what she was doing? The compulsion to make excuses for the other person or blame herself for their behaviour had dominated every relationship she'd ever had – Charles, James, Simon... Had it started with her father? Why had she never realised that before?

'I kicked the door shut with my foot,' she said miserably. 'Doing that must have set the car in motion. I never *meant* to hurt him. Dad had been on the back seat, not the front. He couldn't have driven that car anywhere.'

Was that why she overcompensated now, paying for the best medical care and visiting every week – even though he'd made it clear he didn't care what she did?

When her father had grabbed her at the care home and said, 'I know what you did', was it the accident that he'd meant, rather than Sarah's murder? That would make more sense.

'Had he threatened you before?' Bryn's voice was tight.

'He was mean-spirited, particularly after he'd been drinking. You have to remember, I wasn't used to living any other way. I knew his behaviour wasn't normal, but it was normal for me. When I grew older, I learnt not to do anything that might send him into one of his tempers. It was easier that way.'

'I suppose he was always sorry afterwards.'

Bryn's tone was mocking, but she answered him seriously. 'No, I don't think it ever occurred to him to believe he'd done anything wrong. That's just who he was. His word was law. He expected to be obeyed – like some Victorian father.'

Bryn muttered a curse beneath his breath. 'You saw him recently. Did he say anything of relevance?'

'He tried to deny my mother had been to see him, referring to her as his "nemesis". I asked him who "the gardener" was in Sarah's diary, but he refused to answer. Sir Henry employed several gardeners, many of whom were young and hot, and would definitely have appealed to Sarah. My father said he hadn't wanted to get married or have children, but that my mother trapped him into it. I suppose that explains why he was angry all the time.'

'No, it *doesn't*! Everyone gets angry – but not everyone takes it out on their family. Why didn't you tell anyone about his behaviour?'

'Everyone in the village already knew – it was an open secret – and not one of them did anything about it. I think they saw us as outsiders.'

Bryn was silent and then, as though it was an effort, 'I'm sorry, talking about your dad must be difficult for you, but I need to understand the relationships your family had with each other and with other people.' He rubbed his hands across his face. 'I'm sure everything is connected. Look at what we have: Sarah is murdered, your father's car goes over a cliff, Sir Henry Vyne – who owned the garden where Sarah was found *and* employed your father – died in a shooting accident—'

'They're just coincidences.'

'The way your dad died last night was deliberate. Did someone know he was planning to talk to you or is there some other reason someone would want him dead?'

'He's had fourteen years to talk to me about Sarah's murder. Surely if someone wanted him dead, they'd have killed him before now?'

'We still haven't found out what happened to Geraint,' Bryn said. 'Was there anything *else* your father said? Anything at all?'

'Mostly he ranted about my mother…' She closed her eyes and leant back against the car seat, trying to remember. She pictured her father sat in his wheelchair in that sterile little room – the room now buried beneath the ash and rubble that had once been Rose Court.

Buried ...

'He said I was an idiot for digging over stuff that was better left buried. He said no one would be interested. Sarah was dead and knowing the details wouldn't bring her back. He started quoting the bible at me, talking about revenge, and then he said —' She opened her eyes. 'I wonder...'

'*What?*' Bryn asked impatiently. '*What* did he say?'

'He said the weirdest thing... He said that none of this was about Sarah.'

'She was the one who died. How could it not be about Sarah?'

'I don't know. Do you think we could continue this conversation some other time? Maybe when I've had a chance to think it through?'

'I suppose so.' He undid his seatbelt but then went back to staring at the wall, as though expecting to see the solution written there.

Sarah's murder had haunted her for years. Did he think he was going to solve it overnight?

She made a move to get out, hoping Bryn would take the hint, and noticed another car parked a few spaces along, directly beside the door to the lift. Charles Fitzpatrick had a car like that. A dark-green Range Rover with tinted windows. She sincerely hoped he wasn't paying her a courtesy call after her father's death. It wasn't as though she could pretend to be out. He'd have seen her car as soon as she'd driven into the car park. Unless he was already in reception, waiting for her?

She sighed and hauled her bag onto her lap, scrabbling about until she found a notebook and pen. She wrote her phone number down and handed it to Bryn.

'I've got to go,' she said. 'Maybe we can meet up one day next week?'

He glanced at the paper and frowned. 'Next *week*? Why not tomorrow?'

'I've spent years trying to puzzle out who murdered my sister, for all the good it did me. I'm starting to think my father was right. Maybe I do need to move on.'

Without waiting for a response, she got out of the car.

Bryn did likewise, leaning against the side of it and resting his hands on the roof. 'It's only four o'clock. We could have a coffee? I could buy you dinner? Please?'

'I have another book to write and I'm pretty sure you have a garden to renovate. Goodbye, Bryn.' Locking the car door, Natalie walked towards the lift.

He didn't follow her. Presumably he'd walk out of the car park via the road rather than through reception. It would be quicker.

The Range Rover was still parked beside the lift. The combination of the flickering overhead lighting and the tinted windows meant she couldn't see if Charles was waiting inside.

As she drew level, the driver's door opened and a man got out, but it wasn't Charles. He turned to take something from the back seat, shoving it into his pocket, closing the door and walking straight towards her. He was tall but slightly stooped, and wore a heavy raincoat with a black woollen hat pulled low over his forehead.

A black woollen hat? Where had she seen *that* before?

He moved with an odd, swaying gait, keeping one hand deep in his pocket. Was he drunk?

Unsettled, Natalie glanced behind to see what had happened to Bryn just as something clamped around her waist.

'Got you,' the man said. He swung her around and now she could see Bryn running towards them. 'Tell your boyfriend to back off.'

Bryn abruptly stopped, tentatively raising his hands. What was he doing? Why didn't he knock the man out? Bryn was at least twenty years younger and the way this man was swaying, Bryn could easily overpower him.

'Tell your boyfriend to back off,' the man repeated.

There was a blur of movement, followed by an explosion that hurt her ears. Flakes of plaster showered down from the ceiling.

Natalie froze. 'You've got a gun!'

'Bingo,' the man said. 'Now give me what I want.'

The fight went out of her. 'It's in my bag.'

'Hand it over.'

'I can't reach it. You'll have to let me go.'

After a moment's pause, he relaxed his grip and took hold of her arm instead, swinging her around to face him.

Her first thought was that the gun looked like an antique. Did it even work? Still, it'd be better not to risk it. Her second was that what she'd mistaken for a woollen hat was a balaclava, now pulled down to hide his face.

'Hurry up,' he snapped.

She slid her bag from her shoulder and groped around inside. She thought he'd just grab the bag from her, but he kept glancing at Bryn, as though daring him to do something stupid.

Finally she found her purse and held it out to him.

He dashed it from her hands, sending coins rolling across the concrete. 'Stupid woman! Do you think this is about *money*?'

But if it wasn't about money...

The diary!

Was this the man who'd broken into her apartment; who'd murdered her sister?

He grabbed the bag from her and tipped it upside down. Everything tumbled out – make-up, keys, phone – and when the bag was empty, he shifted it into the hand that held the gun and used his free one to grope around inside.

'Where is it? What have you done with it?'

She was about to answer him when it dawned on her: he was no longer watching her.

For a second, her eyes met Bryn's, then flicked towards the pedestrian exit to the road. Slowly, he shook his head, but, ignoring that, she made a dash for it anyway.

There was a loud bang behind her. She ducked instinctively, as something solid whacked her in the middle of her back, thrusting her behind a parked car and knocking her to the ground.

She pushed herself up, only for someone to take hold of her shoulder and shove her down.

'Have you got a death wish?' growled a familiar Welsh accent. 'Keep your head down.'

In the distance, she could hear the gunman screaming. 'Where have you hidden it?'

'He wants Sarah's diary,' Bryn said, as though he thought her an idiot.

'I know that *now*!' There was grit in her mouth. She spat it out. 'Why didn't he say so in the *first* place?'

'Shh!'

She rolled onto her back and sat up, careful to stay low while she worked out where they were – between a row of the cars and the exterior wall – out of sight, although the man wouldn't have to move far to see them, which he certainly would if they tried to make it to the exit.

'Do you have your phone?' Bryn asked.

'No.' She gestured towards the small heap of her belongings in the centre of the car park. 'Do you?'

'No battery. I've not been home long enough to charge it properly. There'll be no signal underground anyway.' He groaned. 'Why did you have to run *this* way?'

'I was running away from the gun! Why did you knock me over? I could have made it to the road.'

'Sure you could – with a bullet helping you on your way! What were you *thinking*?'

She watched the gunman rip open the lining of her bag. 'Oh, no! That's a limited edition! There's a waiting list!'

Bryn rolled his eyes. 'Give him the diary and maybe we can all go home.'

'You think he'd let us go?'

'Not. A. Chance.'

The pedestrian entrance to the car park, with the steps leading up to the road, was about ten metres away. Was it worth making a run for it while the gunman was distracted? Probably not, but what choice did they have?

She was about to suggest this to Bryn when she noticed a shadow move across the stairwell. Was a car passing on the road or was someone standing there?

Another movement and this time she caught a glimpse of a man leaning back against the wall of the stairwell. He was wearing black, from his heavy boots to the baseball cap on his head. When he realised she'd seen him, he raised his hand and made a gesture towards the ground with his palm.

Beside her, Bryn muttered, 'Oh, hell!' before slapping her shoulder. 'Get down – *now!*'

She closed her eyes as a disembodied voice echoed around the car park.

'Armed police!'

Startled, the gunman fired randomly towards the road before they could finish speaking.

There was a short fast volley, followed by complete and utter silence.

It took a moment before she dared to lift her head.

The gunman was lying on the ground.

The police emerged from the stairwell. One headed over to him, kicking away the old pistol. The other officer stood over her, telling her to stay on the ground, to put her hands over her head where he could see them, and not to move. Beside her,

Bryn did as he was told – in such a practised move she couldn't help wondering if he'd done it before.

She then had to suffer the indignity of being patted down, presumably to check for concealed weapons.

Finally, she was allowed to get up and retrieve her belongings from where they'd been scattered across the car park. One of the police officers escorted her past the gunman. His colleague had already rolled him onto his back to ascertain he was dead and was now tugging off the balaclava. She couldn't help stopping to watch. Was she finally going to see the face of the man who'd killed her sister?

The balaclava was peeled back, but Natalie's view was restricted as the police officer straightened and muttered to his colleague: 'Isn't he supposed to be dead?'

'Well, he is now.'

She tried to move closer, but Bryn was pulling her back. When she tried to push him away, he held her tighter.

'Don't look,' he said.

'I need to see who it is! That man killed my sister.'

'You know who it is, *cariad*. It's your dad.'

TWENTY-THREE

Alicia walked into the sitting room, where her daughter was supposedly doing her homework, although the radio was playing and she was lying with her feet up on the sofa.

'Lexi, do you have something to occupy yourself if I walk down into the village to buy dinner?'

'An essay on Macbeth.' Lexi grimaced and waved the slim paperback in her hand. 'Something wicked this way comes.'

'And can you look after Will?'

'Sure.'

'Where is he?'

'How should I know? His bedroom?'

Alicia raised her eyes to the ceiling. Her son's bedroom was directly above them.

'He's remarkably quiet...'

'Don't knock it. Go to the shops. Buy pizza, *not* asparagus, no one likes it. We'll be fine.'

'I'd better check on him before I leave.'

As Alicia climbed the stairs, it occurred to her that Lexi was right. The smart thing would be to leave Will playing whatever game was keeping him so engrossed. But she couldn't resist opening his door very quietly and peering inside.

Will had the smallest bedroom, although he didn't seem to mind. Despite Alicia's best efforts to keep it tidy, it usually looked as though a whirlwind had raged through it and today was no exception. The curtains were drawn so the small mound hunched up in the centre of the room, which she'd taken to be her son, turned out to be his school bag after she'd switched on the light. With mounting panic, Alicia checked inside the wardrobe, under the bed and beneath the desk, but Will was nowhere to be seen.

She checked the other rooms and then ran downstairs.

'I can't find him,' she told Lexi, trying to keep the rising panic from her voice.

Lexi put down her book. 'I'll help you. I know all his hiding places.'

A quick search of The Old Rectory revealed Will's coat and wellington boots were missing from the cloakroom.

'Maybe he's in the garden?' Lexi suggested.

Alicia looked out the window, as though expecting to see Will standing on the other side. 'But it's raining!'

'Since when would that stop him?' Lexi picked up the keys from the hall table and handed them to her mother. 'We'll check the garden and then walk down to the shops, in case anyone's seen him there.'

Alicia shrugged on her coat. 'That's so kind of you.'

Lexi grinned. 'It's that or Macbeth!'

The rectory garden was large and bordering on neglected. It soon became apparent that Will wasn't in it. Alicia searched the shrubbery at the front, where Will had built a den, and then at the back where he had his tree house.

Lexi scrambled up the ladder. 'He's not up here.'

'Where can he be? We've searched everywhere!'

Her daughter pointed over the hedge into the chapel graveyard. 'How about in there?'

'He's not allowed to go over there on his own.'

'I'm saying nothing.'

Alicia sighed. 'OK, you win. Let's search the graveyard.'

She trekked down the drive, along the road and through the lych-gate into the chapel graveyard, where she found Lexi already waiting, having apparently forced her way through a gap in the hedge. Alicia decided to let it pass.

'There aren't many places to hide,' Lexi said, staring round. 'It's nothing but gravestones.'

'Think like a ten-year-old. We'll start by the road and work our way towards the castle. If we've not found him by then, I'm calling the police.'

The graves were mostly Victorian. Many were less than waist height, although they were still wide enough for a smallish child to hide behind. Away from the main path, the graveyard was overgrown, with long yellow grass and brambles hiding the smaller monuments, making them easy to stumble over.

As Alicia and Lexi passed the chapel, which was thankfully kept locked, the hiding places grew fewer. Alicia was almost sick with panic. How could Will have vanished like this?

Lexi stood still and held up her hand. 'I can hear something.'

It had stopped raining. In the distance was the hum of what passed for rush-hour traffic in Calahurst and, closer still, the gurgling of rainwater surging through the chapel guttering.

Alicia pushed back the hood of her coat. 'I can't hear anything. I'm calling the police. He could have been abducted, anything!'

Lexi was standing with her head on one side, listening intently. 'No, I can definitely hear something... someone shouting...' She swung around. 'It's coming from the castle garden.'

Alicia had already taken out her phone. 'It'll be the workmen Granny hired to sort out the garden,' but when she glanced up, Lexi was darting between the gravestones to where the gate to the castle had swung open and was crashing into the wall with each gust of wind.

Why hadn't she noticed it was open?

Alicia thrust her phone back into her pocket and set off after her daughter, but Lexi was already sprinting along the woodland path in the direction of the castle. As Alicia puffed her way to the top of the hill, leaving the graveyard far behind, she also heard forlorn cries for help and doubled her efforts.

Emerging from the dark avenue of yew trees, Alicia caught her first glimpse of Will. He was sitting beneath the ruined wall of the original medieval chapel, with Lexi beside him trying to calm him down. He had one leg bent awkwardly beneath him and was red-faced and tearful. How long had he been out here on his own, in the rain and the cold?

'He's fine,' Lexi said, before she could say a word. 'He's not hurt at all.'

'I'm stuck!' Will wailed.

'Stuck?' It took a moment for her to understand.

He was sitting directly on top of the old well. While one leg was out in front of him, the other had become jammed through the metal grille covering it. His jeans were dirty and torn, where he'd impatiently tried to free himself and she could see a nasty scratch on his ankle.

'My foot is *stuck*,' he repeated patiently, as though she couldn't understand his predicament. 'I can't get it *out*.'

At least he was calmer now.

She ruffled his hair and gave him a hug. 'Oh, Will! We were so worried about you!'

'Why would you want to stick your foot in there?' his sister asked.

'I didn't do it *deliberately*. I was standing on it, dropping stones to see how deep it went, and my foot slipped and I fell between the bars. Now I can't get my foot back in case my trainer falls off and I lose it forever.'

'It doesn't matter about your trainers,' Lexi said. 'Dad will buy you new ones. Pull your foot out. I'm getting cold.'

'No!' Will screwed his face up again. 'I like my trainers! They're cool!'

Alicia felt her stress levels rising. 'Both of you calm down *please!*'

As they lapsed into indignant silence, she knelt on the grass, rested her hands on the metal grille and peered into the dark cavern beneath.

The well – along with the old chapel, the great hall, the library and the watchtower – was all that remained of the original medieval castle, now hidden beneath the neo-Norman façade. The well was level with the ground and quite wide – over three metres across. There'd once been a winch and pulley system to draw the water up. Now the well was only a hole in the ground, with the metal grille padlocked over the top to stop the unwary from falling into it. Although that had not prevented Will from giving it his best shot. Thankfully, the grille had been strong enough to bear his weight. The alternative didn't bear thinking about.

'OK,' she said to Will. 'Here's the plan. I'm going to ease your trainer off. You're going to slowly pull your foot back through the hole and I'll bring your trainer up separately. What do you think?'

Her son regarded her anxiously. 'I won't lose my trainer?'

'Of course not.' Alicia mentally crossed her fingers.

'OK, then.' He screwed up his eyes and braced himself. 'Go for it!'

Alicia slipped off her coat and laid it on the ground to kneel on. She placed one hand through the bars of the grille and gripped the bottom of Will's trainer. With her other hand, she undid his laces and loosened them – as Will unexpectedly yanked his foot back through the gap and freed himself.

While he ran around the chapel whooping with delight, totally oblivious to the fate of his precious trainer, she snatched at it with her other hand – and caught it.

Only for something small and glittering to slip between the bars and into the darkness.

Alicia shrieked.

Lexi was beside her like a shot. 'What's happened?'

'My engagement ring!' Alicia could hardly form the words. 'You know, the one that used to belong to Grandma Fitzpatrick?'

'The family heirloom that she always checks is still on your finger, before she'll even say hello?'

'Or let me through the door,' Alicia nodded miserably. 'It fell down the well…'

'Are you sure?' Lexi peered into the darkness.

Will attempted to give Alicia a hug. 'I'm sorry, Mum. It's my fault, isn't it?' He looked to his sister, who wasn't quick enough to deny it, and then burst into tears, which was what Alicia would quite like to do but felt that one person having a meltdown was quite enough.

What would Natalie do?

Attempt to get it back.

Seizing the grille with both hands, Alicia rattled it.

'It's *padlocked*,' Lexi said, stating the obvious. At least she didn't add: 'Duh!'

The grille had been made from rods of iron arranged in a grid and welded into a flat metal ring. On one side was a hinge. On the other was the large padlock. Although rusted, it held firm when Alicia shook the grille.

However, the iron ring that had been set into the large stone beneath it moved.

Encouraged, Alicia heaved at it again.

There was a metallic squeal and the grille flew up and over, and slammed into the grass. The padlock, the small iron ring, and even the lump of stone it had been fixed to, still hung off the side.

'Can you see anything?' Lexi asked, yanking Will back by the collar of his jacket as he attempted to peer down the well.

Alicia shuffled forward until she reached the edge. It was difficult to see anything much. Thick green foliage had sprung up between the brickwork, partially blocking the view of the bottom and making it appear even darker than it was. There was an iron rung set into a stone near the top, and she vaguely remembered her father telling her there were others leading to what had once been the water level – another reason he'd installed the gate.

She took her phone from her coat pocket and switched on the torch, shining it into the hole. 'I can see the bottom,' she said. 'It's not far – about nine or ten metres. There's no water, just a lot of rubbish.'

She stuck the phone into her jeans pocket and sat up, swinging her legs over the edge.

Lexi dropped Will to catch hold of her. 'Tell me you aren't serious?'

'It's perfectly safe,' Alicia said, hoping to convince herself as much as the children. 'I can climb down on these rungs.'

'Which are, like, medieval!'

'You could tie a rope around your middle,' Will said, far more enthusiastically. 'The new gardeners have some in their shed.'

Now was not the time to ask how he knew what the castle gardeners kept in their shed. 'By all means, fetch me some rope.'

Lexi waited until he was out of earshot. 'Are you *crazy*? You'll never be able to climb down. Let one of the gardeners do it.'

'Do you see any gardeners?' Alicia said. 'I've not seen a

single one since Granny allegedly hired them. Besides, it's unlikely she pays them enough to risk life and limb.'

'Won't it be super-dangerous?' Will had chosen that moment to return, with a length of rope draped over one shoulder and unravelling rapidly behind him.

'Not at all, darling. It'll be a great adventure.' Alicia tied one end of the rope around her waist and got Lexi to do likewise around the nearest tree. 'Now listen,' she said. 'As the rope isn't very long, I'll climb down the well as far as I can and then untie it. If I fall from that point it won't be any distance at all, so I'll be fine. If I have any trouble, or if it looks the slightest bit dangerous, I'll come straight up again. Do you understand?'

Will, thoroughly overexcited, hopped from foot to foot.

Lexi sighed and nodded.

Alicia returned to the edge of the well, lowering one foot and pressing on the uppermost rung to ensure it would take her weight. It proved to be surprisingly solid, although black with age. She slid onto her stomach and lowered herself over the side until both feet were firmly positioned on the top rung, then felt through the weeds with her toe for the next one. The rungs were set at regular intervals, although each one had a slight slant downwards, presumably from the weight of previous users.

Alicia tried not to think about that.

It wasn't the ring itself, or her mother-in-law's reaction that worried her, but the thought of poor James when he discovered she'd lost one of the few family heirlooms entrusted to him. He'd never blame her, and would probably shrug off the loss with one of his usual jokes, but if there was the slightest chance she could get it back...

She took another step down. She could do this!

The further she went, the colder the air. The rungs were wet, the surrounding walls were moist. She saw each breath forming a little cloud – until she was too far down to see anything at all. She paused to look back up at the circle of light, to reassure herself it was still there.

'Mum, are you OK?' Lexi's voice echoed down the well.

'I'm fine!' Alicia called back, even though she wasn't.

She concentrated on each rung until the circle of light above grew smaller and the tension on the rope grew tighter, until a painful jerk to her ribcage told her it had reached its limit.

Was she there?

Hooking one arm over a rung to steady herself, she took out her phone and was immediately surrounded by a comforting – if dim – light.

The stone wall of the well was stained darker with each subsequent water mark, as its level had reduced over the centuries. No plants grew this far down, even though the occasional fallen bricks had left squares of bare earth and hollows where loose soil had cascaded into the well.

She shone the light towards the bottom of the well. It was about two metres beneath her – jumping distance. There was no water and the ground was uneven, scattered with drink cans and faded food packaging. There was even a football.

'I'm almost there!' she called back to Lexi. 'Only a couple of metres further. I'm going to undo the rope.'

Lexi yelled back a response, but it was unintelligible.

Assuming everything at the surface was still OK, Alicia stuck her phone in her mouth and untied the rope, leaving it swinging against the side of the well. It transpired that there were only two more rungs. She took the phone from her mouth, checked for a likely landing place and jumped.

She fell awkwardly, landing on a pile of broken rocks and bashing her knee painfully, but at least she hadn't broken her phone. She could only imagine how awful it would be to be left alone down here in the dark.

She shone the light around – and something glittered in the beam.

Her ring!

She scooped it up delightedly, making sure that this time it was securely wedged onto her middle finger, where it would take water and soap to get it off again.

Before ascending the rungs, she swept the light from the phone around again and the beam snagged on the football. Someone had drawn a rudimentary face on it and she couldn't help smiling. How on earth it had got through the bars of the grille above? Even she didn't know who had the key.

Perhaps Will would like it as a souvenir?

Alicia took a step closer and bent down, the light shining directly upon it, redefining the curious markings.

Alicia screamed and fell back.

It wasn't a football, it was a *human skull*.

And the rest of the skeleton was right there beside it.

TWENTY-FOUR

The police had rolled John Grove onto his back to check for signs of life and then left him where he lay when it was obvious there were none. The balaclava had been pushed up above his face, revealing tufts of white hair. Natalie was only aware of those pale grey eyes that seemed to stare right through her.

A police car had rolled into the car park and cordoned it off. A multitude of other police vehicles parked along the road above and the car park was soon full of CSIs wearing white coveralls.

Natalie and Bryn were told to wait in the stairwell out of the way. It was poorly sheltered from the elements and, as the sky darkened, the rain began to fall, thudding rhythmically against the stone steps.

'We should get back under cover,' Bryn said, although he didn't move.

Natalie watched a police officer taking photographs of the crime scene, first of the surrounding area and then closer towards her father's body.

Overview, mid-range and close-up, she thought, oddly detached from what was happening in front of her.

Beside her, Bryn shifted uncomfortably. 'Why doesn't someone cover him up?'

As a crime writer she could have told him, but instead she said, 'You don't have to stay. I can give the police a statement.'

'I don't think they're going to let us leave.' He indicated the uniformed officer standing on the stairwell behind them. 'We're witnesses.'

The rain was dripping off her hair and down the back of her neck, icy rivulets finding their way beneath her clothes. Bryn was right, they should've moved under cover, but she didn't want to be any closer to those cold staring eyes than she had to.

A man walked towards them. He wore a dark suit with an unbuttoned trench coat and delicately picked his way around the patches of oil until he came to the edge of the steps where they waited.

Detective Chief Inspector Cameron.

'Ms Grove,' he said, looking up at her. 'My condolences.'

She inclined her head, but didn't trust her voice to speak.

'Someone should take Natalie up to her apartment,' Bryn said. 'It's unfair to keep her hanging around like this, after everything she's been through.'

'You're right,' the DCI said. 'If you'd like to come with me, Ms Grove?'

It was not the answer Bryn wanted to hear. 'I'll take her. It's no trouble.'

'I'm sure, but I need you to make a statement. If you'd honour us with your company for a moment or two longer, I'll arrange for one of my officers to talk to you.'

Bryn muttered something uncomplimentary. It certainly wasn't Welsh.

'Ms Grove?' the DCI said. 'If you'd come with me?'

Natalie reluctantly pushed away from the wall, but before she could make her way down the few steps and back into the car park, Bryn gave her a quick hug.

'I'll call you later,' he said, 'to make sure you're OK.'

'I'll be fine,' she said, surprised by the concern evident on his face.

When she followed the DCI into the lift, she saw him hit the 'R' button instead of the top floor.

'OK,' she sighed, 'where are we really going?'

He regarded her thoughtfully. 'I could drive you to the police station and take your statement,' he said. 'I could do everything properly and record every word you said, whether you meant to say it or not. Alternatively, I could take you to one of the cafés and we could chat informally. What do you say?'

And *she* could have said, 'Why bother to walk along the waterfront to one of the cafés, when I've a perfectly good apartment upstairs?' But he was up to something, so she decided to let it play out.

The lift doors slid open. He waited, regarding her enquiringly.

'Whatever,' she said, walking out into reception.

There were more police officers here. Some were interviewing the residents, others were checking the CCTV; one was taking a statement from Phil.

When Phil saw the lift door open, he raised his hand. 'Are you OK, Ms Grove? He didn't hurt you, did he?'

She shook her head in reply as everyone turned to look. Phil must have been the one to call the police. He'd have seen everything unfold on those CCTV monitors. How could her father have taken such a risk, even wearing the balaclava to hide his face? Had he really thought Sarah's diary was that important? Worth *dying* for?

When they stepped through the door and onto the street, the DCI produced a sturdy black umbrella and held it over her head – even though she was already wet. It wasn't raining as hard now, but the sky was still overcast and the marina lights were popping on, one by one.

She thought they would stop at Tom's Coffee Shop, which was the most popular café on the marina, but the DCI didn't break his stride until they came to the opposite end of the marina and a familiar Victorian boathouse. High above the arched entrance, the word 'Remedy' was picked out in blue neon.

Natalie was surprised the club was even open this early in the evening but supposed the DCI must have phoned ahead to let them know his intent. This was confirmed when they went inside and the barman was waiting for them.

The DCI glanced at her. 'Two coffees?'

'Thank you,' she said. She hadn't even known Remedy sold coffee.

Another member of staff, in the regulation black T-shirt and jeans, was slowly taking the chairs from the tables and putting them onto the floor, ready for opening time. The club had a completely different atmosphere during the day. Silent as a tomb, the overhead lights were on, the fairy lights off – any atmosphere gone.

'Where did you sit last night?' the DCI asked her.

Natalie pointed four tables down on the left hand side. The DCI picked up their coffees and made his way carefully between the tables to the one she indicated.

He should try doing that in a crowded bar in the dark, she thought, and wondered if that was when the sedative had been slipped into her drink.

'Did you get the toxicology report back?' she asked, before he'd even sat down.

'The what? Oh, you mean the specimen we took last night? Sorry to disappoint you but our lab doesn't work that quickly. It's not like the movies.' He pushed one of the cups towards her as he sat down, reached into his jacket pocket and took out a handful of sachets. He dropped them onto the table. 'Sugar?'

She shook her head. 'Do you believe someone put something into my drink last night?'

'Do you?' he countered.

'I kept zoning out.'

'It's likely. The effects can be worse if it's mixed with alcohol.'

'I hardly drank any alcohol. I didn't get the chance.'

'You were extremely lucky.'

'Do you know who put it into my drink?'

He gave her a pitying look. 'Your father. He could have easily obtained some kind of sedative from Rose Court. I suspect he didn't realise the effect would be so immediate. He assumed he could help you home, you'd give him access to your apartment and then fall asleep, leaving him to undertake a thorough search undisturbed.'

'Instead, I didn't drink enough to be affected and didn't go home right away – meaning he had to incapacitate Phil and break in. When I did finally return to the apartment, I walked in and caught him. You know, he could have killed me right there if he'd wanted. He certainly had the opportunity.'

'I don't think he wanted you dead. He only wanted Sarah's diary. His mistake was to start waving a gun around in front of armed police. Those guys don't mess about.'

'Where did he even *find* a gun?'

'It was an old World War Two pistol, registered to Dr Charles Fitzpatrick. I believe it had once belonged to his grandfather. Your father stole his car too.'

Natalie picked her bag up off the floor and unzipped it. The DCI watched, at first interested, and then slightly less so when the only thing she took out was a scrap of screwed-up paper. She smoothed it out on the table and turned it around so he could read it.

'I found this left on my desk after the break-in,' she said. 'It was beneath the bag of liquorice. He wanted me to know the note was from him. The liquorice was a private joke but I automatically assumed it was the *intruder* taunting me – not that he *was* the intruder.'

The DCI frowned. '"*Destroy it*"? Destroy what?'

'Sarah's diary,' she said simply. 'Now it makes sense. He believed there was something in it that revealed who killed her. All those times I visited him and he never said a word! He was going to walk out of my life and I'd think he was dead.'

'That brings me to my next question. Did you know your father could walk?'

'I'd guessed his injuries were not as severe as he made out, but Charles wouldn't believe me. My father was supposed to have a brain injury, yet when I talked to him I could tell he understood me, and not only on a basic level. The last time I saw him – last night, before the fire – he looked and sounded exactly the way he'd done before his accident.'

'Could his injuries have been psychosomatic?'

'Charles said there was always the chance he could improve, but that the more time passed, the less chance there was of it. Dad must have been getting better all the time and hiding it. Why would he do that?'

'You haven't worked it out?'

'You're going to tell me he was overwhelmed with guilt over Sarah's death? That he tried to kill himself by driving over the cliff and faked his injuries to spend the rest of his life in a care home, as some kind of self-punishment? Don't bother, I've heard it before and I don't believe a word of it. What kind of a person would do that?'

'A frightened person,' the DCI said. 'I have a theory that your father was hiding.'

'From whom?'

'That's an excellent question.'

'In other words, you don't know,' Natalie said.

'Find your father's nemesis, find the murderer.'

As she glanced up sharply, he smiled.

'A line of thought you've had yourself?' He raised his cup to his mouth and took a long drink. 'This coffee is excellent. Would you like another?'

'No, I *don't* want another cup of coffee. I'm up to here with cups of coffee, and talk talk talk, and nothing gets done, nothing gets solved. Why are we sitting here? You should be out there, finding my sister's murderer.'

The DCI leant back in his chair. 'You'd be surprised at how much talking can achieve,' he said. 'Far more than a shoot-out where the witness ends up dead.'

'The witness? You mean my father? That doesn't make sense. He made all that fuss about wanting Sarah's diary. Why would he do that, unless it implicated him? I was so sure he knew something. I spent hours visiting him, talking to him, trying to provoke him into telling me the truth about what happened that night.'

'Perhaps you asked the wrong questions?'

'OK, so why do *you* think my father wanted the diary?'

'To protect you from whoever did kill Sarah.'

She nearly laughed out loud. 'You think he'd go to all that trouble? For *me*?'

He didn't reply.

'You know,' she said, 'it occurs to me that every time I get into some kind of trouble the police appear at exactly the right moment. Why is that? Are you following me?'

He smiled. 'Why would you think we were following you?'

'My father brandishes a gun, and two armed response officers instantly turn up to rescue me? Even if Phil phoned you, it would take time to mobilise everyone.'

'Ah, but why would you think we were following *you*?'

It took a beat for her to understand. 'You were following *Bryn*?'

Before he could reply, his phone rang.

'Really?' he said, after listening to the person on the other end say their piece. 'As my old Mum would say, it never rains but it pours. Do what you have to do. I'll be there shortly.' He terminated the call and slid his phone back into his pocket. 'You'll be pleased to know we've finished here.' He indicated her father's note, which lay on the table between them. 'Is it all right if I take this?'

She nodded and he produced a small plastic evidence bag from his pocket and, using the clean end of his teaspoon, batted the note into the bag. Evidence bags, specimen bottles? What else did he have hidden away in that coat?

'We already have your fingerprints from last night,' he said, 'but if you could go down to the station tomorrow and give a formal statement, I would be most grateful.'

'No problem,' she said.

If he thought that was the end of the matter, he was severely mistaken. She had plans of her own.

She reached for her bag, but his hand closed over hers.

'There is one more thing,' he said. 'If you could hand over that diary of Sarah's?'

She looked him directly in the eye and said, 'No.'

'It's evidence for an ongoing enquiry.'

'I can't.'

He tried a different tactic. 'You realise it's not safe for you to be walking around with it in your possession? You've mentioned it in every interview you've given to publicise your book. There will be other people who want it. Unlike your father, they might not give you the choice of giving it up before they kill you.'

When she failed to reply, he added, 'You're going to lose all credibility, not to mention public sympathy, if you make me get a warrant.'

'I couldn't care less about public sympathy,' she began, and then sighed at his dour expression. 'You don't get it, do you? There *is* no diary. Yes, I found a notebook amongst my sister's things, but it contained ideas for the stories she planned to write. It wasn't a diary, with codenames, and suspects, and a signed confession. Wouldn't *that* have been brilliant?'

He frowned. 'But why would you—?'

'I made the whole thing up.' She rubbed her sleeve over her eyes, trying to make it seem casual, trying to make her voice sound steady. She knew she'd behaved badly. She didn't need him to tell her so. Her conscience was already yelling it into her ear. 'The diary was supposed to be bait.'

'Bait?'

Didn't he get it?

'I wanted to catch a murderer.'

TWENTY-FIVE

'Why would you lie about something like that?' the DCI asked Natalie, all trace of his former good humour gone.

'If I could explain?'

'That would be good.'

'The night Sarah died, she met with someone waiting outside the house. I didn't see his face, but Sarah knew him. She threw her arms around him; he picked her up and whirled her around...' Natalie trailed off, lost in the memory.

'What happened then?'

'He took her by the hand and they walked away.'

'In which direction did they go?'

'They walked through the castle gateway and down the hill towards the village.'

The DCI regarded her thoughtfully, as though half-inclined to disbelieve her. 'I've never heard this story. Your mother said Sarah's bed hadn't been slept in, but neither of your parents seemed to know exactly when she'd left the house or where she'd gone.'

'It was about ten o'clock in the evening, on the night of the regatta. There'd been fireworks. I was watching them through my bedroom window when I saw her leave.'

'Sarah was found at nine in the morning. That's eleven hours unaccounted for.'

'She went to the funfair. I climbed out of my bedroom window and followed her – but I lost her. Later, I saw her with Alicia—'

'Mrs Fitzpatrick gave us a statement at the time. She said your sister had seen you enter the caravan of a fairground worker named Geraint Llewellyn and she was concerned for your safety. Mrs Fitzpatrick never mentioned any other man. Are you sure it wasn't the same person?'

So Alicia had been the one to land Geraint in it.

'None of us had met Geraint until that night.'

'You followed this other man to the funfair though. You must have seen something of him?'

'I saw him in the distance. He was tall and had short dark hair. That's all I could see. He could have been anybody.'

'That's more of a description than we've had in fourteen years. Why didn't you tell someone?'

The unfairness of it stung her into retorting, 'I was sixteen years old and no one asked me! You know what my father was like. He hated the police. I thought if I spoke out of turn I'd be in trouble.'

'We requested an interview with you, but it was refused on medical grounds.'

She stared at him in astonishment. 'I didn't know this. What medical grounds?'

'Your doctor thought you were too traumatised to give evidence. It would have been flawed.'

Another piece of the puzzle fell into place. 'This doctor, would he have been Charles Fitzpatrick?'

He was suddenly wary. 'Yes, what of it?'

'It didn't occur to you there may have been another reason for keeping me silent?'

'He was "the doctor"?' The DCI cursed beneath his breath. 'Fourteen years ago, Charles Fitzpatrick would have been in his twenties. Are you suggesting *he* killed her?'

'I've no idea. Sarah did tell me about the men she went out with – and she *did* use codenames – presumably in case I told someone else.'

'So you don't know their real names?'

'I've managed to work some of them out. When Sir Henry Vyne suggested I had counselling to help deal with Sarah's death – and offered to pay – I was referred to Charles Fitzpatrick at Rose Court. As much as I didn't want to see a counsellor, I was happy to see him because I knew he was one of Sarah's ex-boyfriends and I fancied myself as a detective. It took a while, but I was eventually able to get him to admit that he'd had an affair with her. Whether he killed her or not, I don't know. He was threatening to sue me the last time we spoke, because of the book.'

The DCI bit off another curse. 'OK, tell me about "the teacher"?'

'That would be Charles's younger brother, James Fitzpatrick. He's now the head teacher at Calahurst Community School. He told me that he only slept with her once and that they both believed it was a mistake.'

'He was only eighteen when Sarah died.'

'Yes, but everyone knew he wanted to be a teacher after university. They'd tease him about it. Every other kid at school wanted to be a rock star or a footballer. He stood out.'

'What about Sarah's relationship with Simon Waters?'

'She didn't have one! She was in his drama class, but that was all. In those days, the age gap would have been too much.'

'He was almost the same age as Charles Fitzpatrick.' The DCI's dry tone was back.

'Yes, but Simon's always been a bit' – she could hardly say 'fuddy-duddy' – 'sensible, practical... Mature.'

And that made him sound like cheese.

The DCI's patience appeared to be wearing thin. 'Is there anyone *else* I should know about?'

'Sarah mentioned a gardener – presumably one who worked in the castle grounds with our father. She also mentioned a man who worked at one of the clubs here on the waterfront, but I don't think she was serious about either of them. Finally, there was one she nicknamed "the librarian".'

'There's no library in Calahurst. The nearest one is in Norchester.'

'I'd always assumed Sarah was talking about Sir Henry Vyne. The castle has a library. A very big one. She modelled for him during the weekends. A kind of Saturday job, if you like. My parents knew about it and didn't mind. He paid well. He painted lots of the villagers over the years. It was what he was known for – glimpses into rural life.'

'Is that *all* she did?'

Natalie hesitated. 'Why would you say it like that? Has someone else come forward and accused him of... something.'

'I'm talking about his "flower girls" series. We'd heard things about Sir Henry before his death – rumours and gossip, nothing we could act on. No one was willing to make a formal complaint and, in those days, the Vyne family held too much power in the district.'

'But now he's dead?'

'Lady Vyne—' he checked himself. '*Clare*, Lady Vyne, still owns several businesses and properties in the village.'

Natalie sighed. 'And is not someone you'd want to cross.'

'You worked for him too, didn't you?'

She knew what he was getting at. Plus, she didn't depend on the Castle Vyne estate for either her income or her home, and she was independent financially – not wealthy, but comfortable. But did she want to become involved in what would result in a very high-profile case?

Why not? By appearing on television to talk about Sarah, she already was!

'In his library?' the DCI added.

There was no way to avoid it. 'Sir Henry liked painting people. He told me he found it far more interesting than painting landscapes. He'd paint the yachtsmen down at the marina and the staff at the cafés and bars. He was most famous for the paintings he did of the local girls posing with the flowers in the castle garden. He never painted me, but I'd occasionally catch him sketching me when he thought I wasn't looking. By then, the local people were starting to realise that there might be something more to these "flower girl" paintings and suddenly no one was available to pose for him. He gave me the creeps, but he never touched me. If he had, I'd have run a mile. I'd have been too young to appreciate that my family might be unexpectedly made homeless if I hadn't agreed! The money he paid me for the admin work helped fund me to go to university. I could never have afforded it otherwise.'

'He never suggested anything—?'

'Only sketches. My hands, my profile. I assumed it was his equivalent of doodling. There's a lot of work involved in running a castle, especially one that is open to the public. I always had the idea he'd rather have been painting in his studio than doing the accounts in the library.'

As the DCI stared at her, a mixture of disbelief and incredulity on his face – probably for her naïve and rather stupid sixteen-year-old self – his phone rang, making them both jump. Instead of answering it, he took out his wallet and removed a ten-pound note. He dropped the money onto the table as he got up.

'Is that it?' she asked uncertainly. 'Are we done?'

'You've sat on this information for fourteen years; it can

wait a little bit longer. My advice to you, Ms Grove – and please take this *very* seriously – is to go home and stay out of trouble. And bump up your security. Something frightened your father enough to make him break cover. I'm sure you'd agree with me when I say he was not the kind of man to frighten easily.'

Natalie followed the DCI outside. She recognised his car parked further along, on the double yellow lines. She glanced across the marina to her apartment block, grateful that she didn't have far to walk, and saw a man standing on the pavement outside it. Even at this distance, it was easy to recognise Bryn's dark hair and battered leather jacket.

'Your boyfriend?' the DCI observed.

'Hardly,' she said. 'I only met him a couple of days ago. We're...' – how to put this – 'working together.'

Did that mean she finally trusted him?

'Indeed?' He didn't ask what they were working on; he knew. 'In that case, Ms Grove, I suggest you be extremely careful, and leave the police work to us.'

It took a moment for Bryn to notice her approach. He was pacing alongside the length of the apartment block, checking the route up the hill every time he reached the corner. Natalie was unsure whether to feel touched or concerned. When Bryn did finally spot her walking along the waterfront, he hesitated, perhaps unsure of the reception he was likely to get.

'Hi,' she said, stopping in front of him.

'Where have you been?' he asked. 'When there was no reply at your apartment, I was worried.'

She thumbed in the direction of Remedy. 'I've been helping DCI Cameron with his enquiries. How about you? Did you get to make your statement?'

He gave a wry smile. 'We were halfway to the police station and an emergency call-out came over the radio. I was dumped by the war memorial, with strict instructions to stay away from the castle and... er, you.'

'Yet here you are.'

His smile turned into an all-out grin. 'Guess where I'm going next?'

'Aren't you the slightest bit worried you might get arrested?'

'Are you? My truck is parked around the corner. We could go to the castle together. Call it a date.'

She rolled her eyes. 'You only want to use me as an excuse to get past the police.'

'You underestimate my ingenuity. Besides, I have a contract to work in the castle grounds and I'm staying at the Lodge. They can hardly keep me out. You could say that I'd be helping *you* get past the police.'

The sound of a car engine starting up made them both turn, just in time to see the lights of a familiar black Audi disappear from view. Had the DCI been watching them talk? Or only pausing to return his missed phone call?

Why would you think we were following you?

'He had a phone call too,' she said. 'I think it was important.'

'It was,' Bryn told her, his expression suddenly serious. 'They've found another body.'

TWENTY-SIX

Alicia had no idea how she climbed out of the well. A whole lot faster than when she'd climbed down it, that was for certain. When she'd finally crawled over the top, practically kissing the grass in her relief to be back on the surface, it was to find Lexi had already called out the emergency services. Within minutes, a police car, an ambulance and a fire engine were all speeding up the castle drive and Alicia found she had a lot of explaining to do, not least of all to her mother, Clare Vyne.

Alicia sent the children home, promising that she'd join them soon, and then assured Clare that she'd take care of everything personally, and that *of course* the police would make good any damage they caused to the newly returfed lawn.

Meanwhile, the castle grounds were busy with activity. Arc lights were set up to illuminate the garden and a large tent, which had been pitched on the lawn, soon had a muddy path worn through its entrance. A metal tripod was constructed over the well and a man in a hard hat and harness was now preparing to abseil to the bottom.

To think, she'd done it wearing old trainers with a length of too-short rope around her waist.

As Alicia watched the man descend, the local Detective Chief Inspector arrived with his posse. They all wore dark macs and suits, but he was the only one carrying an umbrella. After he'd peered down the well, he swapped the umbrella for a takeaway coffee and disappeared into the tent.

With the hood of her coat up against the persistent rain, Alicia felt invisible; even more so when the skeleton was finally brought up.

The rain fell harder. Alicia moved beneath the shelter of the yew trees. No grass grew here; the ground was quite dry, almost parched, and thickly covered with dull, red berries. Despite her coat, she couldn't stop shivering. Would anyone notice if she left?

Feeling thoroughly fed up, she was about to return to The Old Rectory when she heard footsteps on the gravel path and Natalie emerged out of the woods. She had no coat and was wearing only a black sweater and jeans, yet the rain didn't seem to bother her. Her white-blonde hair was plastered to her head and her make-up had formed panda rings around her eyes. She still looked gorgeous.

She looked like Sarah.

'Hey, Alicia! What's going on?'

Alicia found she couldn't speak. Instead, she threw her arms around Natalie and hugged her.

Apparently taken aback, Natalie patted her shoulder and peered down at her. 'Are you OK?'

Now she really did feel like crying.

Alicia shook her head, fumbling in her pocket for her handkerchief but couldn't find it. She was about to ask Natalie if she had one, but realised her friend's attention had been taken by the huge police operation taking place in the centre of the castle lawn. Natalie didn't even seem surprised. Had she known they were here?

'Has something happened?' Natalie asked, a little too casually.

There was no reason to lie. 'I found a body. A dead one.'

'Where?'

'At the bottom of the well.'

That ensured Natalie's full attention. 'You did *what*?'

'I found a skeleton at the bottom of the well,' Alicia repeated, sincerely wishing she'd left for home when she'd had the opportunity. 'It's a long story. I climbed down the well and found a skull grinning at me.'

'You? *You* climbed down the well?'

Why did everyone find it so hard to believe?

'It wasn't difficult. There's a ladder, of sorts, set into the stone and—'

'Bloody hell!'

'Yes, I *know*. It was a stupid thing to do. I could have been killed. But enough about that, why are you here?'

'We were passing and saw the lights—'

'We?'

A tall, dark-haired man stepped from the shadow of the ruined chapel. Who was *this*? Certainly he wasn't Simon – he was several centimetres taller and a lot better looking for a start. Judging from the state of his clothes, he appeared to have been sleeping rough. So did Natalie. What on earth had they been doing?

Perhaps she'd be better off not knowing.

Alicia waited for Natalie to introduce her and, when that failed to happen, she politely held out her hand. 'How do you do? I'm Alicia Fitzpatrick.'

Natalie frowned. 'I thought you knew each other?'

The man hesitated.

Alicia noticed his eyes were the same greenish-gold as peridot and his skin had the warm glow of someone who spent most of their time outdoors. Definitely *not* the kind of man one would forget, and there did seem to be something familiar about him.

'*Have* we met?' she asked.

He took her hand and shook it. 'I'm Bryn Llewellyn,' he said, as though that ought to mean something. When she continued to regard him blankly, he added, 'My landscaping business was hired to restore the castle garden?'

Perhaps that was why Natalie thought they knew each other? Didn't she realise her mother did all the hiring and firing?

'I'm pleased to meet you,' Alicia said politely, and would have turned back to Natalie, but then he said:

'The body you found down the well? Had it been there for long?'

His voice wasn't quite steady. Was he squeamish? The toughest-looking men often were and she'd rather he didn't faint on her. She had enough to deal with at the moment.

'It was a skeleton,' she said, and saw him flinch. 'But I don't think it was really old. It had fillings in its teeth. I could see them glinting. Are you all right? You've turned awfully pale. Do you want to sit down?' She glanced around, as though expecting a chair to materialise out of thin air. 'Although the ground's a bit muddy...'

'I'm fine,' he said, although he was staring at the well as though hypnotised. 'How did it get down there?'

'It might have fallen, but there's always been a locked grille over the top.'

'Have you spoken to the police? Do they know?'

'I'd rather hoped they would want to speak to me. The chap in charge hasn't even introduced himself. If it hadn't been for me, they'd never even have found the skeleton.'

As though summoning him, the flap of the tent was flung back and the man himself came striding out. 'You,' he said, pointing at Bryn. 'Come here.'

Bryn seemed frozen to the spot. 'Who is it?' he asked, his voice so quiet that even Alicia, standing right next to him, had trouble hearing him. 'Do you know?'

The officer closed the distance between them, holding up a small plastic bag centimetres from Bryn's face.

'We took this from the remains,' he said. 'Do you recognise it?'

Alicia craned forward to see what was inside the bag. It appeared to be a thin metallic chain that might have once been silver but was now tarnished black. Attached to this was a small Celtic cross.

Beside her, Bryn swayed on his feet. 'Yes.' He slipped his fingers beneath the neckline of his plaid shirt and pulled out an identical silver chain with an identical silver cross hanging from it. 'It's his.'

The officer tucked the bag into a pocket inside his coat. 'You need to come with us.' He didn't give Bryn chance to reply but turned his attention to Alicia. 'Are you Mrs Fitzpatrick?'

'Yes, but—'

'Legally, the castle belongs to you?'

'In theory, but my mother—'

'In which case, you need to come too.' Unexpectedly, he smiled. 'Purely voluntarily, of course.'

Alicia didn't find that smile reassuring. 'I can't leave my children on their own for long. My husband is away at a conference and my mother...'

Her mother was not the child-friendly type.

Natalie gently touched her shoulder. 'Don't worry. I'll check they're all right.'

Effectively leaving her without a valid excuse.

'Thanks, Nat.'

Fortunately, no one noticed the sarcasm.

'Excellent,' the DCI said. 'If you'd like to follow me, Mrs Fitzpatrick? We have a car waiting.'

Ride in a police car? Alicia began to panic. What would people think? What if she declined? What would the police do? Would they *arrest* her?

'Mrs Fitzpatrick? This is important. You need to come to the station and answer some questions.'

She forced a smile and attempted to regain the upper hand. 'If you think it would help, then of course I will. Tell the children I won't be long,' she added to Natalie. 'And thank you for offering to look after them.'

'No problem,' Natalie said.

Alicia followed the police officer to a waiting car.

There was no sign of Bryn; perhaps he was travelling separately?

Was he a suspect?

Oh, no...

Was *she*?

TWENTY-SEVEN

Natalie headed back along the woodland path and through the churchyard to The Old Rectory. She didn't even wait for the police cars to leave first, in case DCI Cameron changed his mind and wanted to drag her along for another interview too. She needed to gather her thoughts. It was horrible to think of Geraint dying alone and in pain at the bottom of that well. She'd always assumed he'd been enjoying life on the run, yet for all these years he'd been dead too. Why had no one found him before?

One thing was certain; Geraint's death must be connected with her sister's. Either he'd tried to prevent Sarah's murder and been thrown down the well for his trouble or he was the murderer and had fallen as he fled from the scene.

Yet how had he even fallen down the well when there'd always been a grille locked over the top?

The front door of The Old Rectory was not locked. Lexi and Will were in the sitting room, lolling on the sofa and eating pizza straight out of the boxes. No table, no cutlery, no napkins. Will had one foot draped over the arm of the sofa, with his muddy trainer still attached to it. The huge wall-mounted TV was set to one decibel below deafening and showing a gleefully tacky reality show. Natalie grinned. Alicia would've freaked.

'Hey, kids!' she shouted over the din. 'I came to check you were all right. Any pizza left?'

'Hi, Nat,' Lexi waved her hand but barely glanced up. 'There's loads. Help yourself.'

Natalie headed for the kitchen, which was littered with takeaway boxes from Pizza at Cosimo's. Lexi had apparently ordered for her parents too. Natalie put a barbeque pizza into the oven (probably ordered for James, but he wasn't here), along with a box of breaded chicken, and then set about tidying up the mess the children had made in their enthusiasm, putting leftovers into plastic containers and storing them in the fridge. By the time she'd done, her own food was ready.

Simon had said John's death in the fire had been on the news. Presumably, Alicia hadn't seen it or she'd have mentioned it? Once the media found out Natalie's father had come back from the dead, every juicy bit of gossip about her family would be everywhere.

She'd wanted to stir things up by talking about 'Sarah's diary', to rattle memories in the hope someone would remember *something* about the night her sister had died, but she hadn't wanted *this*.

The kitchen had a small TV and she switched it on to check the local news, but there was nothing about either the skeleton or of her father being shot, so she switched over to an old movie.

By ten o'clock, she'd eaten the pizza and was about to return to the sitting room and assert her authority, when Will wandered in, looking disgruntled.

'Lexi kicked me out of the sitting room. She says it's my bedtime, but I think she secretly wants to watch her vampire show.'

'*Is* it your bedtime?'

Will considered it. 'I suppose so, but Mum always reads me a bedtime story.'

'OK, we'll do a deal. Put your pyjamas on in five minutes *and* clean your teeth, and I'll be right up to read to you. Better hurry!'

He shot off upstairs.

She gave him a fifteen-minute head start before following him.

Will's room was crammed with the latest, most expensive toys, most of which were scattered carelessly across the floor. He was hunched over a pile of plastic modelling bricks but glanced up when she came in, his curly ginger hair flopping over his forehead. For a split second, he looked exactly like Alicia.

'Today was the best day ever,' he said, grinning mischievously.

Natalie tried to appear a responsible adult. 'I think the skeleton gave your mother a bit of a shock. Weren't you scared?'

'No! It was brilliant! Do you think the police would let me go down the well tomorrow and have a look?'

Natalie didn't like to tell him the police had already brought the skeleton to the surface. 'I think that might be dangerous.'

'Mum did it!'

'Goodness knows how...'

'There's no water in it and it's not deep. There are rungs to hold onto and everything. Just like my book.'

Had she missed something? 'What book?'

Will dived beneath the bed and emerged, covered in dust, triumphantly brandishing a tattered hardcover book. It had lost its dust jacket and the spine had been inexpertly repaired with sticky tape, which was already peeling off.

Natalie was tempted to chuck it into the bin but pretended to be impressed. She thought it would be a book about medieval

Britain or an official guide to Castle Vyne. Instead, she found herself holding an old children's book.

'Enid Blyton?' She'd have thought Will would be reading the latest Jeff Kinney.

'It belonged to Mum.' Will's voice was disapproving.

'Why am I not surprised?' She examined the cover again. The book was called *The Ring O'Bells Mystery* and showed an illustration of four children peering into a wishing well. 'I'd have thought you'd had enough of wells, William Vyne Fitzpatrick!'

'No way! Are you going to read it to me? *Please?*' Sensing weakness, Will hopped into bed.

He'd marked his place in the book with an old leather bookmark. It was blue and had the logo of Castle Vyne printed on it in gold. It must date from the time when the castle garden had been open to the public.

Natalie sat on the edge of the bed, opened the book and began to read. Before she could finish the chapter, Will had fallen asleep. She tucked him in and tiptoed out, closing the door softly behind her.

Lexi was waiting for her at the top of the stairs. 'I tried watching TV but kept nodding off,' she grumbled. 'Now I'm going to bed at ten like an old person.'

'OK,' Natalie hid a smile. 'Goodnight.'

Lexi grunted a response. As she entered her bedroom, there was a brief glimpse of black walls and purple fairy lights, and then the door closed.

Natalie remembered her own bedroom back at the Lodge, with its stark white walls, creaking floorboards and ever-present atmosphere of fear. She and Sarah had never been allowed to wear make-up or revealing clothes, which of course they did the moment they left the house. They weren't allowed to have boys as friends either. Perhaps this was why they'd both gone spectacularly off the rails. Did Lexi realise how lucky she was, to have that freedom of choice, to be part of a loving family, when her life could have been so different?

Probably not.

Sighing, Natalie headed downstairs. It was only when she walked into the sitting room that she realised she was still holding Will's Enid Blyton book. She ought to take it back upstairs to him – but what if he woke up? She'd babysat for him before and knew she'd end up reading Enid Blyton all evening. Not that there was much of the evening left. Surely Alicia couldn't *still* be at the police station?

She sank onto the couch, flicking aimlessly through the pages of Will's book. On the cover were a group of children staring down into an old well – definitely the reason he'd chosen it. Something had been written on the flyleaf, in dark spidery handwriting. Natalie tilted it towards the light to read it more clearly. It said:

> *To my darling Alicia*
> *Happy Christmas*
> *with love*
> *Father*
> X

It was chilling to see Sir Henry's handwriting after all these years, as though his ghost had reached out from the grave. It stirred up uncomfortable memories of those cold blue eyes and the way he'd continually puffed on that disgusting pipe, which turned the air bitter and foul, and the constant scratch of his pencil on that pad he carried everywhere, while she gritted her teeth and tried to think of the money she was earning – money that would allow her to go to university and leave Calahurst forever.

She'd been stupid, stupid, *stupid*!

No wonder DCI Cameron thought her a fool – but then

he'd probably never been a desperate teenager from an unhappy home.

While the money *had* paid for her to go to university, here she was, fourteen years later, still trying to impress villagers who didn't give a damn what she did.

Sighing, Natalie closed the book and dropped it onto the coffee table – and then saw the outside security light had come on.

Was someone outside?

Alicia?

The front door swung open as Natalie stepped into the hall to investigate. Due to the poor lighting, it took a moment to realise the man with his back to her, quietly closing the door, was James Fitzpatrick.

What was he doing home? Had Alicia phoned him?

Even though she was some distance away, she heard his sudden intake of breath as he turned and saw her. 'Natalie?'

'Hi, James. How was the conference?'

His dark brows lowered into a frown. 'Where's Alicia?'

'Something came up.'

He regarded her blankly. Should she explain about the well and the skeleton?

Why hadn't Alicia messaged him herself?

His frown was now deepening. 'Alicia asked you to look after the children?'

Who else could Alicia ask? Certainly not the cold-hearted Clare, who Natalie wouldn't even trust with a hamster.

James grimaced. 'I'm sorry, that came out wrong. I've had a long, tiring drive and I thought Alicia would have phoned me if there'd been a problem. I'm not sure why she hasn't...' He forced a polite smile. 'Is her mother being a pain, as usual? Honestly, that woman has all the benefits of living like a queen and still expects Alicia to run around after her like a servant. I don't know how my wife puts up with it. I wouldn't.'

Alicia *hadn't* contacted him from the police station? That *was* odd.

Perhaps she hadn't wanted to worry him?

It might be better to say nothing.

James unbuttoned his coat and slung it over the bannister, then yanked off his tie and threw it in the same direction.

'Stay as long as you like,' he said. 'I've only come home to change and then I have to go out again. If Alicia's stuck at the castle with some kind of domestic disaster, you'd be doing us both a huge favour if you can look after the children until one of us gets back.'

'You're going out again?'

'Yes, to my sister-in-law's.'

Which sister-in-law? He had two brothers: William and Charles. Everyone in Calahurst knew that. The Fitzpatricks were one of *the* local families.

Before she could ask him what had happened, he turned away and headed upstairs, returning ten minutes later, having changed into black cargo trousers and sweater. In the meantime, she made herself a coffee, offering him one when he came into the kitchen.

He shook his head. 'I wish I could, but Hannah's waiting for me. I should have gone straight there, but I needed to get out of that suit.'

Hannah was Charles's wife. They'd only been married a couple of years.

Natalie followed him back into the hall. 'James, has something happened?'

He regarded her strangely as he pulled on his coat. 'Haven't you heard? I thought it would be all round the village by now. The fire at Rose Court—'

'The fire was yesterday—' Natalie broke off as a series of images flashed into her head.

Rose Court in flames.

DCI Cameron telling her they'd found the body of her father.

John Grove, alive and well, holding an old gun to her head that had looked remarkably like the World War Two pistol owned by Charles Fitzpatrick.

Charles's car parked in the underground car park at her apartment block.

And all those unanswered telephone calls she'd made to Charles's phone.

'Charles? He's... *dead*?'

Why had no one told her? Surely DCI Cameron had known about this when he'd seen her earlier?

'Yes, but it's taken the police this long to identify his body,' James said. 'It would have taken longer, but Charles was the only one still missing.'

Had it been *Charles's* body left in her father's room? Did that mean her father had been the one who'd killed him, setting Rose Court ablaze to hide the murder – and the fact he'd absconded?

'How *horrible*! Oh, Jamie, I'm so sorry!'

'Hannah, as you can imagine, is beside herself with grief,' James said. 'She needs me. If you're willing to remain here with my children, at least I can drive over there and be with her.'

'Of course I will. It's no trouble at all. I'll do anything—' But he'd already pulled open the front door. There was a distinct blast of cold air, in direct contrast to the snug warmth of the hall, and then the door swung shut after him.

Natalie was left alone in the centre of the hall, hardly able to believe what had happened. Charles Fitzpatrick was dead. *He'd* been the one to die in the fire.

Meanwhile, her father had miraculously survived.

A little *too* miraculously...

TWENTY-EIGHT

Alicia was taken to Calahurst Police Station, shown into a small waiting room and given a couple of old magazines to read and a coffee, while she waited for someone to deign to interview her. An hour later and she was about to walk out, when the door opened and in came the DCI she'd met earlier.

He sat down behind the desk, introduced himself as DCI Douglas Cameron and, without giving her a chance to speak, added, 'I'm sorry to have kept you waiting. I had a few things I needed to clarify.' He took a notebook from his pocket and opened it. 'You're the legal owner of Castle Vyne?' he asked, pen poised for her reply.

She forced herself to concentrate. 'Yes, I inherited the castle. My uncle inherited the title.'

'Why not the castle?'

'My father owned several properties all over the country, most of which were entailed to the head of the Vyne family. The castle wasn't entailed. It's not old, it's not special – it's basically an overgrown folly built by someone with more money than sense. My father could leave the castle and all its contents to whomever he chose. I suspect that if he'd had a son, he'd have left it to him. My father was very traditional.'

'Was your father still alive when Sarah was killed?'

Alicia stared at him. Why had he said that? Surely he wasn't suggesting—

'Mrs Fitzpatrick?'

'Yes, my father was alive. Sarah modelled for him – she appears in several of his "flower girls" paintings and, when she died, he went to her funeral. I thought you knew that?'

'Were you living at the castle at the time?'

'I was sharing a flat in Norchester with James, but I'd come home for the regatta. We were to attend the same university, but when Lexi arrived I no longer wanted to go. We were struggling financially, so my father begrudgingly gave us The Old Rectory. It meant I could stay at home with the baby.'

She trailed off, wondering if she was talking too much – although the DCI was writing everything down in his notebook, so presumably he thought it was relevant.

When he realised she was watching him, he smiled. Like a shark, she thought, and began to feel nervous all over again.

'Your mother is currently in residence at the castle? With her personal assistant, Robert Dench?'

Did he have to make the word 'assistant' sound like 'lover'?

(Even though Rob was.)

'My mother has the use of the castle during her lifetime, but the estate pays for its upkeep.'

DCI Cameron didn't appear to care for specifics. 'Tell me about the well.'

'There's not much to say. It's only a well.'

'How old is it?'

'I've no idea. We've several plans of the estate, going back to the 1400s, although those ones are kept at the County Archives. We believe it was dug out when the first castle was built. I'm certain I remember my father telling me that.'

'It seems a strange place to sink a well – *outside* a castle?'

'The present building is only two hundred and fifty years old. It's built on the site of an older building, some of which some still remains – the library, the old watchtower and the cellars. There was once a wall that enclosed the entire area and other buildings where the gardens are now.'

'The ruined chapel and the well were originally inside this wall?'

'Yes, but only the foundations of the wall remain and they're hidden beneath the garden. Like the rest of the original castle, the wall was destroyed during the Civil War. For many years, the castle lay in ruins. Much of the stonework was taken to reconstruct the houses in the village, which had also been destroyed. Then an ancestor of mine married an heiress and a new, grander castle was built.'

'How long has the grille been fitted over the top of the well?'

'Since before I was born, although I'm not certain that it's the same one. There might be an invoice for the work in the archives. I'll ask the Estate Manager to look it up for you.'

'Thank you. Now, just to clarify, the grille, as you call it, has been in place for over thirty years?'

'Yes, but not necessarily the same grille.'

'I understand that, Mrs Fitzpatrick. I'm not trying to catch you out. Has the grille always been padlocked?'

'Yes. It's level with the ground, as you've seen. Anyone could fall in. It was always kept locked, otherwise there'd be no point in having a grille.'

It was hard not to sound sarcastic. Why did he have to keep asking the same questions?

'You were able to break the lock quite easily.'

'The stone it was bolted to came loose from the rest of the well. The padlock is still in place. You can check.'

'We already have.'

Why ask, if he already knew the answer?

'Do you know where the key to the padlock is?'

'I'm afraid I have no idea. The estate office?'

He scribbled another note but failed to follow up with a question.

The silence stretched out.

'Was there anything else?' she asked eventually. 'I'd really like to get back to my children.'

'One last thing.' DCI Cameron opened up a folder and took out two large black and white photographs. He laid them on the desk, one at a time. 'Do you recognise either of these men?'

The overhead light reflected on the glossy surface of the photographs and Alicia had to lean over them to get a better view. They were police mugshots, not the most flattering of photographs, of two men who were perhaps in their late teens or early twenties. Both had too-long hair and handsome faces that were marred by defiant expressions.

Something stirred in her memory.

She jabbed her finger at the photograph of the younger man. 'I remember him,' she said. 'That's Geraint Llewellyn. He's the fairground boy everyone said killed Sarah, but he disappeared around the same time.'

'How about the other one?'

'Can I pick it up?'

He nodded. 'Take your time. This is important.'

Finally she was doing something worthwhile.

'There is a slight resemblance between them,' she said. 'Are they brothers? They have the same shaped forehead and high cheekbones, but this man is older, harder – as though he's seen too much of life.'

The DCI's lips twitched. 'Yes... but have you seen him before?'

'Never,' she said confidently, handing him back the photograph. 'And I would remember. I'm good with faces.'

The DCI placed the photographs back into the file. 'That's most illuminating.'

Alicia realised she'd made a mistake. 'Why?'

The DCI stood up. 'Thank you for coming in, Mrs Fitzpatrick. I'll get someone to drive you home.'

'Oh, no. You can't leave me hanging like that! Who's the man in the picture? Is he Sarah's killer?'

'I don't know and that's the honest truth.'

'You must have an idea who he is? That's a police mugshot!'

'I'm sorry, I misunderstood your question. Of course I'm aware of the man's identity. His name is Bryn Llewellyn. He and Geraint were cousins.'

'That's *Bryn*? Our new head gardener? Natalie's... um, friend?'

'Yes.'

'But it can't be! Bryn looks nothing like the man in this picture!'

The DCI's smile broadened. 'I know.'

TWENTY-NINE

When Natalie woke the following day, cold and stiff after falling asleep on the couch, The Old Rectory was silent. Thick velvet drapes had been pulled across the sitting-room window and only the tiniest hint of dawn gleamed through. Someone – presumably Alicia – had covered her with a blanket. She pushed it aside and went in search of her.

She found Alicia in the study, transcribing by hand from a big old book. The door swung shut behind her with an audible 'click' and Alicia glanced up.

'Hi, Nat. You know, you didn't have to sleep on the sofa. We do have a guest room!'

'Yes... that was an accident. I must have nodded off in front of the TV.' Natalie perched on the edge of a small sofa. 'When did you get home from the police station?'

'Around midnight.'

The police must have been *very* interested in what Alicia had to say.

'I heard about Charles. I'm sorry for your loss.'

Alicia sighed. 'We're still processing it. James, as you can imagine, is devastated. Charles's wife is in absolute bits.'

'Would you like me to look after the children again today? I could take them to the cinema?'

'We'll be fine. They're old enough to not need full-on supervision and, if I send them away, they'll feel as though – well, they're being sent away.'

Alicia's eyes had smudges of purple circles beneath them and her face was paler than usual, her freckles barely visible.

Natalie frowned. 'Are you OK?'

'I didn't get much sleep last night. Finding that skeleton, the police telling us that Charles had died in that fire...' She dropped her head into her hands. 'It's just so *awful* and the police seem to think Charles was murdered, which makes it worse.'

Best not to mention her theory about her father's involvement in *that*.

'Why don't we all go out?' she suggested. 'It would be good for you to take a break. We can have lunch at one of the cafés by the marina.'

'That's kind of you, but I wouldn't want to impose. You have your own work to do. Don't you have a deadline for your next book?'

'I'm your friend. I want to help.'

'I should really stay here so James will know where to find me. He might need to discuss arrangements for the... funeral.'

There'd need to be a post-mortem and inquest too, but Natalie didn't like to remind Alicia of that.

'If you need anything,' she said, 'anything at all, *call me*.'

'I will,' Alicia agreed.

Alicia, who never liked to be a bother to anyone, probably wouldn't, but as Natalie turned to leave, her friend said, 'That man you were with last night. Bryn Llewellyn. How well do you know him?'

'Truthfully? Not well at all. Why?'

'I don't believe he's who he says he is.'

That made two of them, Natalie thought wryly, but she left before Alicia could give her a lecture on the importance of personal safety – because Alicia certainly *wouldn't* like what she was about to do next.

After leaving The Old Rectory, Natalie headed into St Daniel's churchyard next door, safe in the knowledge that she was unlikely to meet anyone else this early in the morning. The woods beyond were deserted and, as she climbed the hill towards the castle, the sun slowly rose above the trees, warming the autumn leaves and dispersing the mist.

The castle gardens were empty and silent. It was such a difference to the frantic activity of the night before. The little white tent had been taken away and the immaculate lawn now had a distinct path worn to the well. Police tape still stretched from the castle wall and into the shrubbery, creating a large square around the well. Although no officers appeared to be on duty, a solitary patrol car had been parked on the drive. Perhaps the occupant had gone in search of breakfast?

Natalie took her phone from her bag and stuck it into the pocket of her jeans, then slung her bag over her head and across her body.

It was now or never.

With one final glance towards the patrol car, she ran across the grass to the well, ducking beneath the blue and white tape without breaking her stride. A metal frame had been constructed over the top and there was a length of thick rope still clipped to it, hanging into the hole.

She dropped to her knees, peering into the dark. There were the metal rungs, exactly as Will had described – the same ones Alicia must have climbed down the previous evening.

And if Alicia could do it...

She swung her legs over the edge of the well, flipped onto

her stomach and lowered herself down, feeling for the first rung with one foot.

The well had been built from the same slabs of stone as the ruined medieval chapel. Near the top they were dry, partly obscured by large clumps of weeds. Another couple of metres down, the weeds were fewer and the circle of light above her head had grown smaller. In the confined space, every sound (including her breathing) echoed. It was colder too – her breath was forming into little clouds. The deeper she went, the more slabs of stone were cracked or missing completely – and more than one rung was loose.

Perhaps this wasn't one of her better ideas, but she took her phone from her pocket and switched on the light, shining it down to where she assumed Alicia had found the skeleton. The ground was smooth, with no fallen stones, loose soil, or rubbish. Had it been neatly swept clean by the police in search of evidence?

Damn.

If they'd been over every centimetre, surely they'd have spotted what she was hoping to find? They were professionals. How could they have missed it?

Unless they hadn't been looking for it.

It would never have occurred to her either – if she hadn't read Will's book last night.

She leant into the centre of the well, shining the light over the opposite wall. If the police had concentrated on what they'd found at the bottom, rather than something hidden amongst the stone slabs...

It had to be here, it *had* to be. It would have been impossible for Geraint's body to pass through that grille, or open it if he didn't have a key, which meant—

And *there* it was. A gap in the wall, barely a metre high, the surrounding stones constructed in a deliberate arch.

A *tunnel.*

Geraint hadn't fallen into the well or been thrown from the garden; he'd been crawling inside a tunnel.

What the *hell* had he been doing *inside* the castle?

But as Natalie reached towards the rope, intending to swing across to the other side of the well, a male voice echoed from the surface.

'Hey! Is someone down there?' Shadows flickered over the stones as he shone a torch into the well.

She kept her head lowered, hoping to blend in with the gloom.

Please go away...

When all grew silent and dark, she didn't hesitate. She snatched the rope and swung across to the tunnel. There was another metal rung slightly above it, which she caught hold of before dropping into the gap. She landed painfully on her knees. The rope slithered from her hand and fell back into place.

The powerful beam scooped the inside of the well again. '*Hello?*' the voice repeated, this time with more urgency.

She held her breath. Had he seen her? Had he *heard* her?

But the light disappeared, accompanied by a strange 'swishing' sound.

It took a moment for her to work out what it was – the rope being pulled up to the surface!

There'd be no exit that way. She was now trapped – in the same way Geraint had been, fourteen years earlier.

Best not to think about *that*.

Holding her phone between her teeth, she began crawling down the tunnel.

It was *filthy*. Beneath her palms, she could feel compacted soil, sharp little stones and some crumbly stuff that was possibly rodent droppings – but she'd rather not think about that either.

The tunnel was narrow – barely wide enough for her shoulders – but it grew wider and soon she was able to stand up and walk without hitting her head, until it opened into a wide chamber with the same vaulted ceiling as the castle library.

Was this a storeroom beneath the castle? There were alcoves set into the walls, three for each side, ornamented with a statue. The floor was set with flagstones but crowded with junk – broken furniture, warped paintings and books strewn about in no order at all. The air was damp and cold, and the walls had a tidemark about a metre from the ground. The chamber must have flooded several times before the well had dried up.

In the centre of the chamber were three stone tables, each with another statue reclining upon it. Natalie held her phone above her head and watched the shadows reform until she understood what she was seeing.

Tables? She was an idiot! They were incredibly old *tombs*, with statues of knights lying on top, their hands together as though in prayer. 'Humfreye Vyne' had been carved deeply into the side of the central tomb, but the remainder of the inscription was in Latin.

Beyond that was another tomb and another knight. He held a shield with the Vyne crest upon it. Next to him was a third tomb; the knight's shield lay at his feet, his hands gripping a stone sword.

She'd stumbled into the Vyne family crypt. Abandoned, used as a storeroom, and then forgotten about for several hundred years by the look of it.

More statues were set in the surrounding alcoves, perhaps representing angels or, as there were twelve, could they be apostles? Their heads were bent in prayer, every fold of their robes lovingly recreated. The detail was incredible. Natalie slowly turned, eager not to miss a thing. Alicia would *love*—

One of the shadows moved.

Natalie swung the light back. It was a rat, it *must* be a rat – although she sincerely hoped it wasn't. Little sharp teeth and little sharp claws... It was terrifying to even think about it.

The alternative, however, was far worse.

The statue nearest to her shifted under the spotlight, unfolding, straightening, raising his head, preparing to meet her gaze.

Natalie screamed and dropped her phone.

The light went out, leaving her in the dark.

But unfortunately not alone.

THIRTY

A beam of light illuminated the crypt.

'Sorry,' a rough male voice said. 'It's me: Bryn. I thought you were the police.'

If Natalie still had her phone, she'd have thrown it at him. 'What the *hell* are you doing here?'

'The same as you,' he said. 'Trying to find answers.'

'You were following me!'

'I was here first,' he said mildly.

'It's not a competition! What happened to "working together"?'

She dropped to her knees, scrabbling in the dirt for her phone. She found it lying against Humfreye's tomb. Scooping it up, she checked for damage. It seemed OK, although the screen was now scratched. *Fabulous*.

'You won't get a signal,' he said. 'We're underground.'

And he was now mansplaining too?

'I was using it as a torch.'

'I have a torch.' He held it up.

'Good for you.'

She also noticed he'd had the opportunity to change his

clothes since last night and was now wearing a thick green sweater instead of his usual leather jacket and plaid shirt. It was a small comfort to realise he was just as filthy as her.

'The police have taken the rope away,' she said, 'but I'm not sure if they know we're here.'

'I'm hoping there's another way out.' He flicked the torch around the crypt. 'Did you know about this place?'

She dropped her phone back into her bag. 'No, did you?'

'There was no other way my cousin's body could have got down that shaft. Not with a locked grille over the top.'

It was the same conclusion she'd come to.

Unless someone had a key – and that would point the finger firmly at a member of Alicia's family – and she'd rather not think about that until she'd exhausted all other possibilities.

'Are we beneath the old chapel or the castle, do you think?' he asked.

'The old chapel would make more sense. These tombs are medieval and the current castle wasn't built until the late 1700s.'

'I thought the old chapel was moved?'

'Maybe we're beneath where it used to be?'

He ran the beam of the torch along the wall where he'd been standing. Glimpses of rough-hewn stone could be seen amongst the crumbling and flaking plaster. 'I found some steps in the corner, but they don't lead anywhere.' He spotlighted a flight of narrow stone steps, dark with damp, which led sharply upwards.

'You're looking in the wrong place.' She pushed his arm up a few centimetres and the torchlight flickered towards the vaulted ceiling. 'See that upside down "V" shape? I expect that was the entrance from the chapel.'

'No use to us – it's been bricked up.'

'And it'll be beneath several tons of soil.'

'A cheering thought.' He dimmed the beam and turned back

to face her. 'Do you think the Vyne family know the crypt is here? It's not on any of the estate plans, but then neither was the tunnel.'

'Perhaps the family thought it'd been destroyed when the chapel was moved and they forgot about it?'

Bryn sighed and sat on the corner of Humfreye's tomb. 'Why do I get the feeling I'm wasting my time? That this' – he gestured round at the crypt – 'as beautiful and strange as it is, has nothing to do with anything.'

'You've found out what happened to Geraint. I thought it was important to you to know how he died?'

'It was – *is*.' He ran his fingers through his hair, dislodging a shower of dust and dirt. 'I've come this far—' He broke off, staring around the crypt. 'Who'd have thought it? What the hell was Geraint even *doing* down here?'

Natalie had to agree with him. She'd thought that finding the tunnel would solve everything. Now it'd thrown up more questions.

'Geraint and Sarah died on the same night,' she said. 'That much is obvious. But what links their deaths?'

'This bloody castle.' Bryn kicked out at a stack of wooden chairs. They collapsed, disintegrating into little more than sticks of firewood, sending up a choking cloud of dust. 'And the rich bastards who live here.'

'I'm sure everything will become clearer when we get out.' There was no point telling him that the current Vyne family no longer had money because most of it had been sunk into building and maintaining the castle, and Sir Henry's paintings were no longer in fashion. 'Give me the torch.'

He held it out of reach above his head. 'I've checked everywhere. There's no sign of another tunnel.'

Exasperated, Natalie held out her hand. 'Torch, *now*.'

He slapped it into her open palm. 'Knock yourself out.'

'Charming!'

He rolled his eyes. 'Obviously I didn't mean it *literally*.'

'Good to hear.'

'I'm sorry, I'm feeling... tense.' He flipped open his satchel and took out a small bottle of water, which he offered to her first. But before she could soften towards him, he said, 'You won't find anything.'

That only served to make her more determined.

She took a sip of the water, returning the bottle before glancing back at the tunnel. 'If the well is that way, we've travelled west. The most direct route should be in the north wall.'

For a moment, he said nothing. Then, begrudgingly, 'That sounds logical.' He slid off the tomb, slung his satchel over his shoulder and helped her clear a path through the rubbish.

This wall hadn't been plastered and was set with several large slabs of stone monuments inscribed with the Vyne family name and crest. The dates were entirely from the early seventeenth century. Were there coffins behind them? *Bodies?*

She shuddered.

Bryn glanced back. 'Did you bring a sledgehammer?'

Now it was her turn to roll her eyes. 'Sorry, that'd be in my *other* bag.'

'Luckily I have this.' He produced a small jemmy from his satchel and grinned.

She stared at it incredulously. 'I'm not even going to ask why you thought you were going to need *that*.'

He shrugged modestly. 'I have bolt cutters too. The well had a grille over it. I thought I might meet another one.'

'Let's try something a little more subtle first, OK?' She stepped up to the nearest monument and began to run her fingers over the surface, checking each protuberance for a hidden mechanism.

Once he understood what she was up to, he did likewise. He worked from the right; and she worked from the left. After ten minutes, they met in the middle. Here was the largest slab of all; a two-metre monument to a single family. Each name, along with a date, was listed beneath a large swirly 'V', which had been engraved on a raised stone tile.

'This is the one,' Bryn said confidently. 'The others have the family crest but only this one has a "V".'

'V for Vyne,' she said dismissively.

'It's not a "V", it's an arrow.'

He slammed his fist against the stone tile. The diamond-shaped panel slid back into the stone. For a moment, nothing happened. Then, from somewhere behind the wall, came the sound of stone grating against stone and the whole slab juddered back into the wall, leaving a half-metre gap at either side.

Bryn snatched the torch from her hand and squeezed into the tunnel.

'What happened to "ladies first"?' she called after him.

The only sound that came back was the echo.

As he had the torch, the light faded rapidly. Natalie felt a squirm of apprehension. Any moment now and she was going to be left alone in the dark.

Then, just as unexpectedly, he was back – seizing her hand and pulling her into the hole after him. 'What are you waiting for?' he grinned. 'A royal invitation?'

'You really need to work on your people skills,' she grumbled, but followed him all the same, trying to ignore Alicia's last words echoing in her head:

'I don't believe he's who he says he is.'

THIRTY-ONE

Like the brick tunnel they'd left behind, the passage was not wide enough to walk side-by-side, but it did slope upwards. There were no tree roots poking through because they were walking beneath the lawn. Halfway along, another archway appeared in one side of the wall.

Bryn perfunctorily shone the torch through the gap. 'Priest's hole, going nowhere,' he said.

If Clare Vyne ever decided to open the castle to the public, Natalie thought, all these secret rooms and passages would be a *huge* hit with visitors.

But maybe she should concentrate on getting out of here first.

After another couple of minutes' walking steadily uphill, the air grew stuffy.

Bryn was still holding her hand.

Neither of them had mentioned the events of the previous day.

How to broach the subject?

'I'm sorry about Geraint,' she told the back of his head.

Bryn didn't break his stride. 'I knew he was dead. He'd have made contact otherwise.' His voice was flat, all trace of his former humour erased.

She remembered the horrible things she'd said to him and Siân, at that pub in London. It seemed a lifetime ago.

'Do the police know how he died?'

'A head injury.'

The kind of injury you'd receive falling down a well?

They walked a few more minutes in silence.

'Why did Geraint come to the castle?'

This time there was no response. All she could hear was his breathing, laboured due to the lack of fresh air.

Maybe he hadn't heard her. 'Bryn? Why did—'

'Geraint was with Sarah.'

That didn't make sense.

'Calahurst is full of bars, pubs and clubs,' she said. 'Why would a couple of teenagers want to visit a neo-Norman castle in the dead of night?'

Bryn stopped walking. She thought they'd reached the end of the tunnel, but instead he slowly swung around to face her. The torch pointed towards the ground, leaving his face in shadow.

'There are a couple of things I haven't told you,' he said carefully. 'You saw where we lived?'

It took a moment for her to work out what he meant. 'The caravan at the fairground?'

'We were two ordinary lads with no money and big dreams.'

Where was this conversation heading?

For the first time, she realised she was effectively trapped down here with him.

Did she trust him?

'What do you *think* we were doing at the castle?' he asked, when she failed to respond.

She thought she could almost hear the beat of her heart echoing through the airless tunnel. 'We?'

'Think about it, Natalie. If you need a clue...' He took something from his satchel and held it up.

The jemmy glinted silver in the torchlight.

'You came to the castle to *break in*? Were you *crazy*?'

He dropped the jemmy back into the bag. 'You think we should have started with something smaller? Say, a bungalow?'

'Be serious... please?' Perhaps he relied on humour to deflect emotion but, 'This isn't funny.'

He sighed. 'After you'd left, Sarah told Geraint about the castle and the artist who lived there – Sir Henry Vyne. She told Geraint how to get in and where Sir Henry kept his cash – she knew we weren't interested in anything else. We wouldn't have known an antique if it bit us, even less what to do with one.'

'Why would Sarah do that?' she asked.

'She told Geraint she needed his help. She told him about your father, what a monster he was, and how your mother never stood up for you. Sarah told us Sir Henry had drawn some very dodgy sketches of her – real blackmail stuff – and she wanted them back. She was getting married and knew if her fiancé ever found out what she'd been up to, he'd dump her.' Bryn shook his head. 'To be honest, the fiancé sounded as bad as Sir Henry.'

'Sarah was getting *married*? How would you know this? Why would she confide in *you* and not *me*?'

His laugh was bitter. 'To be frank, she knew we were thieves! She'd seen the stolen gear we had hidden in the caravan. She wanted us to break into the castle for her. She said it would be easy. There were no alarms and no security cameras, because there was nothing worth stealing except for the stuff kept in the safe – and she knew the combination.'

It was as though Natalie's blood had turned to ice. All those hours she'd spent in Sir Henry's library. What had happened to those quick sketches he'd drawn of her? Unlike Sarah, she'd never given it a thought. Were they still in that safe or in someone else's personal collection? At the time, she'd thought they were perfectly innocent, but what if there were more? Was there enough to blackmail *her*? Would they find their way to the Press? OK, so she'd only been sixteen, but why hadn't she taken the time to think it through? Sir Henry had been a respected artist – it had never occurred to her that he might want something more. She'd only wanted to make a little bit of money, just enough to be able to leave Calahurst and never come back.

Like Sarah.

What had she done?

Bryn, unaware of what was going through her head, continued working through his theory.

'Maybe Sir Henry had paid Sarah extra to ensure she kept her mouth shut about the sketches? *That's* how she knew the combination of the safe. She'd have seen him take the money out and seen where he kept his sketchbooks. I guess they weren't the kind of thing you'd want to leave lying around for anyone to see. Were they the kind you'd *kill* for though...?'

Natalie had a memory of that shoebox in Sarah's wardrobe, overflowing with cash.

'How many other girls did Sir Henry secretly sketch?' Bryn was asking. 'If he knew Sarah no longer wanted to pose for him, do you think he had another girl lined up? I suppose we'll never know.'

Natalie had been so flattered when Sir Henry had started sketching her. He was a famous artist. Had *she* been the next girl in line?

'Stop!' She couldn't stand to hear any more. 'I don't need to hear this. I only wanted to know who killed my sister, not all this other... stuff.'

He regarded her pityingly. 'I appreciate it's painful for you to keep going over the past,' he said, 'but how else are we going to get a handle on this?'

She took a deep breath. 'You're right. I'm sorry. Go on.

What happened when you broke into the castle? What did you do?'

'*I* didn't do anything,' he said. 'I was the look-out. My cousin and your sister climbed through the library window. She knew the catch was broken and that no alarms were ever set. For a while, everything was fine. Then it all went to hell. The lights went on, there was shouting and screaming... My cousin stuck his head through the window and yelled at me to run – so I did. It was the biggest mistake I ever made. Geraint went back for Sarah; I ran to the fairground and told Da we had to pack up before the police turned up – but they never did. We thought my cousin would join us on the road, but instead... instead...' Bryn's voice, which had deteriorated into a hoarse whisper, finally gave out.

He shook his head helplessly.

Natalie finished the sentence for him, although it was hardly necessary.

'You never saw him again.'

THIRTY-TWO

Was it better to know for certain your loved one had died, no matter how appalling the circumstances, or to never know – and live in hope that one day they would return?

For Natalie, finding Sarah's body had been worse than knowing she was dead. Worse, because it had been the last time Natalie had seen her and was therefore the last memory she had.

Before she could find the words to comfort Bryn, he'd turned away.

'We've come to a dead end,' he said.

'Are you sure?'

He leant against the wall, angling the torch so she could see the solid wooden panel blocking the passage.

'Do you think it slides?' she suggested, remembering the panelled walls of the castle's entrance.

He handed her the torch and felt around the edge of the wood with his fingers. 'As far as I can tell, it's been deliberately blocked off.' He placed his palms against the wood and shoved. Nothing happened, so he pushed harder and then used his shoulder. 'It may have been bolted into place. Damn, we're never going to get out.'

'Geraint got through.'

Why had she said that?

'Fourteen years ago!' He heaved again at the panel and a gap of a few centimetres appeared on one side. 'You'll have to help me. I think this is some kind of furniture – a bookcase or a dresser. It's been placed to deliberately conceal the passage.' He squashed himself into the corner, indicating a very small space beside him for her to stand. 'Help me push.'

She stuck her shoulder against the wood. This was not going to work, but what alternative did they have? Go back through the crypt and into the well shaft? Where the police might be waiting at the top?

Would that be such a bad thing? OK, they'd trampled all over a crime scene, but they weren't criminals. They'd nothing to hide.

Well, she hadn't.

Bryn had his shoulder to the wooden panel and was ready to heave against it. He stood directly beside her. His chest almost, but not quite, touching her back. She could feel his breath, warm on her neck. It gave her a very strange sensation. Almost like—

'Are you waiting for a countdown?' he asked, amused. 'Because I can do that if you want?'

'Sorry.' She slammed her shoulder against the wooden panel, digging her heels into the stone floor to get a grip, which was almost impossible in her smooth-soled ballet flats.

Bryn cursed in English. Maybe the Welsh didn't have enough swear words?

Incredibly, the bookcase, or whatever it was, moved a few centimetres.

Natalie remembered which room in the castle had bookcases.

'Um... Bryn?'

He didn't hear. His eyes were closed; every muscle was straining with effort.

'Bryn?' she said again, turning around, her fingers lightly touching his chest to get his attention.

His eyes flew open. Beautiful green eyes, far too close to her own.

Whatever she'd been about to say went out of her head. There was a thick streak of dirt across his cheekbone. Without thinking, she licked her thumb and wiped the dirt away. He caught hold of her hand, but then didn't let go, as though unsure as to what he should do next.

'Natalie, I...'

His lips moved to form the next word, but he was drowned out by a massive explosion.

Natalie assumed the roof had collapsed. As Bryn's arms moved protectively around her, dragging her back against the wall of the tunnel, she braced herself for the impact.

But time moved on and only silence settled around them.

She opened her eyes. It was still dark. The only light came from the torch, which lay on the ground where she'd dropped it. The wooden panel had gone, revealing yet another dark chasm beyond, partly obscured by a lingering haze of dust.

Bryn lifted her out of the way and scooped up the torch, pointing it through the gap. His hair was grey with dust, along with the rest of him – apart from a large chunk of his torso where he'd held her to protect her from the sharp splinters of glass that now littered the floor. They'd even become embedded in the thick wool of his sweater.

He shook them off. 'We did it!' He gave her the biggest grin. 'We found the way out!'

'It might be just another vault...'

But Bryn was already clambering over the remains of a heavy wooden cabinet and into the void beyond.

His torch, dimmer now, revealed broken wood amongst the glass, and dark-brown liquid pooling on the floor. The walls were stone, like the crypt, and the chamber had the same low, vaulted ceiling. The only difference was a horrible smell: sweet and cloying, like a rotted Christmas pudding.

'*Not* the library,' he sighed, 'and probably a good thing.'

Natalie, following, recognised the smell. 'It's a wine cellar...'

'What's left of one.'

Glass crunched beneath her feet. 'When someone arrives to investigate the noise, we're going to have some explaining to do.'

'You can, if you want to.'

'What's that supposed to mean?'

'We need to get out,' he said. 'Any explanations can be done later – preferably through a third party.'

'Are you serious?'

'I know you believe these people are your friends, but trust me, they're not. And when they find out what we've done... Well, let's not talk about that. Help me find the way out. You know the castle, you've been inside before. We're in the old part, right? Directly beneath the library?'

He was going too fast. The horrors of the last few days were catching up with her. Everything was taking on a surreal, dream-like quality. She forced herself to concentrate. Perhaps the vault did stretch along the same dimensions as the library. Like the crypt, it had been used for storage. There were wine racks around the walls, still crammed with bottles, but they were blurred grey with dust and cobwebs. No one had been here in a long time either.

We're missing something, she thought, but Bryn had lost interest in her reply and was moving towards a small arch in the corner, where a series of stone steps curled upwards.

'Where do you think this goes?' he asked.

Natalie tried to focus.

A medieval stone staircase? There was only one she knew of.

'I think it's the base of the watchtower...'

'Where's that?'

'It's between the library and the great hall. It doesn't go anywhere above the first floor. It was kept as a curio. The top was demolished when the castle was remodelled in the nineteenth—'

'It goes up,' he grinned. 'That's good enough for me.'

As he slipped sideways, through the arch and up the curving stone steps, the vault became dark once again. And again Natalie was left chasing a light, stumbling over the uneven stone steps as it threatened to disappear completely.

The steps circled once, twice, and then the way was blocked by flat strips of wood above their heads, through which daylight gleamed tantalisingly.

'Floorboards,' Bryn muttered, thrusting the torch at her with a terse, 'Hold that.'

Too tired to argue, she watched silently as he rummaged in his satchel, retrieving his jemmy to lever up the floorboards. But it transpired the floorboards were not nailed down, only slotted together to form a small trapdoor that could be lifted up and out of the way. As he did this, daylight streamed into the gap and Natalie had to turn her head from the brightness.

Bryn ran up the steps.

'All clear,' he called, reaching down to lift her through the gap.

She emerged in the great hall, blinking at the daylight, and standing between the steps of the old watchtower and the heavy studded door leading to the library.

The hall was empty and the castle completely silent. Where was everyone?

Natalie lifted her gaze to the shadowy gallery above, where the portraits of Alicia's ancestors watched them coldly. A sudden movement distracted her. A fat grey pigeon had settled on an outside windowsill, stalking imperiously along its length, before taking flight again.

Had something in the gallery startled it?

Bryn carefully slotted the trapdoor into place. The emptiness of the hall magnified every tiny sound. Natalie's attention was drawn once more to the library door. Was Clare doing the accounts on the other side? How about her assistant, Rob? Where was he?

Bryn took hold of her hand and pulled her across the hall.

Again, she had a sensation of being watched and glanced over her shoulder.

They'd left a trail of wet, sticky footprints on the York sandstone. Coated with a dusting of ground glass, the footprints glittered eerily in the sunlight.

She pointed them out to Bryn, who shrugged. 'What can we do about it?'

'Blame it on the castle ghost?'

He gave a low chuckle. 'I thought you didn't believe in ghosts?'

The years peeled away, the castle vanished and suddenly she was standing beside a ghost train, flirting with a green-eyed boy.

'I *knew* it!' Natalie said. 'It *is* you.'

THIRTY-THREE

The man pretending to be Bryn Llewellyn regarded her stonily. 'This isn't the place for that conversation,' he said.

At least he hadn't denied it.

'You're looking pretty good for a dead man, *Geraint*.'

His expression didn't change.

'Tell me about the skeleton Alicia found down the well. It's obviously not you—'

'It's Bryn. He went into the castle with Sarah and I never saw him again. *Mrawd anwylyd* – he was like a brother to me and those bastards killed him.'

He *was* Geraint... Had she honestly believed any different? The night she'd seen him standing in the shadows of the old chapel, watching the castle, she'd known exactly who he was. It was why she'd run.

She should run now, but she had to know, 'Did you kill Sarah?'

'If I had, would I be going to so much trouble to help you find out who did? Would I even be standing here?'

He'd picked the wrong moment to be flippant.

'Can you prove it?'

'Prove what?'

'Prove that you didn't kill Sarah?'

'I thought you trusted me?'

Something inside snapped. 'How can I trust you when you keep lying to me?'

'Nice to know where I stand.'

He sounded hurt.

But he might have been putting that on too.

Sunlight streamed through the cathedral-like windows of the great hall, warming the back of her neck. There was a dark mustiness emanating from the corridor behind him and the sour scent of alcohol lingered in the air above the stone steps.

'If you want to stay here and fight,' he said, 'if you want to rouse the entire castle, then fine, let's do it. But if you want to find out the truth, I suggest you get a move on because whatever did happen to your sister has a lot to do with this castle and the people who live here.'

He was clever, the way he kept casting doubt, making her search elsewhere for culpability. But what if she was tired of searching?

She wanted it to be over. She didn't care who'd done it. She just wanted to know *why* so that Sarah could be at peace. So *she* could be at peace.

He took hold of her shoulders, dipping his head so she had no choice but to look directly at him. 'Am I making myself clear, Natalie? We need to get out of here and it needs to happen *now*!'

She pushed him away. 'Carry on,' she said tightly. 'No need to wait for me.'

He remained exactly where he was, frowning, apparently reluctant to leave her.

Again, her concentration wandered. The hall was still and quiet. Clare Vyne employed a large team of staff to ensure everything ran smoothly. Where was everyone?

Something wasn't right.

'Natalie?' His voice had softened. 'Why won't you come with me?'

Her attention snapped back. 'You lied to me. You've lied practically every moment we've been together.'

'It was for a good reason. Remember when we met? What if I'd told you the truth? What would you have done?'

'Called the police,' she admitted.

'You see?'

He was about to reach for her again, so she took a step back. 'You've found Bryn. You've learnt everything you need to know. Why are you still here? Go – leave now, before the police work out who you really are.'

Maybe they already had.

'I'm not leaving without you,' he said.

'Now you're being stupid.'

There was the tiniest hint of a smile. 'Probably,' he replied.

A frantic, high-pitched beeping made them both start.

'Have we set off the alarm?' he asked.

'No.' She knew that sound. She'd heard it before. 'It's a pager.'

To be more accurate, it was Rob's pager, coming from somewhere above their heads.

Geraint grabbed her hand again and attempted to pull her down the corridor towards the main door.

Natalie held back. 'Wait!'

By his expression, he clearly thought she was an idiot, but it was too late to argue. As they flattened themselves against the wall of the corridor, footsteps echoed throughout the hall. Slow, measured – it took a moment for her to work out which direction they were coming from.

As they grew louder, Rob came into view. He was moving unhurriedly, across the centre of the hall towards the library, balancing a small tray on his arm. Without bothering to knock, he went straight inside.

Natalie didn't allow herself to relax until the door had closed behind him.

Geraint wiped sweat from his forehead with his sleeve, leaving a distinct streak of clean skin. 'That was close. Too close. Can we go now? *Please?*'

When he turned in the direction of the main entrance, she grabbed his sweater and hauled him back.

'*Now* what's the matter? I thought the exit was this way?'

'So are the new security cameras.'

He winced. 'I'll follow you.'

She led him through the great hall, taking care to keep close to the wall, so that anyone in the gallery above wouldn't see them.

There were many passages and rooms leading from the hall, but the last door on the right, just before the steps down to the kitchen, opened into the breakfast room. It was a small, square, informal room, hung with faded red silk and leading onto a terrace planted with pink roses.

Natalie stepped through the door. A solitary patrol car remained on the drive, so presumably the police were somewhere in the grounds. Unwilling to risk another encounter with the sarcasm of DCI Cameron, she quickly crossed the drive and headed between the rhododendrons opposite, where there was a path of sorts, very overgrown, that emerged into a small orchard. The grass here was long and yellow, and no one had bothered to pick the fruit from the ancient apple trees. They'd rotted where they'd fallen.

Geraint blundered out of the bushes behind her, cursing as usual, but she was already following the slight indentation that was the path, towards a hawthorn hedge, bright with crimson berries, and a small gate. She pushed it open – and found herself staring at the tiny casement windows, the spindly chimneys and woolly thatched roof of the Lodge.

The lawn had been neatly cut and the rusting wheelbarrow had gone, but curiously the old washing line was still there, although someone had given it a fresh coat of black paint.

Geraint walked down the path in front of her until he reached the kitchen door, thrusting a hand into each of his pockets, searching for his key.

'I would kill for a cold beer,' he said – and then saw her expression. 'Is this the first time you've been back here?'

She shook her head, unable to formulate the words. Sarah had died and life had gone on. She'd left for university and, by the time she'd returned, Magda had divorced John and married Richard Vyne – Sir Henry's younger brother. Magda hadn't even bothered to tell her. Natalie had returned to an empty, dusty house. Her key had still fitted, her room was exactly as she had left it, but her mother had gone. If it hadn't been for Simon taking her in...

She owed him *everything*.

The kitchen door creaked open.

'Would you like to come inside and see what's been done to the place?' Geraint asked.

The wind came from nowhere. It shook the oak trees above their heads, scattering leaves like confetti, sending them scuttling along the path. The door was wrenched from Geraint's hand and crashed back against the wall, knocking out a small lump of plaster.

It was then Natalie saw it.

The same table.

All the furniture was the same.

'I've got to go,' she said, attempting her best impression of normal. 'I can't do this any more. I'm going—'

Where? Home? She almost laughed out loud. Nowhere had ever felt like home. And now Simon had broken up with her, there was no one to care what she did, except, maybe Alicia. All Natalie had now was the empty life she'd attempted to fill with her obsession in finding Sarah's killer.

'Natalie?' Geraint's voice was kind, gentle. It was harder to mistrust him when he was being nice.

'Goodbye,' she said, turning away to follow the path around the side of the Lodge

Behind her, the door slammed shut. She was on her own again.

So why did she feel she was being watched? *Was* there something evil about the Lodge? Had all the unhappiness it had seen over the years, imprinted itself upon the bricks and mortar?

Why couldn't Clare Vyne have let the place fall down?

As she rounded the corner, the first thing Natalie saw was the gate onto the castle drive. The latch was closed. There'd be no kicking it open with her foot this time. She'd have to physically touch it. Even though it'd been recently repainted, even though it probably wasn't the original gate at all, she could still see it inside her head as it'd been that night.

Why didn't I call out to her? One word from me and she would've stayed home. She'd have lived. Sarah died and it was my fault.

It had *always* been her fault. That's why she'd spent the past fourteen years seeking someone to blame.

Something brushed against her shoulder and she jumped.

'Natalie? Are you all right?' It was Geraint. When she didn't respond, he added, 'Please come inside. Have a coffee or a sandwich. You'll feel better, I promise. I think you're suffering from delayed shock.'

She shook her head, huddling into her jacket. The sun was shining, so why was she so cold?

'OK... Why don't I give you a lift home? My truck's right there.' He was deliberately speaking slowly, trying to calm her, perhaps thinking she was about to go into some kind of a meltdown.

He wouldn't be far wrong.

'I have to see Alicia,' she said. 'I have to tell her about the tunnel.'

'Don't you think she already knows?'

Geraint believed Alicia's family had killed his cousin. It was understandable. Bryn had been found at the bottom of the castle well and Sarah had been found in one of the castle ponds. But what if someone wanted it to appear that way? What if someone knew Sir Henry's secret and wanted to reveal it?

This isn't about Sarah, it never was.

Another gust of wind shook the surrounding trees, dislodging a shower of dead leaves, whipping them into a whirlwind and sending them dancing down the castle drive.

'Please, Natalie,' he said. 'Let me take you home. I'm worried about you.'

Natalie's attention was drawn towards the leaves. If she concentrated hard enough, she could almost see a girl being whirled around by the man she loved. A tall man, with dark hair...

'You're in shock,' he repeated.

Why couldn't she see the man's face?

'You've just lost your father—'

Perhaps she didn't need to.

'—And you've stirred up all kinds of supressed memories returning here.'

'How long was Bryn's hair?' she asked him.

'What?'

'The night Bryn died? How long was his hair? I'm assuming he was dark-haired, like you?'

Geraint seemed to be struggling to keep up. 'Some people thought we were alike, yes. His dad and mine were brothers, but my mother was Spanish, so—'

'What did he look like?' She could hardly contain her impatience. Did Geraint not realise how important this was? 'What was he wearing the night he died?'

'Jeans, black T-shirt, khaki military-style jacket – the same clothes they found him in, although mostly they'd rotted away. Something to do with natural fibres. If he'd been wearing polyester—'

'Describe him for me.'

'Six foot one or two, the same as me. Brown hair, hazel eyes. He had pale, freckly skin – that was one significant difference between us, that and the colour of our eyes—'

'What about his *hair*? Was it long, short—?'

'I guess you'd call it long. All the men our age had the same style, copied from the bands of the time—' He broke off, frowning. 'You've remembered something?'

'I saw Sarah with a man the night she died.'

'Why didn't you tell someone?'

'I'm telling you now.'

'Was it Bryn?'

Natalie watched the leaves flutter to the ground, completely still. 'No, how could it be? At that point she'd never met him, never met either of you...'

The doctor, the teacher, the librarian, the gardener...

How could she have got it so wrong?

THIRTY-FOUR

'Do you believe in ghosts?' Natalie asked.

A flicker of a smile. 'Please don't tell me you see dead people,' Geraint said.

'For the past fourteen years, I've had Sarah inside my head, stuck on repeat, walking down this path.'

'You think you're the only person to be haunted by a memory? You think I don't blame myself for running away – basically, leaving Bryn to *die* – every single day?'

'I'm sorry, so sorry, but I thought Sarah was murdered by someone she knew – and maybe she was – but, stupidly, I made the assumption that I would know them too. What if I don't?'

'You're going to have to get over the idea that you can solve your sister's murder by yourself,' he said. 'You're not a detective. All you can do is give the police what evidence you have and let them do their job. I suggest we drive to the police station, tell Cameron about the tunnel and let him sort it out. It's his job, not ours. We were naïve to imagine otherwise.'

She could imagine how *that* conversation would go.

'I have to tell Alicia about the tunnel first.'

'You don't have to tell her anything!'

'She's my friend!'

He bit off a curse, turned abruptly, took two paces towards the Lodge and then swung back. 'Look, you already know how I feel about this—'

'I understand, I really do, but Alicia is the only friend I have. I know that sounds pathetic, but apart from Simon, Alicia was the only person who stuck by me after Sarah died. The only person who helped me when I was broke and alone. If Bryn's death implicates her family in any way, she needs to know first.'

For a moment, he merely stared at her.

'Fine,' he said. 'If that's what you want. Let's get it over with.'

She was surprised he'd acquiesced so easily. 'You're coming too?'

'Oh, yes,' was his grim response.

She hesitated. 'You're not going to say anything that might upset her?'

'I think you'll find Mrs Fitzpatrick is a lot tougher than anyone gives her credit for.'

Natalie led him back towards the castle. Two days ago, he'd chased her through these woods, catching up with her outside the Lodge. He'd slammed his fist against the window of her car and called her 'Sarah'. Now here they were again. Fate having the last laugh.

The path to St Daniel's Church was a few metres down on the left. There were several of these little paths leading through the woods. Perhaps they'd once been ancient rights of way, which was why the locals felt they had a right to wander all over them. Although it soon became clear no one walked here any more. The ferns had grown to waist height and spirals of brambles, heavy with ripe blackberries, cascaded over the path. Oak trees weaved their branches together overhead, conspiring to block out all light, their fallen leaves creating a pungently rotting carpet beneath their feet.

A stray bramble latched itself onto Natalie's jacket and, as she paused to carefully un-snag it, a bird shot from out of the undergrowth with a shrieking 'caw caw caw'.

'These woods give me the creeps,' Geraint muttered. 'Every path looks the same. Are you sure we're going the right way?'

She pointed to the ground beneath her feet. Between the rotting leaves was a neat herringbone pattern of brick. 'Follow the red brick road,' she said.

He didn't smile. 'This will take us directly past the walled garden. Are you all right with that?'

'It's the quickest way.'

Aware Geraint was regarding her with concern, she moved quickly on. Sure enough, the path straightened and divided into two, one path leading through a line of clipped yews towards a black, wrought-iron gate. The other path led closely alongside one wall and down the hill towards the church. Natalie took the left-hand fork and walked up to the gate, resting her forehead against the bars, feeling them wet and cold against her skin.

Geraint came to stand beside her. 'What do you think?' he asked.

'About what?' she said, because she was seeing another garden, another time.

'Can you see what we've done to the garden? We based the renovations on the original plans. Incredibly, the estate office still had them. It'll take a while for everything to grow in, but by this time next year, it should look exactly as it did before...' He paused, glancing warily at her.

'Before I found my sister?'

He was swift to make an apology but she was no longer listening.

It was incredible how exactly the garden had been recreated. The original specimen trees had re-emerged from the jungle of weeds and the long terrace had been replanted with neat lines of box. Thick clouds of Michaelmas daisies were already in bloom amongst the stalks of the new rose bushes planted for spring. The past fourteen years might never have happened.

'It's beautiful,' she said.

If she'd not walked through the castle garden that morning, would Sarah's body have been found?

Geraint was convinced Sarah and Bryn had been killed as a result of a burglary gone wrong. If that was the case, why had the killer brought her out here to the lily ponds?

Beside her, Geraint picked something up from the floor. She caught a glimpse of something metallic slithering through his fingers.

'Great,' he muttered. 'Someone's hacked right through it.'

He was holding a metal chain with a padlock hanging from it. The padlock was fastened but the chain had been cut.

'Bolt cutters,' he said in disgust. 'Who takes bolt cutters for a walk in the woods?'

Evidently, he'd forgotten about his own bolt cutters and the jemmy in his satchel.

Geraint leant past her, lifting the latch and pushing open the gate. It swung back noiselessly, leaving her standing in the centre of the path, with no barrier between her and the garden.

'Wait here,' he told her. 'I need to check this. It could be vandals but... Well, you never know.'

What century was *he* living in?

'No, thank you,' she said. 'I'm coming too.'

'I'm serious.'

'Me too,' she said, and followed him as he strode off along the path to the terrace.

She caught up as he climbed the steps – not that he noticed. His attention was directed towards the centre pond.

'What is it?' She took the steps two at a time.

Quickly he turned, blocking her view.

'What's *happened?*'

Why was he behaving so... *strangely?*

'It's nothing.' He caught her hand and attempted to lead her back down the steps.

She pulled her fingers from his grasp and, although he grabbed at her again, it was too late.

The dark water was smooth and unrippled. The petals of the white and pink lilies appeared so perfect they could have been carved from wax. But something protruded through the round glossy leaves. Something shaped like a foot.

Her gaze travelling the length of the pool. Through the murky water, she could discern a knee, a pale thigh, a ripple of green fabric...

'Come away,' Geraint was saying. 'Please, *cariad.*'

Floating a few centimetres below the surface was a young woman wearing a pretty dress, her weight partially supported by the mass of flowers. Her skin was almost as pale as the petals that surrounded her, her hair such a light blonde it could have been spun silver.

Except this time it wasn't Sarah.

THIRTY-FIVE

Summer Ellis's body lay lifeless amongst the water lilies.

Once again, Natalie had that sensation of the past trying to push through to the present.

'It's the same,' she said. 'Exactly the same.'

Geraint, his face blanched white in shock, had turned away.

Natalie moved closer to the edge of the pond. 'Even her clothes are laid out in the same way...' She prodded the pile with her foot and the sunlight caught on the sequins of a green cropped cardigan.

'Don't,' Geraint said.

'You're right. Nothing should be touched until the police arrive.'

'I meant...' His face twisted with the effort of keeping his emotions in check. 'It seems wrong to touch her belongings when she's...'

He must think her very cold-hearted, but how could she explain? She had to keep it together for Sarah. She couldn't collapse. She had to find the thing that would link these two deaths, because that would lead her to the murderer and Sarah could finally rest in peace.

But if she said that out loud, he'd think she didn't care poor Summer was dead, provided her death helped find Sarah's killer. And she *did* care; she *wasn't* that person.

Was she?

Geraint stumbled down the steps and, leaning over the nearest flower bed, began retching.

Natalie took her phone from her bag, dialled the direct line for Calahurst Police Station and asked for DCI Cameron. When told he wasn't available, she explained what had happened and agreed to wait with the body until someone could be sent over. Even then, she sounded so calm the switchboard appeared to think it was a hoax call and insisted on phoning her back. It was only when the call was terminated, and she dropped the phone back into her bag, that she realised her legs were shaking so badly she could no longer stand up.

The nearest seat was in the gazebo, which was little more than a roof supported by stone columns. Around the columns grew a tangled mass of old wisteria, which didn't appear to have ever been cut back. It tumbled right across the flat roof, providing a shaggy curtain where there were no walls. Natalie went inside and sat on the wooden bench to await the police. The curtain of decaying leaves provided no shelter from the chill breeze and she couldn't stop shivering.

Geraint was now sitting on the paved edge of the terrace, his feet resting on the steps, his back turned resolutely away from the pond. He stared out across the garden. The sun shone brightly, the leaves were already turning to gold – it was a beautiful autumn day.

The first police officer arrived almost immediately, walking nonchalantly through the gate and across the lawn to where Geraint was sitting. They spoke briefly. Geraint pointed to the pond behind him. The officer took one glance at it before using his radio to call for assistance, and then the garden was full of people.

It was exactly the same as when Sarah had died.

DCI Cameron was the last to arrive. He walked around the pond, talked with the CSIs and then with Geraint.

The sun, which had been directly overhead when they'd arrived, was now dipping towards the woodland that surrounded the garden. A female officer approached Natalie to ask what had happened. It was hard to know where to begin, so she told her story from when she'd gone down the well, and the officer wrote it all down in a notebook, before advising Natalie that she'd need to come into the station and make a formal statement.

Summer's body was lifted out of the pond.

Unable to watch, Natalie turned her head away and realised the DCI had moved into the shelter of the gazebo and was silently observing her.

'Hello, Ms Grove,' he said. 'I thought I told you to stay out of trouble?'

She thought it best to remain silent.

'May I?' he asked, indicating the bench. Carefully, he arranged his coat over the damp wood before sitting down. 'I understand what you hoped to achieve,' he said, 'writing your book and promoting it on television, but right now you're making my job extremely difficult.'

She'd have protested but he didn't pause long enough to allow her to speak.

'Fourteen years ago, your sister was murdered and left in this very same pond,' he said. 'Questions will be asked and fingers will be pointed. You *will* be blamed for this girl's death, you do realise that? With your talk of diaries and suspects, you've set something in motion. You say you wanted to stir up the past? It appears you have your wish.'

'I didn't want this. I needed to find out what happened to my sister. I never meant for anyone to die...'

He didn't respond.

Summer's body was carried carefully across the garden and out of sight. She was so small, so slight – so *young*.

I was the one who started this. It should have been me.

'It could be the work of a copycat,' the DCI said eventually. 'Fourteen years is a long time to wait between murders.'

That made her feel worse. Not only had she failed to find Sarah's killer, she'd encouraged a new one?

'I should congratulate you on finding the tunnel,' he added.

She was grateful for the change in subject. 'You *knew* about the tunnel?'

'The crypt too. They're clearly marked on a set of nineteenth-century estate plans, now held in the County Archives. There were even photographs taken in Victorian times – a bit blurry, admittedly – before the tunnel was sealed up. It was considered unsafe.'

Those wine racks hadn't been moved in over a century. No wonder they'd been so hard to shift.

'If Bryn didn't escape the castle through the tunnel, how did he end up down the well?'

'Unlike films, the most obvious answer is usually the right one. Someone threw him down there. They wanted to dispose of his body and it was quicker than digging a grave. The poor devil was dead before he hit the bottom.'

'He *was* murdered? It wasn't an accidental fall?'

'He had other broken bones around the facial area and to his hands and ribs.' When she continued to regard him blankly, he added, 'Bryn Llewellyn was in a fight before he died.'

'Did he die the same day as Sarah?'

'Probably.'

'Why wasn't she thrown down the well too?'

'What did Sarah have that the killer thought Bryn didn't?'

'A family.' Apparently even a dysfunctional one like theirs counted for something. 'The killer knew Sarah would be missed,' she said. 'By leaving Sarah where she could be found, he knew it would implicate the missing man as the murderer.'

Well, that answered *that* question.

'There's one last thing I have to ask,' he said. 'Yesterday, when your father threatened you with a gun, you dropped your bag. Are you missing any of your belongings?'

'I don't think so.'

'Would you mind checking?'

'If you're after the diary, it doesn't exist. I've already told you that.'

'Humour me,' he said.

She plonked her bag onto her lap, unfastened it and began to take everything out and lay it on the bench beside her. She didn't have much in there, only her phone, purse, a small make-up bag and her keys.

'It's all here,' she said, looking up at him. 'I'm not one of those women who carry their entire life around with them.'

He pointed to her keys. 'Are those for your apartment?'

'Yes, my front door key and another for my car. After the break-in, I had to have new locks fitted.'

'You have five keys on the fob,' he said.

'They're the keys to the Lodge. The larger one fits the front door; the middle-sized one is for the back door.' She flipped the smallest key with her finger, setting it in motion. 'This one is for my father's old tool shed. I know it's weird but I keep them for sentimental reasons. I thought Clare would have changed the locks, but when I was there recently they still fitted.'

'May I take a look?'

She hesitated. 'That was a trick question, wasn't it?'

The DCI reached inside his coat and took out a plastic bag. Inside was a large padlock.

Her first thought was that it was the one Geraint had found but that had been new and shiny; this one was rusted. She began to sense a certain inevitability.

'May I?' he asked blithely, and held out his hand.

She let the keys fall into his open palm, and watched as he picked out the smaller key; the one she'd always assumed fitted the shed. It slotted easily into the padlock and he twisted it with a flourish. There was a dull click and the padlock sprung open.

'I don't believe it...'

He held the padlock and key out to her. 'Would you like to try it yourself?'

She shook her head. 'That's the padlock from the well, isn't it?'

'Yes,' he said. 'I'm afraid it is.'

THIRTY-SIX

There was a knock on the door. When Alicia went to open it, she found a uniformed police officer on the other side and a stream of cars and vans trundling down the drive, most of which had the County police crest emblazoned on the side.

The *police*? What were *they* doing here?

Before she could go over and ask, a blonde woman in a suit scrunched across the drive towards her. Everything about her was elegant and neat, from her manicured fingernails to the tiny gold studs she wore in her ears.

'Mrs Fitzpatrick?' Her voice was calm and unhurried, with no trace of an accent.

'What is it?' Alicia tried to keep her composure but could hear her voice rising in panic. 'What's going on? Has something happened to one of the children?'

'I'm Detective Inspector Lydia Cavill. Your husband has been arrested for a serious crime. As he was living here when the crime was committed, we have a warrant to search this house and gather any evidence we believe is connected to that crime.' She held out an official-looking form.

Alicia didn't take it. 'What kind of evidence?'

'The nature of the case means we are obliged to seize anything we feel is relevant. If it transpires that it's not relevant, it will be returned.'

'But what's James been charged with?'

'You'll have to discuss that with your husband. He's been taken to the local police station to await interview.'

James had been arrested at *school*?

'Can I see him?' she asked.

'DCI Cameron is the officer in charge. You should speak to him about it.'

'Is it to do with the skeleton I found down the well?'

'I'm afraid I can't comment.' DI Cavill was still holding the search warrant towards her.

As though in a dream, Alicia took it. She tried reading the text, but it was closely printed and the words swam into each other, hardly making sense. How could this be happening?

DI Cavill waited patiently. 'I'd be grateful if you would allow my officers to enter?'

Alicia drew on her last vestige of defiance. 'What if I refuse?'

The DI shrugged. 'You can't.'

Alicia stepped aside. Hardly had she done so, then the police surged into the hall, their feet clattering against the bare floorboards. Alicia, assuming she'd be required to explain the layout of the house, followed – but she was not given the opportunity to speak.

Instead, the DI gave her team a quick briefing, explaining which rooms to search and what to look for, which seemed to cover pretty much everything.

What on earth had James done?

Or, more to the point, what did the *police* think he'd done?

Was it connected with one of his pupils? Had one of them made an allegation? But why? James was the kindest, most decent—

There was a crash above her head, as furniture was clumsily moved. What were they looking for that they needed to move *furniture*?

It was torture, having strangers picking over her belongings.

In the kitchen, she saw two officers emptying cutlery from the drawers, carefully separating the knives and lining them up on the table. They were wearing thin latex gloves and white coveralls.

That meant it was serious, didn't it? Had James been accused of assault? *Murder?*

She slid her phone from her pocket and surreptitiously phoned him.

It went straight to voicemail.

Perhaps it would be more useful to contact the family solicitor.

Knowing James, he'd have done so already.

As she slowly replaced her phone, she realised the DI was standing across from her in the hall, watching her with a strange expression on her face.

It took a moment for Alicia to work out what it was.

Pity.

When Alicia finally arrived at the police station, a uniformed PC showed her into a small interview room where James had been taken to wait for her. His clothes were clean and fresh and he was his usual, almost too-attractive self, but the way he sat sprawled in his seat, the way he barely glanced up when she entered, the almost obsessive-compulsive way he was picking at a scratch in the plastic surface of the table, revealed his confidence had been shattered.

'I'm sorry,' he said, gesturing at the room. 'For all this.'

'It's not your fault,' she said automatically.

Was it?

There were two other chairs at the table. She pulled one out and sat facing him.

'James?' she said, in as calm a voice as she could manage. 'What's going on?'

He didn't reply, just went back to picking at the peeling table.

She tried again. 'The police are searching our house, did you know that? They have a search warrant. They were in my study, taking everything out of my desk and riffling through it, including my notes and files. Then they confiscated my laptop.'

'I'm sorry.'

'Do you know what you've been arrested for? Have you called a solicitor?'

'There didn't seem to be a lot of point,' he said.

What was *wrong* with him?

'Of course there's a point! We need to prove your innocence!'

Taking a deep breath, she tried again.

'The police are presumably searching for something stored electronically?' she said. 'Something more inflammatory than the castle's accounts from the seventeenth century?'

His fingernail kept pick, pick, picking at that bit of curling plastic.

She had to speed things up.

'You're a teacher. Have you been accused of something...?' She could hardly bear to say the words. 'Have you behaved... inappropriately?'

His head snapped up. 'I've got children of my own – a teenage daughter. Why would I do that?'

'You tell me! In fact, it would be great if you could tell me *something*, because at the moment I don't have a clue! *Why* have you been arrested? Surely the police have told you the reason?'

He put his head in his hands. 'The police believe I've killed

Summer Ellis and I expect they were at The Old Rectory to find evidence that would confirm that.'

The interview room became darker, the air more close. Alicia remembered the CSIs, with their white suits and gloves, going through her knives, comparing sizes, and felt sick.

'Summer's... *dead?*' In her head, Alicia saw another young woman, laughing, smiling. 'How?'

'I've no idea. They won't tell me anything. All I know is that her body has been found and they're linking her death with Sarah's.'

'That was fourteen years ago.' Alicia stared at her husband. Handsome, confident, good-natured James. Seeing this broken man in front of her, it was like looking at a stranger. *Had* he killed Sarah?

No, it was impossible. They'd been together for almost fourteen years. She *knew* him. He'd made mistakes, *big* mistakes in his past, but he wasn't a cold-blooded killer.

Although the police seemed to think so...

'They must be quite certain you're guilty. Do you think they'll find some kind of' – she hardly dared to say the word – 'evidence?'

'I don't know. I don't *know.*' He rubbed his hand over his face. 'You and the children should go away. I don't want you mixed up in this. I don't want you hurt. This is going to get nasty. Once the press get wind of it, and they will, trust me – it's too good a scandal for them to pass up – "*Local Head Teacher Accused of Murdering Ex-Pupil*" – your lives will be hell.'

'What about *you?*'

'I'll be fine.'

She almost rolled her eyes. 'You're not going to be *fine*, James. You need legal representation and you need it quickly. I can send the children to stay with my mother and we'll work through this together.'

'No, you need to distance yourself—'

'For goodness' sake, James! You're my husband – for better, for worse – do you remember that bit? You think I'm going to go skipping off into the sunset at the first sign of adversity? I'll call William's wife, Olivia. She's a solicitor. If she can't help, I'm sure she can recommend someone. That's what families are for.'

'I don't deserve you,' he muttered. 'I really don't.'

'Probably not, but it looks as though you're stuck with me. I'll call Olivia, I'm sure once she arrives she'll be able to update me. The police won't be able to hold you indefinitely. There must be rules about that.'

'They can if they have evidence.'

'*Do* they have evidence?'

He shrugged again. 'They must do. Why else would they have arrested me?'

Why indeed.

THIRTY-SEVEN

'Does this mean I'm a suspect?' Natalie asked.

DCI Cameron shook his head. 'How many sets of keys to the Lodge were there?'

'I've no idea. This set belonged to my father. After the accident he had no need of them, so my mother gave them to me.'

'As the head gardener, it's logical that John Grove would have a key to the well. Unfortunately, we don't know how many copies were in circulation.'

Geraint was convinced one of the Vyne family had been complicit in his cousin's death; now DCI Cameron was suggesting the same thing. Her father had worked for them. Had he killed Bryn? Had *he* disposed of the body? Was that why Sir Henry had paid his medical bills – to ensure her family's silence? It was too horrible to contemplate.

'I'm sorry, I'm having trouble processing—' She broke off to wave her hand in the direction of the pond. 'You understand? Finding Summer, my dad's death – and now you're suggesting Dad might have been behind Bryn's murder, or at least the disposing of his body? Can I take a break?'

'Of course,' he said smoothly. 'I understand. Why don't you

go home, have something to eat and take some rest? We can continue this conversation later.'

Later? Natalie was close to tears. Hadn't she said all there'd been to say? But the DCI's attention had been taken by Geraint, who was heading across the terrace towards them. Sitting on the damp ground had cleaned some of the dust from his clothes, but the rest of him was filthy, much like herself.

'Your knight in shining armour,' was the DCI's dour comment.

'He told me everything, you know.'

The DCI raised an eyebrow. 'Everything?'

'I know his real identity – and I know you do too – and that he didn't kill Sarah.'

The DCI's expression didn't change. 'You're sure of that?'

'Yes,' she said. 'I am.'

Geraint also appeared to have reached his limit. 'May we leave the garden now?' he asked the DCI, perfectly politely but with a definite edge to his voice.

'Of course,' the DCI said. 'Thank you once again for all your help.'

If he was being sarcastic, Natalie decided she no longer cared.

Once the DCI had walked out of the gazebo and was safely out of earshot, Geraint turned to her and said, 'Do you still want to visit your friend Alicia?'

Natalie remembered the way her key had slotted so easily into the padlock. 'I'll call her later.' Once she'd got her head around everything that had happened. 'That might be best.'

'I'll give you a lift home.'

'Thank you,' she said. 'I appreciate it.'

They walked along the woodland path, to where Geraint's truck was parked outside the Lodge. Natalie hadn't paid it much attention earlier. She knew it was painted green and had black letters on each side, advertising his landscaping business, but she'd never bothered to read it. This time, while she waited for Geraint to fish his keys out from his pocket, she did. It said:

Llewellyn Brothers
Landscaping
The Old Mill
Raven's Edge

Raven's Edge? It was less than ten miles away. A pretty little village in the centre of the forest, with thatched medieval cottages huddled along the main street and half-timbered houses clustered around a square.

'You only live in the next village!' she said.

'Did I imply any different?'

'There was a huge police search, yet all the time you were *here*?'

'Not all the time, but you're right. It's curious how people never spot something right underneath their nose. My uncle gave up the funfair after Bryn disappeared. His heart was no longer in it. I returned a few years ago. I'd always loved this part of the country. I went to work for a landscape gardener. When he retired, I took over his business. I now employ twenty staff and we're doing brilliantly – otherwise I could never have bid to renovate the castle gardens at a loss. I was so keen to win the contract, I even recreated the walled garden at the Mill. I wasn't sure if the ponds were still here, you see.'

'You called your business Llewellyn Brothers?'

'In memory of the old funfair, my da and uncle, and, of course, Bryn.'

The drive to Calahurst marina took only a few minutes. Geraint brought the truck to a rumbling halt directly opposite the entrance to her apartment block.

Natalie felt awkward. She'd spent fourteen years wondering if he'd murdered her sister and up until two days ago he'd been a stranger. Now they'd spent so much time together, they were becoming friends.

'Is everything OK?' he asked, when she didn't get out.

'Thank you for the lift,' she said, fully intending to cut and run.

Her speedy getaway was foiled by the seatbelt. Even pressing the release button hard had no effect. She blinked back the tears. The combination of shock and tiredness had left her at breaking point.

'Here, let me.' He leant towards her. 'It can be tricky. I don't carry passengers very often, sometimes it sticks.'

He was very close. She remembered how he'd held her when they'd been in the tunnel. How he'd protected her from the flying glass. How every time she'd been suspicious of his motives, he'd proved her wrong by doing her a kindness.

She was starting to like him, but how did he feel about her?

There was a click and the seatbelt slithered across her body.

'There you are,' he said. 'Call me if you need anything – and don't go getting into any trouble!'

He sounded like DCI Cameron.

She rolled her eyes. 'I don't think I'm going to get into much trouble in my own home!'

She heard him laugh good-naturedly as she slid out of the cab.

THIRTY-EIGHT

Even though the school was less than five minutes' drive away, Alicia knew she was going to be hopelessly late collecting the children. But as she drove between the large silver gates, she was cheered by seeing one of the other mothers shoot past in the opposite direction, with two squabbling children on the back seat.

At least she wasn't the only one to be late.

She found Will sitting at the top of the short flight of steps outside the main door. He was so engrossed in his book, he'd not noticed her arrival. Alicia felt a little less guilty.

'Hello, darling.' She walked over and ruffled his hair. 'Sorry I'm late.'

'I've been waiting here for an hour and a half,' he announced, sending a resentful glare in her direction. 'Drama Club was cancelled. Mr Waters never turned up.'

Because he'd been covering for James...

Damn.

How much did the children know about why their father had been called away? Had anyone told them?

'I tried phoning you *and* Dad, and no one answered,' he added.

Her heart cracked as his voice wobbled on the last word, but she could hardly tell him the truth. She'd rather save that conversation until she'd had chance to process it herself and decide on the best approach to take.

'Where's Lexi?' she asked instead.

'Talking to a *boy*.' He sounded thoroughly disgusted.

Despite everything, Alicia found herself smiling. Well, Lexi *was* thirteen. It had been only a matter of time.

As though her thoughts had summoned her, Lexi walked through the door, happily chatting away to a boy the same age, who appeared to share her love of all things gothic.

Any other time, Alicia would have suggested inviting him home for tea – something that would have horrified Lexi. Hopefully – Alicia closed her eyes – *hopefully*, next time.

'I don't want to do drama class any more, Mum,' Lexi said, sliding into the car. 'It's boring.'

'That's fine, if that's how you feel.' Lexi should probably be concentrating on her schoolwork anyway, if she wanted to realise her dream of becoming a vet. 'What about you, Will?'

'Whatever,' he shrugged, and then seemed to consider it for a moment. 'It *would* give me more time to do my homework...'

Alicia didn't believe *that* for a second.

Hiding a grin, she started the car and pop music automatically came blaring out of the speakers. Both children groaned. Alicia sighed. It wasn't as though she was about to start *singing*.

It was only as she drove through the huge gates of Castle Vyne, ten minutes later, that Will lifted his head from his book. 'Are we going to visit Granny Vyne?'

'Is that all right?'

With the police currently taking The Old Rectory apart, where else could they go?

'Will we be having dinner there?'

'I think so.' Her mother employed a very efficient cook, so feeding them all at short notice wouldn't be a problem. Whether Clare would be *pleased* to see them was another matter – and Alicia would probably have to suffer a lecture along the lines of 'I *knew* this would happen if you married one of those Fitzpatrick boys.'

Her family would have to sleep at the castle too, if the police didn't finish soon. Once she had the children settled, she'd return home and find out what was happening – perhaps take the shortcut through the graveyard.

And then she'd have to tell Lexi and Will the truth...

'Mum?' Will's voice broke into her thoughts. 'What are we waiting for?'

How long had she been sitting here, parked outside the castle entrance, staring into space?

'Sorry,' she said, unclipping her seatbelt. 'I have a lot on my mind—'

But the children were already out of the car and running up to the door.

By the time Alicia joined them, Will was banging on it.

'Where's Rob?' he grumbled. 'I want to go inside. I'm cold.'

Where indeed? Hopefully *not* kissing Clare in one of the castle's sixteen bedrooms. Honestly, why didn't they formalise their relationship? Was being 'Lady Vyne' and living in this castle so important to her mother?

Rob must be an *extremely* tolerant man.

Or he preferred living in a castle too.

'Perhaps Rob didn't hear us,' she replied. 'We'll go through the breakfast room.' That door was usually kept unlocked during the day, to allow easy access to the garden.

Hardly were the words out of her mouth before Will had sprinted off across the terrace and through the rose garden. By the time Alicia managed to catch up with him, he was halfway across the breakfast room.

She made a grab for the collar of his jacket. 'Will, please don't rush into the library unannounced. You know how Granny hates to be disturbed when she's... working. Why not go downstairs into the kitchen? I'm sure Cook will be able to rustle up some sandwiches to keep you going until dinner.'

'OK.' Will swung round and vanished down the steps to the kitchen.

Lexi, however, hesitated. 'Where's Dad? The kids at school were saying some weird stuff – that the police had taken him away in handcuffs!'

Alicia winced. Would the DCI really have been that crass?

'He's... helping them with an investigation.'

Well, it wasn't a lie...

Lexi patently didn't believe her but didn't argue, running up the main staircase and leaving Alicia standing outside the library door.

She knocked. Once the children were settled in, she'd return to the house and see what kind of a mess the police had left it in and how soon they could all return.

Realising her mother had failed to answer, Alicia knocked again, louder this time, and then pushed open the door.

Her first thought was that the library was empty. It was so still and quiet. Then she saw Clare at the other end, a picture of cool elegance in black trousers and sweater. She was sitting at Henry's old writing desk in the window, as she always did, but leaning back in her chair, apparently lost in her own thoughts.

Alicia hesitated, unwilling to interrupt.

She tried clearing her throat and, when that didn't work, lightly touched Clare's shoulder.

And then screamed.

Her mother's eyes were wide open, staring sightlessly into

the garden, and there was a trickle of blood on the side of her head.

Alicia didn't need to check for a pulse.

Her mother was quite obviously dead.

THIRTY-NINE

Natalie unlocked the door to her apartment.

It was exactly as she'd left it.

After all she'd been through, its familiarity was oddly surreal.

She dropped her keys onto the hall table, switched on the overhead light and let the door swing shut behind her. Without Geraint's constant presence, she felt lonely. Had her apartment always been this quiet, this empty?

Simon was right; living here was like being in some ivory tower far away from real life. But wasn't that why she'd chosen the most expensive apartment at Calahurst Marina? To show how far she'd come from being 'little Nat'?

Except, lately, it didn't feel as though she'd come very far at all.

Despite the bare floorboards, her shoes made no noise as she walked into the sitting room.

The silence was almost... oppressive.

She switched on the radio.

The last of the afternoon sunshine flooded through the windows, giving the white walls of her apartment a rosy glow.

She pressed her nose to the tinted glass and peered at the street below. Geraint's truck was still there. She could even see his jean-clad legs and the glow of his phone.

She turned and picked up her own phone to order a takeaway. Delivery was promised to arrive in an hour, so she left her phone on the coffee table and went to run a bath.

As the bathroom began to fill with steam, she eased her shoes from her feet. There were angry red welts on her skin where her shoes had rubbed, and walking across wet grass had made the dye run. It was a shame, because they were her favourites, but there was no way she could wear them again. She dropped them into the bin.

Both her jeans and sweater were filthy, and the sweater glittered with tiny slivers of glass. She tried picking them out, but they'd snagged into the wool and she only succeeded in cutting her finger.

Another candidate for the bin.

A little ball of blood oozed from her cut, so she stuck her finger beneath the tap in the basin and watched as the tiny streak of crimson swirled briefly against the white porcelain.

Tonight she was going to have a long soak in a scented bath. She was going to eat her favourite chicken korma, watch a bit of mindless TV, and go to bed and dream of nothing.

Tomorrow she'd deal with reality.

Turning off all the taps, she wrapped a tissue around her finger, placed a fresh towel on the heated rail and left the bathroom to turn up the music.

She'd forgotten to lock the front door and it hadn't closed properly. There was a gap of a few centimetres, through which she could clearly see the lobby and the lift. She leant against the door, hearing the catch 'click', before deadlocking it. She'd left the hall light on, but there was no need to switch on the one in the sitting room. The sun had disappeared beneath the horizon, in a blaze of pink and orange, but there was enough light to see by.

She couldn't resist looking out of the window again, down to the road below. Geraint's truck was still parked there, but she couldn't see him.

Had he gone to the pub?

Should she call him and invite him up to share her takeaway?

There was a creak from the hall.

She glanced back. The front door remained locked and the chain was across it.

She was spooking herself.

Really, she was a bag of nerves – and was it any wonder after the day she'd had? Maybe dinner and an early night *was* the most sensible option.

Returning to the bathroom, she closed the door. The sooner she bathed and changed, the sooner she could make a mug of strong coffee.

She *really* needed that coffee.

Taking hold of the hem of her sweater, she pulled it up and over her head, catching sight of her dishevelled reflection, wearing a T-shirt and jeans, in the bathroom mirror as she emerged – and the reflection of the man standing behind her.

The man who, when he saw her open her mouth to scream, clamped her arms to her sides and pressed a cloth to her face, holding it tightly over her mouth and nose while she struggled.

Until she struggled no more.

FORTY

Natalie drifted in and out of consciousness, unsure what was real and what was a dream.

It was dark.

She lay curled on her side with something warm and soft against her cheek. Fabric of some kind? Its scent was familiar and reassuring. When she attempted to stretch out, her feet hit something painfully solid.

Ow, ow, ow.

Where were her shoes?

Her head throbbed, echoing the beat of her heart. She wanted to sleep, but something kept nagging at the edge of her conscious. There was something she had to do. It was vitally important, but she couldn't, for the life of her, remember what it was.

Snatches of memory tantalised her.

A man's silhouette.

A lid closing on a coffin.

An angel with a starburst of light creating a halo around its head.

Were they hallucinations, brought on by tiredness and stress?

This certainly wasn't a coffin – that would have been smaller, narrower, longer – and she hadn't been buried beneath cold damp earth. It was too warm and there was a sensation of movement and a low buzzing. The white noise of an engine?

Although it *was* becoming harder to breathe...

Ignoring the stab of panic, she rolled back – and her shoulder hit a wall. She tried lifting her head – and cracked it on something hard and metallic.

The pain sharpened her senses, bringing her firmly into the present, enabling her to focus.

What did she remember?

A man in her apartment, a cloth being held over her face, the sense of disorientation as she struggled for breath. He'd moved too quickly for her to see him properly. There'd been a gap – presumably when she lost consciousness, and then she'd been thrown into this... space... She'd caught a quick glimpse of bright lights shining behind his head – again, shadowing his face – before some kind of lid had been slammed down.

The lights had been yellow...

The car park beneath her apartment block had yellow fluorescent lighting.

Had she been thrown into the boot of a car? Her *own* car? The keys would have been right there on her hall table. Was that why her surroundings smelt familiar?

OK, so she'd been abducted and had no idea where she was heading.

The important thing was not to *panic*.

Really? Her brain mocked. Because what could make *this* more terrifying?

Hearing someone breathing beside her.

FORTY-ONE

Alicia was in the great hall.

She was sitting on a chair someone had taken from the library, because the great hall didn't have furniture, just a grand piano and a few desultory suits of armour.

DCI Cameron crouched beside her, his long coat splayed out over the flagstones like a cloak.

She hoped the flagstones were clean. It was a fallacy that black hid the dirt. Having children had taught her that.

'Mrs Fitzpatrick,' he said. 'I appreciate that you've had a terrible shock but—'

'Mum had a panic alarm,' Alicia said. 'It was beneath the desk. Why didn't she press it?'

'We believe Lady Vyne knew her killer. She let them in. She didn't bother to rise from her chair to greet them. We need to know who that person was. Did your mother have enemies?'

'Of course not!'

Although Clare had never been particularly popular...

'Were there any firearms kept on the premises? We've no record of a licence but—'

'No, Mum hated guns, ever since my father's accident. She got rid of them all. Even the antique ones.'

His words were beginning to sink in. Her mother hadn't got out of her chair. Either the murderer had caught her unaware or, as the DCI had suggested, she'd been killed by someone she knew. But who?

'What about the staff?' she asked him. 'Did they hear anything? I know the castle walls are thick, but surely they'd have heard a gunshot?'

'I don't know how many staff your mother employed, but most appear to have gone home for the night. The kitchen staff are still below stairs, but they didn't hear or see anything. We'll take statements, of course...'

'What about my mother's assistant – Rob?'

The DCI hesitated.

What did that mean? That Rob was a suspect, or a victim?

'Robert Dench? He was my mother's personal assistant.' And personal everything else too, since her father had died. 'Where's he?'

'We're not sure. We've searched everywhere, but, well, Mr Dench seems to have disappeared.'

Alicia sat back in the chair and stared at him. 'You think Rob killed her? That's impossible! He's been with my family since I was a child. If he'd wanted to kill my mother, he's had plenty of prior opportunities.'

The DCI stood up. 'We believe the motive was robbery. The safe in the library was open.'

Alicia hadn't even known there *was* a safe in the library.

'I wouldn't have thought it contained anything of value. All the paperwork pertaining to the castle is kept in the estate office. My mother's jewellery is held in a safety deposit box at her bank.'

Sadly her father's paintings weren't worth anything any

more. She suspected they'd only sold well in the first place because he'd been a baronet and lived in a castle.

'It contained some old sketchbooks and not much else.' The DCI beckoned towards another officer hovering nearby with an armful of books. 'Two were in the safe; the others had been abandoned on your mother's desk. One was on the floor, as though it had been dropped. There were pages torn from it, quite roughly, as though the person was in a hurry. We think the robber may have been disturbed before they could find what they were looking for.' The DCI took one of the sketchbooks, opening it at the beginning, and held it out to Alicia. 'Perhaps you'd be kind enough to take a look? Please? It would help with our investigation.'

'You think my mother was murdered because of some *old drawings*?'

Alicia almost snatched at the sketchbook – but then nearly dropped it when she saw what it contained. Sketch after sketch, some drawn quickly, just a few rough lines, others with more care. But *all* of them were of young women wearing very few clothes.

Shocked, her first instinct was to slam the book shut and hand it right back to DCI Cameron. Then one picture caught her attention.

The woman was in her early twenties, wearing a diaphanous white dress and leaning against a huge old desk.

Alicia recognised that desk. It was Victorian and hadn't been moved since it had been placed in the library over a hundred and fifty years ago. It was her father's desk. The one he always worked from, the one her mother had been sitting in front of when Alicia had found her lifeless body.

'There are six books in all,' the DCI was saying, 'so it's quite a collection. We're going to need some help tracing the women. Do *you* recognise any of them?'

'Yes.' Alicia found she couldn't even look at him. She

pointed to the drawing instead. 'That's Jade Dickens. She was the daughter of the local vicar.'

Jade had been such a shy little thing. Not the kind of girl you'd imagine...

Alicia swallowed. Jade wouldn't have had a choice. Sir Henry would've held all the power.

'What about the other women?' the DCI asked.

Did he honestly want her to look at every single picture?

Alicia thought she might be sick. How could her father have *done* this?

'Please, Mrs Fitzpatrick? It's important. These women are potential witnesses.'

Witnesses to what?

As though he could read her mind, DCI Cameron said, 'Your mother was killed because someone wanted one of these drawings. We're working on a theory that she might have been blackmailing one of the subjects.'

Was that true? Chilled, Alicia remembered how a series of 'good investments' over the past few years had brought money flowing into the castle's finances for the first time. Was *this* where the money had originated? From one of these women, terrified that their past had come back to bite them?

'What do you need to know?' she asked.

'Do you recognise any of the women?'

'Apart from Jade, no.'

As she spoke, the enormity of it began to sink in. Her *father* had drawn these pictures. Her father had drawn these pictures *in their home* and she'd been completely oblivious to it. What had he given these women in return? *Money?* It would explain why there had been so very little of it left in the bank after his death.

And now it was coming back in again – because her mother had been blackmailing them.

Alicia could hardly turn the pages of the sketchbook, her hands were trembling that much.

The DCI leant over and did it for her.

Behind him, the other officer stood poised with a notebook and pen, presumably hoping for her to reel off a list of names.

Forcing herself to concentrate, she tipped the sketchbook she held, angling it to avoid the reflected light from the cathedral-like window behind her.

This drawing was of another girl in a thin summer dress, reaching up to take a book from one of the library shelves. The sun shone through the window behind her, casting her face into shadow and creating a halo of light around her hair. The drawing blurred, and at first Alicia couldn't understand why, and then she realised it was because she was crying.

'That's Natalie... Oh no, it's *Natalie*...' She shoved the book back at the DCI, but it dropped to the floor before he could catch it, hitting the stone floor with a thud that echoed around the cavernous hall. 'I can't do this. I can't. I'm sorry. I know it's important...' She tried to stand, but the DCI already had his hand on her shoulder and was forcing her back into her seat. 'How could my father have done such a thing?'

The DCI scooped up another sketchbook, pressing it into her hands and flipping over the pages. 'One more, Mrs Fitzpatrick, and then I'll take the book away. Just one more, please.'

Alicia glanced down, steeling herself, trying to keep her thoughts objective as she saw another young woman, this one lying against a bed of flowers. The flowers were such large, exotic-looking blooms it took a moment for Alicia to place them.

Water lilies?

Such was the angle of the drawing, no water could be seen at all. Her father must have lain on the flagstones, to be level with the pond.

'*Sarah?*'

Sarah's eyes stared right at the artist, an enigmatic smile curving her lips.

Alicia could hardly credit what she was seeing.

Sarah, floating in a lily pond – and *smiling*...

'That's *impossible*...' she said.

'Why's that?' he asked, even though she was sure he already knew the answer.

'Because in this drawing, Sarah's *alive*.'

FORTY-TWO

Natalie bit her lip, forcing herself not to scream, not to lose it completely, but to work through this *rationally*. If she could hear breathing, it meant someone was in here with her. If they were breathing, they weren't dead and, as they were unlikely to be here through free will, she had a potential ally.

She reached into the dark, her fingers touching a warm body – the body her cheek had been pressed against when she'd woken. The person appeared to be unconscious, but not dead. Exploring further, she found broad shoulders, short silky hair, and a cheek with rough stubble. There was also the faint odour of a scent she recognised but couldn't put a name to, mixed with one she could.

Geraint.

He lay on his side with his back towards her. His legs were bent, the same as hers, but he didn't seem to be bound or tied in any way. Shaking him elicited no response, not even a groan, but least he was alive.

How long had they been unconscious? She didn't have a watch and had no idea where her phone was – probably back at her apartment – but what about Geraint? Did he have a phone?

Gingerly, she felt for his pockets. There was a wallet in one back pocket of his jeans, and something rectangular in the other—

A dim light illuminated the boot.

A phone screen! She'd found it!

It took more than a few minutes to get it out, not helped by the car jolting as it drove over an uneven surface. Geraint rolled back, partially squashing her. She gently pushed him away as the car slowed down and made a sharp turn. Had they reached their destination?

She yanked the phone from his pocket.

The light had gone out, but as soon as she pressed the screen it came back on. The battery was charged, the signal was good, and the screen was locked with his fingerprint – easily opened because he was right there with her, albeit unconscious.

Once she'd done that, she brought up the keypad and hit 9 three times.

It didn't even ring before it was answered.

'Hello?' She asked for the police, careful to keep her voice low. The first obstacle was when the switchboard operator asked her to confirm the number she was calling from.

'I don't know; it's not my phone.'

'Where are you calling from?'

'I'm trapped in the boot of my car.'

'In which case, may I suggest you contact a garage or a locksmith?'

'No!' Her stomach plunged in panic. 'Please don't hang up! My name is Natalie Grove and I've been kidnapped.'

Didn't *that* make her sound like an absolute crank?

Why hadn't she phoned Alicia?

'Can you give me the make and model of the car, and the registration number?' the operator said, after only a brief pause.

Yes! She was being taken seriously. Natalie reeled off the

details, praying that she'd been correct in assuming this was her own car – which had now begun to slow...

Oh, no...

'Ms Grove?'

'He's stopped the car!'

'Please stay calm. I've passed your details onto the local patrol. They're looking for you right now.'

'I could be anywhere!'

The car vibrated with the slam of a door.

'He's coming!' she hissed.

'You must stay on the line, Ms Grove. It's important.'

How could the woman remain so calm? Didn't she understand how serious this was?

There was a click as the lock on the boot was released.

Natalie tried to shove the phone beneath Geraint to hide it, but as a bright white light was shone into the boot, dazzling her, the phone was snatched from her hand and she was dragged out of the car.

Her legs had cramped and she couldn't stand upright, landing painfully. Instead of a tarmac road, she was kneeling on the shingle of a private driveway. Directly in front was Geraint's mobile phone with the screen still lit. A tinny voice, barely audible, was saying, 'Hello? Hello?' When she'd have snatched it up, a man's foot ground it into the gravel.

Natalie stared at the shattered pieces of metal.

That was it.

Her last hope.

The lid of the boot slammed.

Was Geraint still unconscious inside?

What would happen to him?

What would happen to her?

'Get up,' a man's voice said.

'Stuff you,' she said bitterly.

He dragged her to her feet and held her there. 'Do as you're told, Natalie.'

She lifted her head at the familiarity of his voice.

It *couldn't* be...

And, like that, her defiance ebbed away as she recognised the man who held her.

FORTY-THREE

'*Simon?*'

He didn't reply. He tightened his grip on her arm and dragged her away from the car.

Her bare feet couldn't get a grip on the gravel. 'Where are you taking me?'

'You'll find out.'

She stumbled and fell onto her knees. 'Let me go. I promise I won't tell the police.'

In response, he took something shiny from his pocket and held it up. '*You're* not in a position to negotiate.'

Simon had a *knife*?

'Now, are you going to behave yourself?'

She closed her eyes. 'Yes.'

He slid the knife back into his pocket. 'Up you get then.'

She had to stay strong. The police knew she was in trouble and they were looking for her car. They might even have traced the phone's location – *if* she was lucky. All she had to do was keep her cool, not antagonise Simon in any way, and delay him for as long as possible.

They were on the drive of a detached, medium-sized Victorian house. It had a large garden to one side, with a derelict windmill in the distance. While Natalie couldn't see any other houses, she did have a clear view of what looked like a main road. *If* the police drove past, and *if* they took a glance down the driveway, they'd see her car.

She'd be relying on a whole bunch of 'ifs' though.

'Where are we?' she asked.

'You don't know?' He seemed genuinely amused. 'You've never been here before?'

What was she missing?

The house appeared deserted. There were no lights and, although it was dark, none of the curtains were drawn shut either.

'Are we going inside?'

'No.' He flipped the beam of the torch to a stronger setting. 'We're going for a walk.'

A *walk?*

Somewhere more isolated?

Simon seemed to know where he was going, leading her through a maze of flower beds and herbaceous borders until the house and road could no longer be seen.

Occasionally she caught glimpses of a surrounding stone wall, older than the red brick of the house, perhaps linked to that derelict windmill? But as they passed between a gap in a neatly clipped yew hedge and into another garden beyond, Natalie had a horrible sense of déjà vu.

Oh, no...

That was *impossible!*

He lifted the torch to illuminate the garden ahead, where a terrace had been created against a tumbledown wall. A terrace which was bordered with roses and Michaelmas daisies and, leading up to it, two sets of stone steps.

No, no, no...

She cast a glance behind. There was no surrounding brick wall, only a hedge of dark yew, albeit newly planted.

'What's going on? Why have you brought me here?'

He took hold of her arm, half dragging her over the grass and up the steps to the top of the terrace. Ahead was a glimmer of moonlight on water. Three ornamental pools, filled with white and pink water lilies.

As she tried to back away, Simon moved behind her, resting his cheek on the top of her head. '*Now* do you know where you are?'

'Simon... Let me go. *Please*? I won't say anything! I won't! Just let me go...'

He kicked a short wooden post. It must have contained a power switch because the garden was immediately illuminated. There were banks of lights along the back wall, fairy lights sprinkled amongst the trees and pretty glass spheres staked in the flower beds.

'This is what we're going to do,' he said. 'I want you to walk over to the middle pond and get into the water.' He took hold of her hand, leading her towards it. 'I'll help you...'

Whatever sick game he was playing, perhaps if she went along with it, taking as long as possible, the police might still turn up? They knew what'd happened. Hopefully they'd spot the car or calculate her position from Geraint's phone.

The phone that now lay smashed on the drive.

'Natalie?'

She'd never hated him so much as she did then, but she could draw strength from that. Fear paralysed and she had to stay strong.

'All right,' she said, feigning a confidence she didn't feel.

He released her.

She dipped one toe into the murky water but couldn't stop herself from shivering.

It was like ice. How deep was it?

'Hurry up,' he said.

She lowered herself onto the paving stones, swinging her legs into the pond. The mirror-like surface was instantly broken. For a moment she didn't move, her fingers gripping the edge of the pool. Then, as she heard movement behind her, she held her breath and hurriedly slid in, gasping at the cold water as it came up to her waist. Not too deep then...

'Lie back.'

That wasn't as easy as it sounded. She had to push aside the clusters of water lilies and avoid stumbling over their roots, packed tightly into little plastic baskets beneath the surface. She glanced over her shoulder to ensure he really meant her to go through with it – an indifferent thumbs-down was her answer.

Slowly, she immersed herself in the water, bringing her legs up to float on her back, trying not to wince as the sharp-edged leaves of the lilies scratched the exposed skin of her arms and ankles. There were trails of slimy pondweed caught on her clothes and her left foot was stinging. She must have trodden on something sharp, buried beneath the silt.

It was impossible to remain afloat. The mass of lilies helped, but every time Natalie moved, the water would ripple across the pond, splashing her face and going up her nose, and weighing down her clothes. But it was the water in her ears, deadening all sound, which was the most disorientating.

Where was Simon? He'd watched her get into this pond without showing any kind of emotion, when he *knew* she'd find it traumatic. How could she have shared her life with him for all these years, yet apparently not have known him at all?

And where were the police? Somewhere in the shadows of the garden, waiting for the perfect moment to strike? She'd heard no sirens. Was she going to have to face this alone?

'Simon?' she said. 'Are you still there?'

There was silence. She brought her legs down, struggling to

find a place on the bottom of the pond to put her feet. It was crammed with those blasted containers. She turned, trying to see where he was.

'What are you doing?' he asked.

He'd been crouched on the edge of the pond, so close she could have touched him.

'I'm sorry!' She tried to feel a path through the lily baskets with her feet, to subtly move away from him. 'It's so hard to float. I was never much good at swimming.'

He didn't reply.

Maybe playing the victim would help?

'Why are you doing this to me?'

'Because I can.' His tone was dry.

Obviously he couldn't take her to Castle Vyne, because the police were still there, but how had he known about *this* garden. Was it his? Had he recreated it? If not, to bring her here was a risk. They were still in the King's Forest District, so they couldn't have driven far. They weren't in Port Rell, because she couldn't hear seagulls or smell the sea. They hadn't got as far as Norchester, because it was too quiet. They must be in one of the villages between. The home of a keen gardener, someone who knew and admired the landscaping of Castle Vyne.

Oh, no...

Someone who needed to prove they could recreate it to win an important contract.

Except anyone who *didn't* know about that contract might assume the garden was the sign of a dark obsession.

The final piece of the jigsaw puzzle fell into place. The garden, that derelict windmill – and the signage on the side of Geraint's truck:

Llewellyn Brothers
Landscaping

The Old Mill
Raven's Edge

Did the police know about this garden? Was that why they'd been following him?

Oh, Geraint, what have you done?

'This is Geraint Llewellyn's house,' she said out loud.

'Well done.' Simon hardly seemed to be paying attention. Instead, he trailed his hand in the water, amongst the flowers, as though hypnotised.

'You're going to set him up. You failed the first time because the police were never able to find him, but now he's back.'

'Aren't murderers supposed to return to the scene of their crime? I thought it was mandatory.'

'The police already know who Geraint is. They're watching him. I expected they've been following him 24/7. They'll know he didn't kill Summer.'

'Are you sure? What *else* do they know?'

'I don't under—'

'How about that he's staying at the Lodge, a two-minute walk from where Summer's body was found?'

'The police will be able to prove that he didn't do it.'

'You're assuming that they *want* to prove him innocent, instead of closing this case, once and for all.'

He was right, damn him. If the police were sure that they'd found their man...

She hoped Geraint had a good lawyer.

'Forensics—' she began.

'Ah, but that's the beauty of water. It washes everything clean.' Simon looked up, his hazel eyes finally meeting hers. 'The police won't find any forensic evidence because I've never left any. But when they can't find you, they'll come here to interrogate him and find the house locked up and your car on the drive. They'll find you lying here in the pond – and him strung up from the nearest tree. Murder/suicide. A nice neat ending for the detective chief inspector. It's what you and everyone else have wanted for fourteen years. Closure.'

But not like this...

What a fool she'd been. What an utter, utter fool.

Why couldn't she have left the past buried?

'You're the man I saw waiting beneath the trees, the night of the fair.'

Simon paused, lifting his hand from the water. 'You saw me? You never said.'

'I was watching from my bedroom window. I didn't know it was you at the time.'

He shook the droplets of water free from his skin. 'Did you tell anyone?'

'Yes: Geraint and DCI Cameron.'

Simon's smile was chilling. 'No, you didn't.'

She tried to take another step back, but the bottom of the pond was too tightly packed with those stupid baskets.

'We were going to run away together,' he said. 'We were going to get married – did you know that? Then the fair arrived in Calahurst and Sarah wanted to go. I didn't. We had a fight and she went anyway. I went to the pub.'

She remembered. It had been his alibi and several villagers had corroborated that.

'When I arrived home,' he said, 'I found Sarah crying on my doorstep. I thought she'd come to beg my forgiveness. Instead, she told me this wild story, about how she had broken into Castle Vyne with a boy she'd met at the fair. They'd been caught by Sir Henry. He'd chased them, but the boy didn't know the castle as well as Sarah and he'd fallen down some stone steps, hit his head and died instantly.'

It had been an accident?

'I could hardly believe what I was hearing,' Simon said. 'Why would Sarah break into the castle when she had thousands of pounds saved from modelling? Then she confessed – she hadn't earned the extra money from the paintings, she'd earned it by allowing Sir Henry Vyne to draw more... personal sketches – and she had the cheek to say she'd done it for us.'

Natalie, who'd been hoping for a police siren or even a patrol car to turn up on the drive by now, was distracted by a rustling behind the yew hedge. Was this it? Was this her rescue? They were certainly cutting it fine.

'We went indoors,' Simon was saying. 'We went into the kitchen. Sarah picked up the phone to call the police. She said she was going to tell them everything. There must have been a knife left on the draining board. I don't remember. Then it was in my hand.

'I made her tell me every last detail. I made her take me to his secret garden. She told me he liked her to float in the water amongst the flowers. I told her to get into the pond to show me – and that's when I must have killed her. I don't remember doing it, but there was no one else, just us.' Simon stared at the knife in his hand, turning it over, and then over again. 'Sarah slipped quietly into the water and was gone.'

'You loved her,' Natalie whispered. 'How could you do that?'

'She didn't love me. How could she, when she had all those other boyfriends? She was eighteen. I thought she was pure...'

Pure?

Was *that* what this was about?

If she'd been terrified before, that took her to a new level.

How fast could she get to the other side of the pond? How long would it take to scramble out and start running through the garden, how long to find her car?

Then what? She didn't even have her keys!

'I thought you were different,' he sighed. 'You were very

young, very impressionable. You only wanted someone to love you. I understood that. I was happy to be there for you, to coach you, to wait for you to leave university so that we could be together properly. But you didn't tell me about Charles or James. In the end, it turned out you were exactly the same as Sarah.'

He made his move then, before she had the time to react. Leaning out over the water, he grabbed her hair and pulled her back to him. She was knocked off balance, sent splashing beneath the surface, but he hauled her up.

His eyes softened as he gazed down at her. 'I'm sorry,' he said. 'You do understand this is for the best?'

There was a flash of silver.

Instinctively, she raised her hands.

Bang!

He flinched. The knife dropped silently into the water beside her.

For a moment, he seemed to be leaning over her, as though searching for the knife. But his eyes were unfocused and his expression frozen. The grip on her hair relaxed and he fell into the pond, landing directly on top of her.

Natalie was sent plunging beneath the icy water, her struggle beginning again, Simon's weight keeping her pinned below the surface. The more she pushed against his body, the further down she went.

She couldn't breathe...

She was losing consciousness.

Couldn't breathe...

She grabbed his shoulders, giving one final, desperate push.

For a second, it was as though an invisible presence was in the water, helping her. Then, as Simon's body floated to the side, she broke the surface, taking a huge gasp of air. Her arms flailed; one hand smashed against the side of the pond. She curled her fingers around the stone, dragging herself to the edge, pushing her hair from her eyes, forcing herself to look round.

Simon was drifting on his front, half-supported by the water lilies. He'd been shot – but by whom? She searched the darkness beyond the terrace for her rescuer – Geraint or a police marksman perhaps?

But the garden was deserted.

FORTY-FOUR

One month later

'So sorry for your loss.'

How many times had Alicia heard that today?

'How are you coping?'

Another favourite.

The funeral for Clare, Lady Vyne, was a popular event. Held at St Daniel's Church, exactly one month after her death, Alicia had been slightly disconcerted to discover her mother had left detailed instructions for the arrangements, including contact numbers for the companies she'd chosen to arrange the flowers and provide the catering for the reception afterwards. There'd even been sheet music provided for the organist.

Alicia had envisaged a small, private, family ceremony. Clare had other ideas. She'd provided a list of people she wanted invited, who all expected to be put up at the castle, presumably expecting the comforts to be on a level with a five-star hotel.

They were to be severely disappointed.

The murder charge against James had been quietly

dropped, along with the investigation into his alleged relationship with Summer Ellis. The consensus was that Simon had set him up, sending him messages from the dead girl's phone before deliberately drawing the attention of the police with fake concern, hoping to step into James's job once he was out of the way.

As the funeral service finished, and their little family walked back up the aisle, James took hold of her hand and squeezed comfortingly.

They had to accept their lives had changed. The castle and its responsibilities were now hers. Yet, as the car drove back through that huge stone archway and she caught a glimpse of the castle, stark grey against the blue skyline, Alicia couldn't quash that little thrill of excitement.

It was all hers...

FORTY-FIVE

'Are you sure you want to do this?' Geraint said.

'If I don't,' Natalie told him, 'I might never get the chance again.'

The huge chestnut trees in front of the Georgian manor were almost bare. Autumn had arrived with a vengeance following a stormy week. There were no fallen leaves, or children playing on the tennis court. Even the net had been removed.

Natalie stared at the house, psyching herself up. There was no sign it was even occupied, but she knew their arrival had been noted.

'Geraint,' she said, 'would you mind very much if I asked you to wait out here?'

'Is that a good idea?'

'I'll be able to see you from the window and you can see me. You'll be my insurance, so to speak.'

'So pleased I'm useful for something!'

She patted his shoulder. 'Useful is good, trust me.'

He caught her hand, holding it close. 'Be careful, *cariad.*'

His smile was wry, but when she walked towards the house he didn't follow.

As usual, the door opened before she got there. The butler politely asked her to enter and showed her into the same little sitting room as she'd been in before, overlooking the empty tennis court – *exactly* what she'd been hoping for.

Before the door closed, she heard the sound of 1940s jazz music wafting along the hall, along with the faint aroma of tobacco. Sir Richard Vyne must be home. Would she have the opportunity to finally meet the man who was her stepfather?

She doubted it. Magda had been careful to leave her old life – and her old family – behind.

Restlessly, Natalie moved over to the window. Geraint was leaning against the side of her car. When he saw her, he relaxed somewhat, raising his hand in acknowledgement. She was about to do the same when the door opened and her mother walked in.

Magda was wearing an exquisite black cashmere sweater and matching trousers – overly smart for a day spent at home. Perhaps a reaction to her first marriage, where she'd been forced to watch every penny?

Her mother wasted no time on preliminaries. 'What are you doing here?'

Natalie slid her bag from her shoulder and took out a brightly wrapped parcel. She held it out to her mother, pleased that her hand remained perfectly steady.

'This is for you,' she said.

Magda didn't take the parcel. Indeed, she regarded it as though it were something slightly nauseating. 'I told you not to come here again. You're not welcome.'

Natalie swallowed, her throat dry. 'After today you'll never see me again, I promise.' She kept her hand outstretched. The parcel wavered slightly.

For a moment, Magda hesitated, her attention caught by the

sunlight glinting off the metallic wrapping. Then she turned away, looking instead out of the window, catching Geraint unable to resist pulling a weed from the flower bed.

'You brought your bodyguard?' she sneered.

'Do I need one?'

'What you do is of no interest to me.'

Natalie felt a pang of hurt, but had she expected any different?

'I'll leave this on the table, shall I?' she said, holding up the parcel again.

'I'd rather you didn't.'

Natalie made a point of placing the parcel, perfectly square, in the centre of the table, before beginning on her rehearsed speech.

'Before I leave,' she said, 'I think I have the right to know why you've shut me out of your life so completely. You went to pieces when Sarah died, yet you seem quite happy to pretend I don't exist. I don't understand why you would behave this way. Even if you loved Sarah better than you did me' – she stumbled over the word 'loved' – 'I'm your daughter too. We could have worked through our grief together.'

There. After all those years of having those words festering inside her, she'd finally said them.

But when she gathered her courage to look at her mother directly, it was to realise Magda was watching her with increasing distaste.

Instead of the usual fine platinum chain about her neck, today Magda wore a narrow black ribbon with an ornately gothic cross suspended from it – the universal symbol of personal sacrifice.

How ironic.

'Why can't you move on, as I have done?' Magda began twisting the sliver of ribbon around her fingers. 'Why do you keep coming back? I've put that part of my life behind me. I have a new life with Richard and the boys. The police have already been to see me. They know who killed Sarah; it was that teacher boyfriend of yours – and then he tried to imply James Fitzpatrick was having an affair with Summer Ellis. It's all over the village. Everybody knows. I said at the time Simon was no good. You should have listened to me. But you never listen, do you, Natalie? You do exactly what you want to do and never mind how much you hurt other people with your behaviour; it always has to be about *you*. You were the same as a child.'

The unfairness of this stung Natalie into retorting, 'It's not about *me*, it's about justice for *Sarah—*' but even as she said the words, she heard her father's voice inside her head.

This isn't about Sarah, it never was.

So she said instead, 'I suppose you have everything you want now? Richard and your boys, a lovely house, a happy family life? You don't need me reminding you of the past.'

Magda didn't respond. She didn't have to. They both knew she spoke the truth.

'Was it true that you only married Dad because you were pregnant with Sarah?'

Even though Natalie knew Sarah had been born a year after their marriage.

But Magda kept to her story. 'I had very little choice in the matter. My parents threw me out and John offered to marry me. I thought he was my hero, but he turned out to be a bad-tempered misery who made my life hell. You were so terrified of him, you sent his car over the cliff. And you wonder why I want to leave my past behind?'

'I didn't *mean* for the car to go over the cliff! It was an accident! Dad was drunk. He hadn't put the brake on properly.'

'So *you* say. You seem remarkably quick to forgive him, to listen to him, to take his side in all this.'

'I don't *want* to take sides; I just want to find out the truth!'

'We *know* the truth! Sarah was murdered by her drama

teacher because he was jealous. Detective Chief Inspector Cameron explained everything.'

'Did he explain why Simon left Sarah's body in that lily pond?'

'Simon was psychologically disturbed. He didn't need a reason.'

'Simon thought Sarah was having an affair with Henry Vyne.'

Magda's fingers around the cross were instantly still. 'That's not true,' she began, then checked herself. She unravelled her finger from the ribbon and then, as though she couldn't help herself, began to wind it up again. 'How can you say such terrible things? Sir Henry was an honourable man, a kind man. He set up that trust after your father's accident to pay for his healthcare. He let us stay at the Lodge, rent free. He didn't have to do that.'

More likely, Sir Henry was paying for John's silence after he helped him dispose of Bryn's body.

'The police found a collection of sketchpads,' Natalie said out loud. 'They date from a few weeks before Henry died, right back to the early 1990s. Drawing after drawing of young women taken in almost identical poses, in his studio and the walled garden, probably the only places he knew he'd never be disturbed. Sarah was one of them.'

Magda's fingers tightened over the jewelled cross. 'You'd better leave now. Radley will see you out.'

Natalie placed herself directly in front of her mother, preventing her from pressing the bell set beside the door. Unless Magda was willing to make an undignified detour around the sofa, she was trapped beside the window.

Predictably, Magda stayed put.

'Sarah hated her life,' Natalie told her mother. 'She planned to leave Calahurst with Simon and never come back. They were going to be married, but she knew he'd flip if he ever found out about those sketches, so she arranged to steal them back, with the help of two brothers she met at the fairground. The three of them broke into the castle, but before they could remove the sketchbook from the safe they were caught. In a panic, Sarah ran to Simon's house for help, but, just as she knew he would, he flipped. He forced her back to the castle and into the walled garden, where he killed her, leaving her body in the lily pond as a message for Sir Henry. Perhaps he hoped Sir Henry would be charged with her murder.'

Natalie paused, but there was no reaction.

'What did you believe, the morning you realised Sarah had gone?' she asked her mother. 'When they found Sarah's body in that pond, *did* you think Henry had killed her? Did you think he'd left her there as a message for *you*?'

Magda glanced at her watch. 'Have you finished wallowing in the past? Because I'd rather live in the present.'

'One last question.'

'That's enough—'

'How did it feel to kill the man you loved?'

Now she had Magda's full attention. 'I don't know what you're talking about.'

'*You* shot Henry. It was never an accident. You'd loved him for all those years and at first he'd loved you back. Then he jilted you for Clare and you had to watch as he became obsessed with increasingly younger women until finally, in what must have been the biggest blow of all, he noticed Sarah. How hard it must have been for you, seeing him become infatuated with another teenage blonde, yet knowing all along that *you* had been the original. When Sarah was murdered, you believed he'd done it. You kept quiet, assuming that would be the end of it, but then you realised he'd noticed me. So you killed him before he could go further.'

'And *you* got to live.' Her mother's blank expression didn't change and for a moment Natalie wasn't even sure she'd spoken. 'You lived and Henry died. I chose you over him and it's *still* not enough for you? You want me to "love" you too? Well, I can't, because I love *him*. No matter what he did, or the kind of person he became, Henry Vyne was the only man I've ever loved. Perhaps now you'll understand why I can't bear to look at you, and if you *ever* try to contact me again I'll have you arrested for harassment.'

At that moment, which should have been the worst in her life, Natalie felt nothing. This was the woman who'd given birth to her and she felt absolutely nothing.

She was finally free.

There was one task remaining.

Natalie picked the parcel up from the table and ripped the paper from it, letting it float to the floor. Inside was a book; a glossy hardback. It had a black dust jacket with Natalie's name written along the top and the outline of a bluebell picked out in silver.

'This is a copy of my book,' she said, holding it out. 'I've even signed it for you.'

'I don't want it,' Magda said coldly. 'Simon's dead. They're all dead. That's the end of it.'

The end of it.

A score settled?

Not quite.

'I nearly died too,' Natalie said. 'Did you know that? Simon was about to kill me, but someone shot him. What do you think of that?'

'I think you were extremely lucky,' Magda said.

'The killer had been following Simon. The fact that I was there too, the fact that I was saved, was coincidental.'

Natalie paused, to give her mother the opportunity to speak, but Magda remained silent.

'I've always thought it odd that none of the other girls in Henry's sketchbook came forward after Sarah died, despite a police investigation. Apparently they preferred to remain silent, hoping no one would find out what they did when they were young and foolish. So if someone found those sketches, and was able to put names to all those faces, it would make a perfect blackmail opportunity, wouldn't it? Particularly if you were the kind of person who had a lot of expenses – such as a castle to run, shall we say? Is that why you killed Clare? Was she blackmailing you too?'

Magda said nothing.

Natalie sighed. 'Dad called you his nemesis, but I don't think he understood who she really was. He seemed to think Nemesis was some kind of goddess of revenge, someone who was determined to get the better of him. In reality, she's the spirit of retribution – retribution against those who show arrogance towards the gods. You know, you might do well to consider that.'

Still her mother remained silent and, as Natalie had nothing more to say either, she placed the book back on the table and left, closing the door quietly behind her.

Magda watched through the window as her daughter left the house. A man stepped from the shadow of the chestnut tree and Natalie ran towards him, flinging her arms around his neck. He lifted her up, whirling her round before setting her back on her feet and hugging her close. But there was another man too, emerging from a car. A man in a familiar black overcoat, accompanied by two others in suits.

That damned detective back again.

Infuriated, Magda turned away from the window, knocking against the table where Natalie had left her book. Before Magda could stop it, the book slid across the polished wood and hit the floor heavily, causing something to flutter free from its pages. Without thinking, Magda bent to pick it up and found she was holding a copy of a drawing of herself as a teenager, wearing a pretty summer dress, smiling seductively, floating amongst a mass of white and pink water lilies.

Scrawled in thick black pen, right across the drawing, was one word.

Nemesis

A LETTER FROM THE AUTHOR

Dear reader,

Thank you so much for reading *Murder at Castle Vyne*! I do hope you've enjoyed it. I had a lot of fun writing it. If you'd like to be the first to hear about new releases and bonus content, you can click on the link below to sign up.

www.stormpublishing.co/louise-marley

If you've enjoyed this book and could spare a few moments to leave a review that would be hugely appreciated. Even a short review (or a star rating) can make all the difference in encouraging a reader to discover my books for the first time.

When I'm writing a book, several ideas need to collide inside my head to provide the spark of inspiration. The first idea came while walking around the garden of an old house. The garden was very run-down. It had a large pond filled with water lilies and was overshadowed by huge gothic-looking trees, which made it look quite depressing. I've never cared much for water lilies. To me they seem creepy. Their petals are too perfect and they look fake – as though they've been made from plastic. I made a joke about the scene only needing a dead body to make it complete, and then promptly forgot about it.

Around the same time, I visited Tate Britain and saw the very famous painting of Ophelia by John Everett Millais. This painting shows a scene from Shakespeare's *Hamlet*, of the unfortunate Ophelia, floating in a river, surrounded by flowers.

So there you have it: three ideas collided to create my story: a gloomy pond, masses of sinister water lilies, and a beautiful girl floating amongst them.

If you've read my *English Village Mystery* series, you may recognise the village of Calahurst! All my books are set in the same 'world' (the fictional King's Forest District) and some characters do 'book hop' – in this case, DCI Doug Cameron. However, this story is set *before* the events in *Murder at Raven's Edge*.

The castle mentioned in *Murder at Castle Vyne* is partly inspired by Penrhyn Castle in Gwynedd, Wales, although I substantially 'remodelled' it to fit my plot.

Louise x

You can contact me at louise@louisemarley.co.uk. I'd love to hear from you!

You can also find me here:

> Website: https://www.louisemarley.co.uk
> Raven's Edge: https://ravens-edge.co.uk

facebook.com/LouiseMarleyAuthor
x.com/LouiseMarley
instagram.com/louisemarleywrites
bsky.app/profile/louisemarley.bsky.social

ACKNOWLEDGMENTS

Huge thanks to Kathryn Taussig for her patience, unerring insight and brilliant suggestions to help keep my stories on track. Also, a big thank-you to Oliver Rhodes, Alexandra Begley and the fabulous team at Storm for all the hard work that goes on behind the scenes – without whom you wouldn't be reading this book!

Thank you to my wonderful family for their support, particularly when everything has to be dropped for a deadline, but especially to my poor husband, who has to suffer daily updates on my characters' lives and *exactly* where I am on my edits.

Thank you to Novelistas Ink for the writerly chat and pep talks. We always have the *best* fun at our book launches!

Finally, a big hug to my lovely readers for the support, the kind-hearted messages and the wonderful reviews. You are all brilliant!

Printed in Dunstable, United Kingdom